A Killer Edition

Berkley Prime Crime titles by Lorna Barrett

MURDER IS BINDING

BOOKMARKED FOR DEATH

BOOKPLATE SPECIAL

CHAPTER & HEARSE

SENTENCED TO DEATH

MURDER ON THE HALF SHELF

NOT THE KILLING TYPE

BOOK CLUBBED

A FATAL CHAPTER

TITLE WAVE

A JUST CLAUSE

POISONED PAGES

A KILLER EDITION

Anthologies

MURDER IN THREE VOLUMES

A Killer Edition

Lorna Barrett

BERKLEY PRIME CRIME
New York

BERKLEY PRIME CRIME
Published by Berkley
An imprint of Penguin Random House LLC
1745 Broadway, New York, NY 10019

Library of Congress Cataloging-in-Publication Data

Names: Barrett, Lorna, author.
Title: A killer edition / Lorna Barrett.
Description: First Edition. | New York: Berkley Prime Crime, 2019. |
Series: A booktown mystery; 13
Identifiers: LCCN 2019011733 | ISBN 9781984802729 (hardcover) |
ISBN 9781984802743 (ebook)
Subjects: | GSAFD: Mystery fiction.
Classification: LCC PS3602.A83955 K55 2019 | DDC 813/.6—dc23
LC record available at https://lccn.loc.gov/2019011733

First Edition: August 2019

Printed in the United States of America
1 3 5 7 9 10 8 6 4 2

Cover art by Teresa Fasolino
Book design by Laura K. Corless

For Nancy Cooper

Acknowledgments

I'm so grateful that so many of my readers have become my friends. They let me pick their brains for details that help bring my books to life. Thank you, Mare Fairchild, for schooling me on high school procedures. My cruising pal and good friend Nancy Cooper reminded me that candy is *important*. And Darcy Fechner is a walking reference for information on New Hampshire and its wildlife.

Cast of Characters

Tricia Miles, owner of Haven't Got a Clue vintage mystery bookstore

Angelica Miles, Tricia's older sister, owner of the Cookery and the Booked for Lunch café and half owner of the Sheer Comfort Inn. Her alter ego is Nigela Ricita, the mysterious developer who has been pumping money and jobs into the village of Stoneham

Pixie Poe, Tricia's assistant manager at Haven't Got a Clue

Mr. Everett, Tricia's employee at Haven't Got a Clue

Antonio Barbero, the public face of Nigela Ricita Associates; Angelica's stepson

Ginny Wilson-Barbero, Tricia's former assistant; wife of Antonio Barbero

Grace Harris-Everett, Mr. Everett's wife

Grant Baker, chief of the Stoneham Police Department

Marshall Cambridge, owner of the Armchair Tourist

Joyce Widman, owner of Have a Heart romance bookstore

Russ Smith, owner of the *Stoneham Weekly News*

Nikki Brimfield-Smith, owner of the Patisserie; ex-wife of Russ Smith

Midge and Muriel Dexter, elderly twin sisters who reside in Stoneham

Donna North, cake decorator and candy maker

Cindy Pearson, a member of the Stoneham Police Department

Toby Kingston, president of the Pets-A-Plenty Animal Rescue

Adelaide Newberry, president of the Booktown Ladies Charitable Society

Bonnie Connor, secretary of the Pets-A-Plenty Animal Rescue

Rebecca Shore, executive committee member of the Pets-A-Plenty Animal Rescue

Mrs. Randall, principal of Stoneham High School

Cori Haskell, volunteer at the Pets-A-Plenty Animal Rescue

A Killer Edition

ONE

Tricia Miles gripped the steering wheel so tightly, her fingers were white. A death grip like that wasn't healthy, not if one intended to use one's fingers for other purposes—like turning the page of a book or holding a cup filled with coffee. Or perhaps strangling someone.

Okay, strangulation was perhaps too harsh a punishment for someone who supposedly had your best interests at heart, but of late, Dr. Kendra Vought had inspired thoughts of little else. Her specialty was grief counseling, but she didn't seem particularly good at her profession. Though she said things like "Time is your greatest friend," her body language, bored expression, and an eye on the clock conveyed another message: *"Move on, already."*

Moving on was proving to be a lot more difficult than Tricia had anticipated. Not that she hadn't already experienced a prolonged period of grief when her beloved grandmother had died—and at far too young an age. But she had been older than Tricia's ex-husband, Christopher Benson, who hadn't died of disease but had been murdered.

Maybe that was why after almost two years, Tricia still thought about him daily. And it wasn't like he had been an everyday part of her life. After their divorce, it got so that she thought of him only now and then—until he'd reappeared practically on her doorstep with requests to "get back together," all of which she had ignored.

But it wasn't Christopher who was on her mind just then. After that morning's session, Tricia and Dr. Vought were officially through. Her last piece of advice had been ludicrous, to say the least. "Go read a sexy romance novel, and then visit your friend with benefits."

Friend with benefits? That wasn't how Tricia thought of her relationship with Marshall Cambridge. Okay, they were friends, and they did sometimes have the occasional sleepover, but that didn't mean . . .

Good grief, Tricia realized. She and Marshall *were* friends with benefits!

And oddly enough, that was all Tricia really wanted from the relationship.

At least . . . for now.

But read a sexy romance?

Forget it.

Tricia braked as she approached the Stoneham municipal parking lot, which was pretty full on that sunny morning in late June—a morning that was quickly slipping toward noon. After locking the Lexus, Tricia headed for the sidewalk along Main Street, but first she had to pass the Have a Heart romance bookstore, run by her fellow shopkeeper Joyce Widman.

Tricia paused in front of the big display window.

Romance.

It had been a long time since romance had been part of her life. For her, romance had died when Christopher had asked for a divorce.

Not counseling, not a trial separation, but divorce. Then he'd gone to the Colorado Rockies to contemplate his navel for several years until he realized what and whom he had discarded.

Tricia took in the book covers of the paperbacks that populated the display. Bare-chested Scottish heroes with six-pack abs dressed in bold tartan kilts appeared to ravish long-tressed heroines in flowing gowns that flaunted their heaving bosoms. Bold romances reflecting a bolder time. But she wasn't into historicals and knew the store stocked more than just that subgenre.

Romantic suspense . . . now, that she would enjoy. A kick-ass story with an adventurous heroine who could not only take care of herself but save the day *and* have a successful romantic relationship as well. Not with a man who'd abandon her. Not with someone who would turn on and stalk her. Not with a man who feared commitment.

And not with somebody like Marshall Cambridge?

That was a tougher question. Their relationship was satisfying in so many ways—but mostly because Marshall let her do her own thing because he was busy doing his own thing. For both of them, it meant running their businesses and their lives without asking permission and without making excuses.

But if she was honest, Tricia did miss the romance. The weekend trips to quaint locales. Dinners in exclusive restaurants. Snow skiing in the winter, water-skiing in the summer. Giving and receiving little gestures of affection that made her heart sing.

Tricia sighed. Maybe Dr. Vought was right. Maybe what she needed was to lose herself in the pages of a romance novel. At least temporarily. Because she knew what the real problem was.

Tricia Miles was bored. Ever since she had given her assistant, Pixie Poe, the job of assistant *manager* of her vintage mystery bookshop, Haven't Got a Clue, she'd felt rather lost. And oddly enough,

Dr. Vought just couldn't seem to accept that. Well, it wasn't *her* problem.

Heaving another sigh, Tricia entered the bookshop.

Joyce had done a nice job decorating her shop with pastel-colored walls, comfortable upholstered chairs in reading nooks, romantic prints decorating the walls, and lots and lots of shelves filled with paperback novels, stock that had been carefully sorted according to genre.

"Tricia, fancy seeing you here."

The voice had come from behind the cash desk. "Hi, Joyce. I came by to find a little reading material."

Joyce did a classic double take. "Really?"

Did she have to sound so skeptical?

"Yes. Something a little—"

"Racy?" Joyce suggested and giggled.

"Not exactly. Something with a lot of suspense and with a heroine who can take on the world."

"I should have known you'd like some intrigue."

Tricia nodded.

"I can recommend a number of different series and stand-alone books by a variety of wonderful authors."

"I'm listening."

Before Joyce could walk around the counter to help Tricia, the door burst open and a matronly woman with a mop of gray hair and an expression filled with fury bounded into the shop.

"You *had* to call that tree surgeon when I specifically asked you *not* to!" the woman protested in what was definitely an outside voice.

"Hello, Vera," Joyce said politely, if curtly. "And yes, I did. We talked about it and I told you what my insurance company said. That limb was over my yard and fence and legally I had the right to trim it and its branches."

Tricia started to edge away from what might well become a confrontation, but Joyce's voice stopped her. "Vera, have you met Tricia Miles? She owns the Haven't Got a Clue mystery bookstore down the street."

"No, I haven't—and why would I care? I don't have time to read stupid books."

Them was fightin' words, but Tricia didn't respond to them. She simply said, "Hello."

Vera ignored her.

"That giant limb could have come down in my yard during the next windstorm, and when it did—!"

"You would have been compensated by insurance. I spoke to my insurance agent, too. But I specifically asked you to wait—"

"Well, my garden *couldn't* wait. It needs full sunlight if I'm to grow vegetables to can for the winter."

"Don't give me that bull. You can buy vegetables at the grocery store or the farmers' market for a lot less money and effort."

Joyce let out a sigh of disgust and looked away.

"If you touch anything else that grows in my yard, I will sue you for every penny you have. I'll take this precious shop of yours, too, you—you smut peddler!"

Vera may as well have slapped Joyce across the cheek as insult her beloved romance novels. Joyce's mouth dropped open and her cheeks went a vivid pink, but despite that, she did not raise her voice. "I'm afraid I'll have to ask you to leave."

Vera defiantly crossed her arms across her chest. "I'm not going anywhere."

It was then that the newest hire at the Stoneham Police Department stepped around one of the tall shelves. "Is there a problem here?" asked Officer Cindy Pearson. She looked to be in her mid- to late twenties and stood five ten or so, with a blonde ponytail that stuck out the back of her ball cap with the Stoneham Police Department emblem emblazoned on the front, and her thumbs hooked on her thick leather belt, her service revolver resting on her right hip.

Vera's eyes widened in anger, and for a moment Tricia thought the woman might explode, but then she averted her gaze. "The problem is Joyce's."

"I believe Ms. Widman is correct about her right to take care of her property as she sees fit. If you have questions, feel free to contact the Stoneham Police Department to clarify your homeowner rights," Officer Pearson said.

Joyce let out a breath and gave the officer a grateful smile. Vera, however, wasn't placated. She turned her baleful gaze on the bookseller. "You haven't heard the last of this, Joyce." And with that parting shot, she turned and bolted from the shop.

For a long moment, Joyce and the officer just looked at each other, and then the cop spoke. "My lunch break is over. I need to get going. I'll come back another time to get some books. Feel free to let me or the department know if you have any other problems with your neighbor."

"Will do. And thank you," Joyce said gratefully.

Officer Pearson touched the brim of her hat and headed out the door.

"Wow," Tricia said, "that was uncomfortable. I'm glad the officer was here to defuse the situation."

"So am I," Joyce said. She gave herself a little shake. "Living next to Vera has been a trial. She's angry that her good friend no longer lives next door and that I bought the property."

Frannie Mae Armstrong, who had been Tricia's sister Angelica's assistant at the Cookery for almost six years, had had to sell the house in order to pay her legal team's fees. They had so far not been able to get her released from the county lockup after she'd killed someone and then attempted to kill another. Joyce had swooped in to buy the property and had moved in just after the vernal equinox. Since then, she'd been taking time off from work to make the house and garden her own. Like Tricia, she had a dependable assistant in Lauren Squire.

"So, you enjoy gardening?" Tricia said, eager to change the subject.

Joyce nodded. "My parents were organic gardeners long before it became a trend. Their flower gardens were magnificent, but they weren't much into growing vegetables. I like to do both."

"I'm afraid I don't have much of a green thumb," Tricia admitted. "I have a couple of pots of herbs on my balcony, but I'd like to try something more ambitious. Would you be willing to give me some pointers?"

"I'd be happy to. I have some errands to run this afternoon but will be home around three. Why don't you drop by then and I'll give you some lettuce and herbs fresh from my garden."

"That's very generous of you. Thank you. See you then."

"Wait! What about that book you wanted?"

Tricia laughed, having forgotten why she'd come into the store in the first place. "Yes, please pick out a few titles for me."

"I'm happy to do so," Joyce said and led Tricia to the nearest bookshelf.

It was almost noon when Tricia entered her vintage mystery store, Haven't Got a Clue. As usual, her former assistant and now assistant *manager*, Pixie, was speaking with a customer. Tricia's sister, Angelica, also known as the owner of Nigela Ricita Associates—albeit by not too many—had wanted to poach Pixie, whose checkered, lady-of-the-night past couldn't belie the fact that she was an extraordinarily talented woman. So Tricia had elevated Pixie from assistant to assistant manager, giving her the responsibility that went with the title, and Pixie had excelled far beyond Tricia's expectations. So much so that Tricia now felt like an extraneous cog in the machinery that was Haven't Got a Clue. Tricia had no husband, and now she didn't seem to have a store to run, either. Oh, she still handled the bookkeeping and other sundry tasks for the business, but Pixie had quite successfully taken over the rest of the operation.

With more free time on her hands, Tricia's original idea had been to volunteer at the local animal shelter—and she'd hoped to become an integral part of the operation. Unfortunately, her overtures to help had been met with a cool—one might even say glacial—reception, despite the fact that she'd been a generous donor in the past. Had they thought she was trying to buy her way into a position of authority? That hadn't been the case, but that seemed to be the assumption. The fact that she had successfully run a nonprofit for nearly a decade in Manhattan gave her credentials most organizations could only hope to exploit.

Tricia closed the store's door behind her and saw that her cat, Miss Marple, was asleep on her usual perch above and behind the glass display case that doubled as a cash desk. No welcome there. As it was Monday, her other employee, elderly Mr. Everett, had the day off.

Tricia stood near the register, pretending to inspect the stuffers that went into the bags that would hopefully be filled with vintage and current mysteries. A minute or so later, Pixie had finished speaking with the customer and joined her.

"Thanks for opening this morning," Tricia said by way of greeting.

"It's never a problem," Pixie said cheerfully, her gold canine tooth sparkling under the halogen lights above. That day she was dressed in a pumpkin-colored vintage dress that mimicked the carrot color of her hair, which changed with the seasons or Pixie's whims. "We had a bus at ten and scored at least eight pretty good sales."

"I'm sorry you had to handle it on your own," Tricia said sincerely.

Pixie waved a hand as though to brush off the apology. "It wasn't a problem. I always feel psyched when we have a good influx of customers. It's so invigorating," she gushed.

Tricia *used* to know that feeling when she'd been the one ringing up the sales, but Pixie insisted that it was now *her* job to take care of customers so that Tricia could concentrate on the more important parts of the business.

Like what?

Okay, Tricia had invested in some additional promotional materials, but that had happened long before the tourist season had commenced over Memorial Day weekend. Instead of laboring over promotion, she'd often found herself exiled to her lovely apartment, where she'd restlessly paced or indulged in a new hobby: baking.

During the previous three or four years, Tricia had depended on purchases of cookies from the Patisserie to accompany the complimentary coffee she provided to her customers. But after a particularly nasty conversation with the bakery's owner, Nikki Brimfield-Smith, some months before, she decided that she would no longer frequent the business and would bake the treats she gave to her patrons as a thank-you for their support.

"The mail's on the counter," Pixie said, and pointed.

Tricia had completely missed it. She picked it up and leafed through the envelopes and circulars. Buried within it was yet another flyer for the upcoming Great Booktown Bake-Off. Her gaze lingered over the text.

"You know, you ought to enter," Pixie said, her tone sincere.

Tricia looked up. "Why?"

"Because you've come so far this past year cooking and baking. I think you could give Angelica a run for her money."

No way, Tricia thought. Then . . . "Really?"

"Definitely!" Pixie said enthusiastically.

Of course, most of what Tricia knew about cooking and baking had come because her sister had mentored her. But then, once you got the hang of it, following a recipe to the letter usually made for a pretty foolproof result. That is, if you could trust the recipe.

"The deadline is tomorrow," Pixie pointed out. "I really think you should enter. I mean, what have you got to lose?"

What *did* she have to lose? Since Tricia was already known as the village jinx, perhaps some might think her entry could be looked on with suspicion—maybe even poisonous. Then again, maybe if she did well in such a competition, perhaps coming in third or fourth, it might help to repair the unfortunate reputation she had never deserved. It wasn't her fault that she seemed to be a corpse magnet or that since her arrival in Stoneham, once the safest village in New Hampshire, it had become homicide central—at least when compared to burgs with the same population.

"I'll think about it," Tricia promised, folding the flyer and pocketing it.

"Do you mind if I take off for an hour or so this afternoon? Joyce over at the Have a Heart bookstore invited me to come over to her house and score some fresh vegetables. I thought it would make a great salad for dinner tonight."

"Go right ahead. And if you're late, closing won't be a problem. You go ahead and have fun. You deserve it," Pixie said.

"I should probably text Angelica to tell her I'll be contributing to our dinner."

"Good idea."

Tricia pulled out her phone, tapped the keys, and sent her sister a quick message. Almost immediately she got a reply that said,

Yay! I never turned down fresh veggies. You can make a salad. It'll go great with pasta.

Tricia and Angelica—her sister, fellow bookseller, and entrepreneur—tended to have dinners together so that they could not only share a martini or two but talk about the trials and tribulations of the day as well. In fact, it had become Tricia's favorite part of the day. They usually had lunch together, too, but that day Angelica had canceled because she was interviewing potential employees for the day spa she intended to open in just weeks. After dinner, Tricia would be seeing Marshall, too. She couldn't help the smile that crept over her lips. Yes, she certainly had a lot to look forward to.

The door opened, bringing in a fresh wave of customers. Before Tricia could greet them, Pixie sprang into action. "Welcome to Haven't Got a Clue. I'm Pixie. Let me know if you need any help."

Tricia sighed and decided to retreat to her basement office until Pixie's lunch break to see what trouble she could get into there, as she didn't have to be at Joyce's house for at least another three hours. And she might just peruse the Bake-Off's rudimentary web page once again to remind herself of the rules and think about what recipe she might potentially enter. No doubt about it, with Pixie's encouragement, she felt better about the idea of entering the contest. And despite the unhappy beginning of her day, Tricia was pretty sure the latter part would be well worth waiting for.

Of course, every time she thought along those lines, something usually went drastically wrong.

TWO

Tricia arrived at Joyce's house no more than two minutes late. She rang the bell and it was only seconds before Joyce answered. "Hey, come on in." She threw back the door and motioned Tricia to enter.

Although the house had been familiar on the outside—Tricia passed by it many times on her walks with Angelica's dog, Sarge—she'd never been inside the little Cape Cod when it had been owned by Frannie Armstrong. Joyce had furnished the place with contemporary pieces, heavy on a particular shade of beige. That is, except for the art that decorated the walls. They were prints of the same sort that hung in her romance bookstore, by artists such as William Waterhouse and Alphonse Mucha. It was definitely a woman's home, and why not, since Joyce was divorced and lived alone. Perhaps she'd been looking forward to decorating her new home for herself with only objects and pictures she loved. Or maybe she just went to Target and furnished the place in a weekend. Who knew? Maybe one day

Tricia would ask; right now they weren't close enough for that kind of a conversation, but maybe that would change, too.

"I don't want to keep you," Tricia said, "but I'm dying to see your garden—especially your vegetables. I almost wish I had a little garden of my own. I think it would be fun to grow food that I could eat and share with friends and family."

"But you can. Before I bought this place, I had a fine container garden. I grew cherry tomatoes, peppers, and plenty of leaf lettuce, as well as herbs. Although I must admit my patio was bigger than your balcony. Have you thought about hanging window boxes?"

"No. What a great idea. Maybe I'll go to the garden shop tomorrow and buy something like that. I wonder if I could have someone install them, too."

"What about your friend Marshall?" Joyce asked with the hint of a smile.

Tricia shook her head. Marshall was a man of many talents, but she wasn't sure he would be up to that task.

"Come out back and I'll show you my little farm," Joyce said, and led the way through the small but updated kitchen to the door that led to the backyard.

The smell of sawdust was heavy in the air. While the north side of the yard had obviously been raked, the evidence of wood chips in the grass was unmistakable. So was the raw wound on the now lopsided maple in the yard next door. No wonder Vera had been upset. The once symmetrical tree looked as though it had been butchered. A couple of purple finches hopped from limb to limb, chirping away as though to disparage the destruction. Tricia shook her head and turned away.

Joyce must have started her garden early, for there were tendrils of beans winding their way up sturdy green metal poles that acted as a curtain in the middle of her yard. In front of them was a row of six tomato plants, which were already standing at least eighteen inches high. Had she grown them from seed or bought half-grown plants at the nursery? At each end of the row were what looked like pepper plants, and, of course, the plot along the fence on the south side of her yard was her herb garden. The chives, parsley, and several large basil plants grew in full sun, as the center garden would now do also. When the basil fully matured, Joyce would be able to make a heck of a lot of pesto. Roses were just about to bloom along the back of the house, but they had obviously been established years before.

"Oh, my," Tricia said. "You really *are* into gardening."

Joyce laughed. "But of course." Then her brow furrowed and she looked to one side.

Tricia turned. "Is something wrong?"

Joyce frowned. "The fence gate is open."

Tricia looked and saw that indeed there was a gate in the fence between Joyce's and Vera's yards and it was ajar.

Joyce said nothing, but her expression was anything but pleased. Without a word, she stomped over to the gate, slammed it shut, and threw back two shiny silver-hued bolts at the top and the bottom. Then she turned on her heel and started, her mouth dropping open as she let out a stifled scream. Tricia rushed forward, but Joyce pushed her aside, her shaking arm raised and pointing at what could only be a body lying in the grass. Unfortunately, there was a pitchfork thrust through its midsection.

Joyce seemed frozen in place, and Tricia crept forward, but it was obvious the person was no longer alive.

And that person was Vera Olson.

It was Tricia, of course, who reported the body. Joyce was far too upset to be thinking or speaking coherently. Tricia pulled Joyce over to the patio and pushed her into a seat before the poor woman fainted.

And of course, the 911 dispatcher didn't seem at all surprised when Tricia identified herself. Tricia gritted her teeth but managed to stay calm and gave what few facts she knew, and then ended the call to wait for the sirens of the police cruisers she knew would soon arrive.

Joyce was too upset to make conversation, and Tricia took the time to go back to look at the body once more. Surprisingly there was very little blood, which could have meant two different things. Either Vera had died very quickly, or she'd been dead before she'd been run through. The dead woman didn't look much different than she had in life. Her features were twisted in what was either anger or fear or terrible pain when she died—not unlike the angry expression she'd worn at the Have a Heart bookstore earlier that day. Tricia frowned. Could that mean she'd been surprised by the identity of her attacker? Bending low and squinting, Tricia saw that Vera's neck was ringed with red blotches. Strangulation?

Trying hard to be dispassionate, Tricia took note of the position of the body, the area surrounding it, and the state of the back side of the garden, which had been hidden from sight when they'd first entered the yard. She was about to walk the perimeter when Joyce called, "Tricia?" her voice sounding shaky.

Tricia returned to stand beside her business neighbor. "It might be a good idea for me to wait in the driveway for the police. Will you be okay on your own?"

Joyce looked terrified and reached for Tricia's arm, clasping it in what could only be called a death grip. "Please don't leave me alone with that—that—" But she couldn't seem to finish the sentence.

"Why don't I stand by the gate to the front yard. I'll only be a few feet away. You wouldn't want them breaking down your front door."

Joyce looked horrified, as though she'd already been through enough and couldn't bear the idea of having to repair the entrance of her home as well. "Go ahead. I guess I'll be all right. I *have* to be all right."

Tricia knew exactly what she meant.

As expected, the first police cruiser came screaming down the street and stopped in front of the house, leaving a patch of rubber. The siren was cut off and the armed officer bounded toward the house. Tricia called to him, diverting him to the backyard, but the gate was locked. Ready or not, Joyce was going to have to pull herself together and help the officers begin their investigation. She produced a key and handed it to the officer, who opened the gate and entered the yard. Tricia led him to where Vera lay. With his hand resting on the unfastened clasp over his service revolver, the officer took in the body, pursed his lips, and looked around the yard as though seeking the perpetrator, but said nothing.

"She can't have been dead long," Tricia said.

"Is this how you found her?"

"Yes. We both found her."

The officer looked from Tricia to Joyce and frowned.

His question about finding the body was to be asked at least another ten or twenty times during the next hour by a number of sources, and more than once by each. But of course, upon arriving, it was Police Chief Grant Baker who seemed to ask it the most. Tricia and Baker had a history, which everyone seemed to know about, and he was once again very unhappy to be standing by her side and near yet another corpse.

"You really are a jinx," he said unkindly. It was an unwelcome word and an equally unwelcome reputation that Tricia seemed to have to bear.

"And you are a—" But Tricia didn't finish the sentence. Instead, her blood came near the boiling point.

"What am I going to do with you?" Baker asked, chagrined.

"Nothing." Tricia turned and started to walk away when something on the ground caught her attention. She was about to investigate further when Joyce called her and she headed back to the patio, where the woman still sat huddled in one of the padded lawn chairs. Standing next to her was Officer Cindy Pearson, the same woman who had been in the Have a Heart bookshop earlier that day. There hadn't yet been an opportunity for either Joyce or Pearson to mention Vera's visit to the bookshop and her threats. Was it up to Tricia to relay that information?

Looking at her feet, Pearson seemed as though she wanted to say something but didn't.

A male officer Tricia knew to be named Henderson pulled Baker aside and spoke to him in a low voice. Baker looked up and turned his gaze toward Joyce, then nodded. He came to join the women on the patio.

"I understand you and your neighbor, Ms. Olson, weren't the best of friends."

"Everyone around here knew that," Joyce admitted.

"And what was the nature of your problem?" Baker asked.

Joyce looked outraged. "*My* problem was that my neighbor didn't respect my property lines. She was friends with the former owner and was used to coming and going through the gate in the fence whenever she pleased. That changed when I bought the house this spring, and she didn't like it and she didn't like *me* because I objected to her trespassing."

"And why was that?" Baker asked.

"You had to know who lived here before me," Joyce said.

Frannie Armstrong, Tricia mouthed when Baker turned to her for clarification.

He turned back to Joyce. "I'm assuming you own the pitchfork that pierced her?" Baker asked.

"Yes."

"And why would you own such a tool?"

Joyce gestured toward her patch of vegetables. "I'm a gardener. It's a tool I use on a regular basis to turn over the soil and work with my compost pile."

Baker frowned, as though unhappy with the explanation. "Perhaps we should talk about this in more detail down at the station."

Joyce looked astounded. "Don't tell me you think *I* killed her."

"I'm willing to hear your story."

Joyce shot out of her chair. "*My* story?"

Pearson spoke up. "Chief, I happen to have been at Ms. Widman's bookstore this morning when Ms. Olson paid her a visit. The woman was abusive and rude. Ms. Widman treated her with respect, although there appeared to be some kind of underlying tension."

Joyce looked at the officer in disbelief, anger clouding her features.

"I was there, too, Grant," Tricia volunteered.

"Of course you were. You've always got your sticky fingers in situations like this."

"I beg your pardon," Tricia said, none too pleased. "I may have only met Vera Olson once, but it was obvious to me that she had a disagreeable personality. I'm sure the officer who just spoke to you told you many of her neighbors felt the same way as me."

"He did," Baker grudgingly agreed.

"Then I hope you'll cut Joyce some slack. Plenty of people knew the reason for the discord between them. Someone who did could have used that to try to pin the blame on Joyce."

"And Ms. Widman will have plenty of time to defend herself." What he didn't say was whether it would be in court.

Tricia sighed. Cops always believed the worst of everyone. Of course, she supposed they had to. It was their job. But it became very tiresome. She spoke to Joyce. "Do you have a lawyer? Is there someone I can call for you?"

"Just the guy who prepared the paperwork for the closing on my house, but he isn't the kind that's going to be able to help me if I'm in trouble—which I shouldn't be because I did not kill Vera Olson," she said emphatically.

"I know of someone."

"She doesn't need a lawyer if she's prepared to tell the truth," Baker said flatly.

"I intend to, but I also watch a lot of TV shows and read a lot of romantic suspense novels. The cops can't wait to pin a crime on an innocent person—just so the district attorney can get a conviction," Joyce said.

"Ms. Widman," Officer Pearson warned.

"I'll handle this," Baker told his subordinate.

Pearson looked away, dutifully admonished.

"What about my house?"

"You can grab your purse and lock it up; then you will accompany Officer Pearson to the station and wait for me."

"Yes, sir," Pearson stated.

"I'll call my friend to see if he can meet you there as soon as possible," Tricia promised. She had attorney Roger Livingston's contact information stored on her cell phone.

"Very well," Joyce said, but Tricia could tell by her tone that she was anything but pleased.

"I'll make sure the chief knows to close and lock the gates before he and his team leave," Tricia promised.

Joyce nodded and she headed for the house, with Officer Pearson bringing up the rear.

Tricia didn't envy Joyce. The next few hours would be extremely stressful for her.

Unfortunately, much as Tricia wanted to believe her business neighbor was innocent of Vera Olson's death, it didn't look like Joyce had much in the way of an alibi.

THREE

Tricia trudged up the steps to her sister Angelica's apartment. Thankfully she only had to make it to the second floor, since during the past few months Angelica had reconfigured her living space to mirror what Tricia had done with her own home. The second floor was now Angelica's entertainment area, with a brand-new state-of-the-art kitchen with all the bells and whistles that a professional chef would require, and the third floor had been reconfigured as well.

Of course, Angelica was *not* a professional chef—even if she thought she was as talented.

As she topped the landing, Tricia was greeted by the sound of enthusiastic barking from Angelica's Bichon Frise, Sarge. That happy little pup was always glad to see Tricia because he knew she was a soft touch and would toss him at least one if not four dog biscuits during any given visit.

"Come on in, the door's open," Angelica called.

Tricia entered the apartment but had to fuss over Sarge before she could make her way to the newly expanded kitchen. In comparison, Tricia's kitchen seemed almost makeshift. Angelica had had to reinforce the flooring to accommodate the large stainless steel behemoth of a stove she'd had installed. With its six burners and a pot-filling faucet over it, she could produce restaurant-quality fare for the family she loved.

"Good grief, you are a noisy boy tonight," Angelica scolded Sarge. She grabbed a couple of biscuits from the crystal jar on the counter and tossed them to him. He caught one in his mouth and snatched the other before running to his bed to devour his snack.

The chilled martini glasses sat on a tray on the counter. Angelica turned to the fridge and took out the glass pitcher of martinis she'd already prepared. Setting it on the counter, she picked up a long glass spoon and stirred the contents. "My goodness, you're late tonight, Tricia. How many veggies did you pick at Joyce's house?" Then she looked at her sister and seemed to realize Tricia had arrived empty-handed. "Where are the veggies?"

"Unpicked," Tricia said succinctly.

"What?" Angelica said as she poured the first martini.

Tricia sighed. "Bad news, I'm afraid."

"Oh, no," Angelica wailed. "Don't tell me you found another body."

Tricia frowned. "Now, why would you automatically think that of all things?"

"Because I know you. And when you have bad news to report, you've usually found a corpse."

Tricia's frown deepened. "As it happens," she said. "I sort of did."

"Not Joyce, I hope," Angelica cried, appalled.

"No, but she was there at the time. It was her neighbor. Or should

I say, it was Frannie's neighbor. Frannie's friend. Apparently, this woman, Vera Olson, never took to Joyce and resented the fact that she now lives in Frannie's house."

"And just where did you find this woman? Inside Joyce's house?"

"No, behind her vegetable garden. Someone had run her through with a pitchfork."

Angelica shuddered. "Ouch. That's not the way I want to go." She handed Tricia one of the glasses. "So who killed her? Certainly not Joyce."

"I don't think so. I happened to be at Joyce's store this morning when Vera showed up berating Joyce for having a limb removed from a tree that hung over her yard. It could have gotten ugly, but the village's new policewoman, Officer Pearson, was also in the store at the time and defused the situation."

"I haven't met her yet. Is she nice?"

Tricia shrugged. "She seems to be. She showed up at Joyce's house, too, as part of the police show of force after I called nine one one."

"Yes, the whole department seems to show up whenever there's a problem."

"I'd say murder was a major problem," Tricia agreed.

"I assume Joyce is the prime suspect," Angelica said.

"They did haul her off to the police station for questioning, but it seems Vera was not a favorite among the neighbors. Frannie may have been her only friend."

"And now Frannie's in the pokey—and probably will be for life," Angelica said, and took a sip of her drink. It wouldn't have seemed proper to have toasted after Tricia's announcement of yet another death within the village limits.

Tricia sipped her drink, too. "I called Roger Livingston. He agreed to go to the station to advise Joyce, who practically accused Grant of trying to railroad her."

"Not the best approach so early in the investigation," Angelica observed.

"No, but the poor woman was badly frightened, and with cause. I mean, who wants to find a dead body in their backyard? And it *does* look suspicious."

"All deaths with pitchforks are terribly suspicious."

"That's not what I mean," Tricia said. "I can't put my finger on exactly what—but something wasn't right about the murder scene."

Angelica looked thoughtful. "Leave it to Grant. It's his job to discover the truth, although you're probably right that it was almost certainly a disgruntled neighbor. But who else was in Joyce's store at the time of their disagreement?"

"I thought of that, too, but I didn't recognize anyone. But then why should I? Our bookstores attract a different clientele. I didn't even see Joyce's assistant, Lauren. It was too early for her lunch break, but she might have been running an errand or getting stock from the storeroom. Joyce's customers are voracious readers and her shelves empty incredibly fast."

"Would that that would happen to us," Angelica lamented.

"A bus came through this morning and Pixie said we did well." Tricia frowned and took a bigger slug of her drink. She used to keep a mental tally of the day's sales, which wasn't as easy to do now that Pixie often closed the shop.

Angelica set down her drink, picked up the large, shiny pot on the counter, and filled it with water. "What are we going to do now that we don't have a salad?"

"Pasta is enough for me. Do you have any Italian bread?"

"Of course. I got it fresh from the—"

There was only one place to get fresh-baked bread in the village: the Patisserie. Nikki didn't seem to hold a grudge against Angelica, who still regularly patronized the bakery. That was all right. There were several wonderful bakeries in Milford, just a few miles up the road, and they were only too happy to sell their wares to Tricia.

"The loaf isn't tainted," Angelica assured her sister.

Tricia wasn't going to be a pill about eating it, either. But she didn't have to enjoy it.

"I guess what I should have said is, are *you* okay? I mean, it is upsetting to find a body."

"I'm okay," Tricia assured her sister, although it was partly the nearly finished martini that was doing the talking for her. "Let's change the subject, okay?"

"Name it," Angelica said.

Tricia thought about the flyer that was still in her pocket. "I'm considering entering the Great Booktown Bake-Off," she said offhandedly.

"Really?" Angelica said, her tone tinged with incredulity.

"You know I've practiced my baking skills throughout the winter. My customers certainly haven't been complaining about the quality of the cookies and cupcakes I've provided in the store these past few months."

"Yes, Grace mentioned that she's gained at least five pounds because Mr. E keeps bringing home your goodies."

"Perfect proof. If they're eating my efforts, then they can't be horrible."

"No," Angelica agreed. "And I've eaten your muffins, cakes, and cookies, too. You're much improved."

Tricia knew that was as close to a compliment as she was likely to get from her sister.

"Um, just what recipe were you thinking of making?" Angelica asked, her tone light.

Tricia looked at her sister shrewdly. "Oh, no. You just want to know so that you can one-up me."

Angelica batted her lashes innocently. *"Moi?"*

"Oui, vous."

Angelica shook her head. "I think we both know who's going to win the contest."

"You?"

"Of course—in the amateur division. I've been baking since I was seven. You've been baking less than a year."

"I can follow a recipe," Tricia assured her.

"Yes, darling, but I *create* them. I know the chemistry of baking. I could bore you to tears on the subject of leavening agents alone," she said, and checked to see if the pasta water was boiling.

That was probably true, but Tricia wasn't going to admit it to anyone, least of all Angelica.

"You'd better get the paperwork in first thing in the morning, then," Angelica said. "The contest registration closes at eleven."

"I'll get it done," Tricia said.

"Then it seems we're competitors."

"It isn't the first time," Tricia said, remembering Angelica's power serves from when they had taken tennis lessons together as children. Being five years older, Angelica had never taken their age difference into consideration when she'd obliterated her sister during practice.

"What charity are you representing?" Tricia asked.

"It was a tough choice, but I decided to go with the White Mountain Farm Sanctuary."

"Why?"

Angelica shrugged. "I figured that horses, goats, and chickens could use as much love as cats and dogs, and not many people think about supporting them. Cats and dogs come first in most people's hearts."

"Says the dog owner." Sarge seemed to know he was being mentioned, for he hopped out of his bed and trotted over to sit in front of Tricia, looking hopeful.

"You've had enough treats," Angelica admonished him.

Sarge's tail stopped wagging.

Tricia continued. "You're right. I thought I'd go with Pets-A-Plenty. Maybe I should rethink that choice."

"It won't matter because you're *not* going to win."

"I might."

"Pullleeese," Angelica said with disdain. But then her demeanor immediately changed.

Tricia didn't take her sister's insult personally. "I guess that depends on how many people I can get to sponsor me."

"You've left it late, dear. The rest of us have been signing up sponsors for weeks."

Tricia hadn't thought about that when she'd delayed entering the Bake-Off. Depending on where one landed in the competition, the sponsor would pay a dollar. Tricia had no idea how many contestants had entered.

"Did you know that Chef Larry Andrews from the Good Food Channel is one of the judges?" Angelica asked.

"I saw that on the flyer."

Angelica seemed to be waiting for a better response.

"So?" Tricia obliged.

"I met Larry on the Authors at Sea cruise on the *Celtic Lady*."

"And?"

"Well, of course he's going to remember me."

"And is that supposed to give you an edge over the rest of us?"

Angelica shrugged. "It's a possibility."

Considering how many people on the cruise had fawned over the celebrity chef, it was doubtful he'd remember one of the cruisers, but Tricia decided not to mention that to her delusional sister. Instead, she said, "You haven't mentioned setting up a signing for the great chef. I suppose he does have a couple of cookbooks out."

Angelica's mouth dropped in horror. "Good grief! I've been so busy with getting ready to open the day spa, I forgot all about it!"

"There really isn't time to set one up at this late date."

"Says you! First thing tomorrow, I'll have June see what she can do to make it happen."

"Has she ever set up a signing before?"

"No, but this will be a good chance for her to learn." Angelica shook her head. "I could kick myself for not thinking about this sooner."

"Do you really have time to devote to the Bake-Off when you're about to open a new business?"

"I admit, the timing is tight, and since I'm opening my day spa under my own name, instead of Nigela Ricita Associates, it's proven more difficult than I expected. I don't have the same human resources at my command. But I perform well under pressure. I do wish you'd show more interest in the enterprise."

"I want to see it when it's finished. I mean, transforming that ugly cement-block building into a glamorous spa is truly a feat. I know how nice the outside of the building looks—I want to be surprised by the inside's transformation, too."

The truth was, Tricia hadn't wanted to enter the building formerly owned by the man who'd killed her ex-husband. She had too many memories of her encounters with Bob Kelly in that building. She knew once Angelica was finished with the renovations it would bear absolutely no resemblance to the former Kelly Realty. With the old sign gone, there were fewer and fewer triggers to remind her of that part of her past.

"You still haven't told me the name of your salon."

"Day spa," Angelica insisted. "It's going to be much more than a hair and nail salon. And the name is a surprise."

"Why?"

"Because that's more fun!" She flashed her perfectly manicured nails, which were a dark plum in color. "I interviewed a manicurist today. Tomorrow, I've got another—who does pedicures, too. The two pedi chairs were delivered this afternoon."

"Did you test them out?"

"Of course!" Angelica practically squealed. "It's like a Jacuzzi for your tootsies."

Tricia had soaked in such a chair but didn't feel the need to remind her sister of it. Instead, she changed the subject.

"What kind of pasta are we having?"

"Farfalle with pesto sauce."

"Is the basil from your balcony pots?"

Angelica practically had an herb farm on her new balcony. She'd built one more than twice the size of Tricia's so that she could entertain their little makeshift family during their summer Sunday dinners.

"Yes."

"We should go out there and sit with our drinks some evening."

"That's not a bad idea. We'll do it tomorrow."

"Sounds good to me." Tricia turned her gaze to the sliding glass doors of Angelica's balcony. "Joyce suggested I hang window boxes on my balcony rail so that I can grow herbs."

"It's not too late in the season. You could also get a few tomato plants in pots. Cherry, grape, or Juliet tomatoes are small and tasty."

"I'll have to look into it," Tricia said, and looked down at her empty glass. "Another?"

"Of course," Angelica said, and poured.

This time, they did raise their glasses but said nothing in the way of a toast. Tricia gave a little shudder as she remembered the sight of Vera Olson lying dead with that pitchfork through her middle. Whoever had killed her must have been very, very angry.

* * *

Twilight was falling and the Dog-Eared Page was crowded when Tricia entered through its front door. She looked around and saw Marshall standing at the bar. He raised a hand to wave to her, giving her one of his widest smiles, and something inside her tingled. If they were only friends with benefits, why did she often feel a thrill of excitement when she saw him? That the thrill didn't last for more than an hour or two said something, but that didn't mean it wasn't real.

They walked toward each other and met on the open floor; he gave her a quick kiss on the lips and then clasped her hand and led her to one of the open booths on the side of the room, where they sat opposite each other. "Didn't you get a drink?" she asked, looking around the room, but nobody seemed to be focused on them.

"I was waiting for you."

"I hope you haven't been here long."

"Maybe five minutes. But I'd be willing to wait a lot longer if I had to."

Tricia couldn't help but smile, but Marshall's expression sobered. "I heard about what happened earlier today. I'm guessing you could use a good stiff drink."

"Oh, believe me, I've already had two."

"Angelica does take good care of you. Was it too bad?"

"A little gruesome. It's not every day you see someone with a pitchfork through them."

Marshall winced. "Sorry about that."

"I'm sure Vera Olson was even sorrier."

"I don't suppose you want to talk about it."

"Not now, and especially not here. I need a little time." He nodded, but she also knew that he knew that she had already discussed it in detail with her sister. True-crime buff that he was, Marshall would just have to be patient if he wanted to hear the same story.

"I don't suppose you knew Vera?" she asked.

"As a matter of fact, I met her just a few days ago. She came into my shop looking for a book on whale watching in New England's waters. I asked if she was going on vacation and she told me to mind my damn business."

Tricia couldn't help but feel amused. "Good old Vera, spreading joy wherever she went."

"Not on that day," Marshall said.

Bev the waitress arrived at their table. "What can I get you two? The usual?"

Marshall adopted his best English accent. "Of course, dearest Bev, and some crisps for dear Tricia, too, please. Pip-pip, cheerio, and all that rot."

Bev giggled. "You crack me up, Marshall."

"It's my way with women, darling."

Again, Bev giggled. "If I was only ten years younger."

Tricia made as though to get up from her seat. "Would you two like to be alone?"

"We'll have to meet in secret some other time," Marshall told Bev, and waggled his eyebrows.

Bev blushed and looked away. "I'll go get your drinks."

Marshall rested an elbow on the table, his chin on his cupped hand, and gazed into Tricia's eyes, giving her one of his enigmatic smiles. "Let's get drunk and go back to my place and fool around."

She didn't give him the satisfaction of a smile but simply said, "I thought that was a given."

"Before we do, what would you like to talk about?" Marshall asked.

"Something innocuous."

"Like what?"

"Like tomorrow I'm going to enter the Great Booktown Bake-Off."

"Really?" Marshall asked, although he didn't sound at all surprised.

"Pixie thinks I can win."

"And can you?"

"I'd sure like to try. Being a runner-up wouldn't hurt. I'd like to give Angelica a run for her money. She seems to think she *will* win the amateur prize."

"And just what is the prize?"

"I have no idea—at least when it comes to the amateur division. The winner of the professional division gets a shot on celebrity chef Larry Andrews's TV show."

"Who do you think will win that?"

"I'd be happy for any of the contestants." But that wasn't exactly true. Nikki Brimfield-Smith and Tricia were no longer friends, although it wasn't by Tricia's choice. The woman was a skilled French-trained pastry chef. She was also younger than Tricia by at least a decade and very pretty, just the kind of person who would positively glow under hot klieg lights. She might even be ruthless enough to scheme her way into a TV show of her own—should she win, of course.

"Did I mention I was one of the sponsors of the amateur division?" Marshall said.

Tricia raised an eyebrow. "No."

"I'm rather surprised you didn't step up to the plate," he said.

"I don't think it would look good if one of the contestants offered to help underwrite the event."

"Then it sounds like you've been contemplating entering all along."

Tricia frowned. "Well . . . maybe."

Marshall shook his head. "Then why wait 'til the last minute to sign up?"

Tricia shrugged. "I guess I've been preoccupied. I've got a lot going on," she lied. The truth was she had far too little going on, which was good in one way. It would give her more time to prepare for the competition.

"What does your sponsorship entail?" she asked.

"Giving the Booktown Ladies Charitable Society a big fat check to defray costs."

"Such as?"

"I'm not sure. Maybe flyers, posters, postage—stuff like that. They're supposed to plug my shop in return."

"Would you personally consider sponsoring me in the contest?"

"How much is this going to cost me?"

"I don't know how many contestants there are. It could be ten or twenty dollars."

"And I can write this off?"

"Of course."

"Okay, I'll be your sponsor."

Tricia gave him what she hoped was a warm smile. "Thanks."

Bev arrived with their drinks, setting them down on white paper cocktail napkins. "I'll be right back with your crisps," she said, and giggled again.

They watched her go; then Marshall raised his glass. "To your success in the Great Bake-Off."

Tricia raised her glass, too. "Thank you." To best Angelica, she was going to need all the luck and good wishes she could get.

FOUR

Sometimes you're just not in the mood. And after Tricia had arrived at Marshall's apartment in the building that also housed his bookshop and travel sundries business, the Armchair Tourist, she realized that, after the day she'd had, making love was the last thing on her mind. But she also knew that despite her previous assertion, maybe what she really needed to do *was* talk about Vera Olson's death. Since Marshall was a true-crime fan, he was probably the best sounding board she'd get—besides Angelica, of course.

Marshall poured hot water into two cups and stirred until the cocoa powder had completely dissolved. "Are you sure you want to have cocoa after a martini?"

Tricia nodded. "It's a comfort thing. My grandmother used to make me cocoa when I was upset. Have you got any cookies?"

"Fig bars."

"I haven't had one since . . ." Had Tricia *ever* had a fig bar?

Marshall retrieved an already opened package and set several of the cookies on a plate. "Let's go sit in the living room." He picked up one of the cups and the plate and led the way. Tricia grabbed her cup and followed.

They sat in adjacent chairs, and Tricia kicked off her shoes, drawing her legs onto the seat. Marshall pushed the plate toward her and she picked up one of the bars, taking a sniff. "Oh, my, it almost smells like perfume." She inhaled deeply. Absolutely intoxicating.

"I heard a little about the situation. That there was an argument between the dead woman and Joyce Widman earlier in the day."

"Yes. And I was there."

He nodded. "Now, what is it about Vera Olson's death that's got you spooked?" he asked.

"Besides seeing the woman with a pitchfork in her belly?"

"You've seen worse."

Unfortunately, he was right, but she also knew that he wasn't being callous about her reaction.

"There was very little blood."

"So she was already dead before she was run through."

Tricia nodded. "The grass was pretty much undisturbed, which had to mean that she wasn't dragged to the spot where she was dumped."

"Were there any other signs of trauma on the body?" Marshall asked, and picked up his cup.

"Possible bruises on her neck."

"So strangulation?"

Tricia nodded.

"Did she and the woman who owned the house have a recurring problem?" he asked.

Tricia nodded. "Joyce and I really didn't talk much about Vera before we went into her backyard. After seeing the tree, I can understand why the woman was upset. The people who cut it really butchered it. But it's odd. During their hot discussion this morning at Joyce's shop, it sounded like Vera would have been okay with the limb coming down if it had happened under other circumstances," she said, and took a bite of her cookie, surprised by the crunch of seeds but not put off by the texture.

"What do you mean?"

Tricia chewed and swallowed. "Vera said to Joyce, 'I specifically asked you to wait.' Wait for what?"

"Why did Joyce have the limb cut today of all days?"

"She wanted her vegetable garden to get full sunlight and the tree gave too much shade. The limb they took down had to be eighteen inches or more in diameter, and it must have hung pretty low, too."

"Then it could've been an obstacle for whoever had to cut the grass—Joyce or someone she hired."

"It was probably Joyce. She has a shed full of gardening tools. It was her pitchfork that was run through Vera. Her vegetable patch took out quite a swath in the middle of the yard."

Marshall nodded and grabbed a cookie for himself. Tricia caught him studying her, his expression enigmatic. "What?"

He shrugged. "I can tell by the set of your mouth that something else is bothering you. What is it?"

"I don't know. I'm pretty sure I saw something in that yard that was of significance, but I don't know what it could be."

"Don't try to think about it. That way, it might come to you when you least expect it."

Tricia sipped her cocoa and nodded. Then yawned.

"It looks like someone needs to crash."

"It's been a long day," Tricia admitted.

"Come to bed with me. I'll hold you all night—make you feel safe."

"No, you won't. You'll hold me until you nod off, and then you'll roll over and I'll be on my own."

"Really?"

"That's the way it usually works," she said mildly.

"Are you sure?"

She nodded.

He looked chagrined. "Well, at least I don't snore."

"That you know of," she said pointedly.

Marshall scowled but then seemed to realize she was teasing him. "Can I at least walk you home?"

"That I would enjoy. And if you don't mind, maybe you could even hold my hand."

He gave her another of those thrill-inducing smiles, which almost made her change her mind. "I wouldn't mind in the least."

Not only had Marshall walked Tricia to the door of her store, but he'd also given her a pleasant kiss that promised more at a future date. She saw that he waited until she switched off the last of the lights before he started for home and had been grateful for his patient company.

Still, it wasn't at all surprising that Tricia didn't sleep well that night. Restless dreams with frightening themes caused her to wake up several times and were frustrating because, while she couldn't remember them, she'd been terribly upset, which was silly. She knew the genesis of those nightmares—Vera Olson's death.

She'd finally fallen back to sleep around five and hadn't awoken until nearly eight. After coffee, and a light breakfast for her and her cat, she was ready for her daily exercise. That day she chose to take a walk around the village, without Angelica's dog, Sarge.

She left Haven't Got a Clue, locked the door, and headed north.

The Patisserie was already open and was crowded with customers, with Nikki herself behind the counter bagging bagels, scones, and doughnuts. Tricia bypassed the shop but soon stopped when she saw the lights were on in Joyce Widman's Have a Heart bookstore. Joyce stood behind the cash desk looking like she hadn't slept much the previous night, either.

Although the sign on the window said CLOSED, Tricia knocked on the jamb to get Joyce's attention. Joyce got off of her stool and came around the desk to open the door.

"My, you're at work early today," Tricia said.

Joyce sighed. "Right now, home is not my favorite place. I can't bear to look out the back window to see my garden."

"I'm so sorry you're going through this," Tricia said.

Joyce merely shrugged.

"When I saw the lights on, I thought I'd ask how you're doing."

"Not well," Joyce admitted, which was evident by the weariness in her voice.

"If you'd like someone to talk to . . ." Tricia left the sentence hanging.

"Actually, I would."

"Our stores don't open for at least another hour. Why don't you come over to my place for coffee."

Joyce looked around her empty shop. "Actually, I would like to escape to somewhere quiet."

"Then let's go. I've got an almost bottomless coffeepot."

"You've got a deal," Joyce said, relief coloring her tone. She turned off the lights, then locked the store, and the two women walked briskly toward Haven't Got a Clue.

Once they'd reached the apartment, Joyce settled on one of the stools at the kitchen island while Tricia made a fresh pot of coffee. "Thanks for inviting me. I couldn't muster the energy to make anything for breakfast this morning."

Tricia hit the switch on the maker and took out a couple of pretty floral bone china mugs she'd received as a housewarming gift from her former assistant and now niece-in-law, Ginny Wilson-Barbero. She set one in front of Joyce and pushed the tray of cream and sugar closer to her. "Sorry I don't have muffins, but I've got some snickerdoodles. It's my grandmother's recipe."

"That sounds great. Did you make them yourself?"

Tricia nodded. "I've been doing a lot of baking lately."

"Did you sign up for the Bake-Off?"

"It's on my list of things to do this morning. How about you?"

"I signed up, but now I'm not sure I want to compete. I mean, it would just draw more attention to me and what happened to Vera."

That wasn't a subject they needed to harp on—that is, unless Joyce wanted to talk about it.

Joyce sighed. "Thanks for sending Roger Livingston to the station last evening. I don't think I needed him, but it felt good to have someone with me who was on my side."

"I'm sorry. I should have gone with you."

Joyce shook her head. "I don't think Chief Baker would have appreciated it. He sure likes to ask the same questions over and over again. It was almost as though he was trying to trip me up."

"That's exactly what he was doing," Tricia said.

"I'm sure he'll be hounding me in the days to come—but I sure would like to put this behind me. As it is, I'm not sure I ever want to go in my backyard again."

It was time for Tricia to steer the conversation to another subject, but then she found she didn't need to, as Joyce started another topic.

"When I think of how my life has changed these past few years, I have to say that—except for yesterday—I don't have any regrets."

Tricia's main regret was that Christopher had been murdered, but there wasn't anything she could have done to change that—or how she still felt about the loss.

"I was one of the first booksellers to answer the ad to relocate to Stoneham," Joyce recalled.

Tricia had heard the story before, but she wasn't about to interrupt Joyce, who seemed to need to talk. "That had to be a big leap of faith for you."

"Yes. Especially since I'd only been in business for a year and was fresh off a divorce," Joyce admitted. "But I was looking for a new start. And for the most part, I've been very happy here in Stoneham—at least professionally."

"And what part of your life wasn't so happy?" Tricia asked.

"Being Vera's neighbor."

Tricia wasn't sure if they should return to that subject, but then Joyce continued.

"You saw that gate in my side yard that opens to Vera's property. It was there when I bought the house. I just assumed that Frannie and Vera—or maybe even whoever lived there before Frannie—had been good friends. But the truth was it made me feel uncomfortable. Especially when I caught Vera in my yard pinching my herbs last month."

"She stole them?" Tricia asked, surprised.

Joyce nodded. "It took me a little while to catch on. I set up a stakeout and caught Vera in the act just after dawn. That very day, I visited the hardware store in Milford and bought a couple of bolts to seal the door between our properties. Vera never apologized, and since then she's been downright hostile toward me and tried to make my living there as unpleasant as possible."

"That's terrible," Tricia said. "Did she have problems with other neighbors?"

"Of course, but she turned her wrath against me, trying to turn everyone on the street against me."

"And how has that gone?"

Joyce managed a small smile. "Thankfully, not all that well." She broke a piece off of her cookie and ate it. "Wow, these are good."

"Thanks. They were one of Angelica's favorites when we were growing up." Tricia's mother had discouraged her from eating sweets, but she had recently learned just how much she savored the taste.

They discussed the upcoming Bake-Off, but Tricia's mind kept wandering back to something Joyce had said about the bolt on the gate in her yard. If it had been bolted on Joyce's side of the barrier, and the gate to the front yard had been locked, too, how had Vera gotten into the yard in the first place?

FIVE

By the time Joyce left Tricia's place, it was already past ten o'clock. Tricia didn't bother loading the dishes in the dishwasher but set them in the sink, then grabbed her purse and cell phone and hurried down the stairs. Pixie was helping a customer and Mr. Everett was hard at work dusting the bookshelves with his beloved lamb's wool duster, while Miss Marple sat nearby and attentively admired his work.

"Sorry, but I've got to run," Tricia said. "The deadline for registering for the Bake-Off is in less than an hour."

"Hop to it, then," Pixie said. "We'll hold the fort."

Tricia dashed out the door and headed up the street toward the municipal parking lot. She had to get to the Chamber of Commerce office before eleven if she was going to be a part of the competition. The Chamber was not sponsoring the Bake-Off, but it was handling the registration for the Booktown Ladies Charitable Society. Of course, the last person Tricia wanted to see was the man who had beaten her for the Chamber presidency the previous fall.

She and Russ Smith had a history that wasn't made of fond memories. She and the owner of the village's small-time newspaper, the *Stoneham Weekly News*, had been lovers for a short time, but then he had dumped her when he thought he was about to be hired by the *Philadelphia Inquirer*. When that didn't happen, he decided he wanted her back—and she wanted nothing to do with him. That's when he'd stalked her. Eventually, he'd courted and married Nikki Brimfield, who'd previously been very friendly toward Tricia—until she'd developed an unhealthy and unwarranted jealousy of her. After two years—and one child—the couple had parted, and Russ and Nikki were in the process of divorcing, but that hadn't tempered Nikki's animosity toward Tricia—and Russ's blatant campaign against her for the Chamber presidency hadn't endeared him to her, either.

Russ had certainly put his stamp on the Stoneham Chamber of Commerce in the months since he'd become its leader—by doing everything he could to dismantle the improvements Angelica had made during her two-year tenure. He'd moved the Chamber from a lovely office in a brand-new building on Main Street to a much cheaper location in what was essentially a run-down warehouse. He'd slashed the budget for the flowers that had decorated the village streets and put them right out of the running for Prettiest Village in New Hampshire. He'd also fired the Chamber's receptionist and had been making do with temporary office help ever since. The problem was he made the job so uncomfortable for the temp workers that they tended to last a few weeks—and often only days—before quitting in disgust.

Tricia only hoped that Russ was minding the shop for his crappy little fish wrapper and that she wouldn't run into him at the Chamber office.

Unfortunately, that wasn't the case.

Tricia parked her car in the warehouse's dirt lot and got out. She opened the big steel door that was the front entrance to the new Chamber office and immediately saw her foe standing over the desk of the harried-looking young woman with blonde hair and a streak of blue that cascaded down the left side of her head. She sat in front of a tiny computer screen. What had happened to the state-of-the-art equipment that had been available to the former receptionist? Had Russ sold it on Craigslist to the highest bidder and replaced it with a crappy laptop several computer generations older?

"What do you want?" Russ growled, his voice full of venom.

"Excuse me, but I'm a longtime member of the Chamber and I'm here to sign up for the upcoming Bake-Off."

"Well, then do it and get the hell out of here," he groused and then turned back toward the horrible little office that had been partially walled off with bare plywood just steps away from the receptionist's desk. He made a point of slamming the unfinished hollow-core door.

Tricia said nothing.

The young woman at the receptionist's desk looked over her shoulder to the office behind and seemed to shiver. "Sorry about that," she apologized sincerely. "Mr. Smith is . . ." But then she didn't seem to have a reasonable explanation for her boss's rudeness.

"Don't worry about it," Tricia said. "As I said, I'm here to sign up for the Bake-Off."

The young woman smiled. "This is like something out of the Good Food Channel. I hear it may even be televised on local cable. I can't wait to see what happens—and who will win."

Tricia smiled. "Well, I can't lie. I hope it will be me. How are things going?"

The young woman looked around, as though someone might be listening. "You didn't hear it from me, but there aren't as many applicants as everyone thought there'd be. A lot less than the Booktown Ladies Charitable Society figured. It's too bad only one person can win in either division."

"Then it's kind of like the Olympics."

"Oh, yeah?"

"Someone is going to feel the thrill of victory—while the others experience the agony of defeat," Tricia sort-of quoted.

"Wow. That is *so* profound," the young woman spouted, looking awed.

Ah, to be so young, Tricia thought.

"Please, I need to sign the paperwork right now—before the deadline."

"Of course," the young woman said, and shuffled through her desk to come up with the appropriate forms.

"What's your charity?"

"Is anyone doing it for Pets-A-Plenty?"

"Three, actually."

"Is it okay for me to sign up for the same one?"

"Oh, sure. That just means they've got a better shot at raking in the most dough."

It took only a couple of minutes for Tricia to fill in the paperwork. The receptionist stamped it and then filled in the time: ten forty-five. Tricia had made the deadline by a full fifteen minutes.

"Congratulations. And I hope you win," said the young woman, handing Tricia a copy of the rules and her sponsor sheet.

"Thank you. Will you be attending the competition?"

The young woman's expression said, *Are you kidding?* and Tricia wished she hadn't asked.

"Uh, no. And I'm going to ask the temp agency not to send me back here. It's not a fun place to work," she said, and again eyed the closed door behind her desk.

Tricia nodded. She couldn't blame the woman. "Thanks for helping me sign up."

"You're welcome. And I'll make sure nothing happens to your forms before the auxiliary ladies come to pick them up," she promised.

Would Russ be petty enough to sabotage Tricia's chance of competing?

It was entirely possible.

"I appreciate that," she said sincerely. After Russ's not-so-warm welcome, she didn't want to contemplate just what he might have been tempted to do with them.

Just then, the door to the office opened and a silver-haired woman with pink cheeks and a face filled with wrinkles born of years of smiles entered. "Hello," she called brightly, and walked up to the desk. Tricia backed away and was about to leave but paused when the woman introduced herself. "I'm Adelaide Newberry, head of the Booktown Ladies Charitable Society. What happened to Belinda?"

"Uh, I'm afraid she left the Chamber," the young woman said. "But I can help you. I assume you've come to pick up the entries for the Bake-Off."

"I certainly have. Oh, dear. It looks like I'm a few minutes early. I just power walked all the way from Oak Street—great for the old ticker," she said, and chuckled.

Tricia stepped forward. "Hello, I'm Tricia Miles. I own the vintage mystery store here in the village—Haven't Got a Clue."

"I've never been there. Very busy with my charity work—so much to be done in this big cruel world. I don't even own a television set so I won't be distracted from my efforts."

"That's very noble of you," Tricia said.

"Well, somebody's got to do it," Adelaide said, and gave a theatrical sigh.

Tricia wasn't sure if the woman was putting her on. "Um, I guess I'm the last entrant in the contest."

"That's splendid, splendid. Happy to meet you," the older woman said, and offered her hand. "I'll be the third judge in the competition. It's going to be *so* much fun!"

"Are you a chef?"

"Oh, goodness no. But I can tell a good cupcake when I taste it. In fact, some of our members have lost their sense of taste because of the medications they take. Me, I don't take any. That's the benefit of regular exercise. That and a glass of red wine every night with dinner, but don't tell my doctor that. *He* thinks he's been keeping me fit for years. It would hurt his ego to know I've been taking care of myself *by* myself."

Tricia smiled. She liked Adelaide Newberry. "It was very nice to have met you. I guess we'll see each other at the competition next week."

"Best of luck," Adelaide said, then seemed to catch herself. "Oops. Maybe I shouldn't say that. Others might think I have a bias."

Tricia's grin widened. "I doubt it. Until next week."

"Good-bye, dear," Adelaide called, and waved as Tricia left the makeshift office.

She started toward her car and decided—*what the heck*—and began to swing her arms. If power walking was good enough for Adelaide, it was good enough for her, too.

It was almost eleven when Tricia returned to Haven't Got a Clue. Once again Pixie had everything in hand and was waiting on a customer, while Mr. Everett helped two more people select books in a new-to-them series. Once again, Tricia knew he didn't need her help, so she climbed the stairs to her apartment to go through a couple of cookbooks. It was then she realized that she had an appointment for later in the afternoon that she needed to keep, and in fact, it would conflict with her lunch with Angelica. Pulling out her cell phone, she texted her sister and asked if they could meet an hour earlier than usual.

Okay with me, came the reply.

Tricia bent down to inspect her kitchen bookshelf, which was filled with cookbooks. Angelica had picked out most of them for her, and she'd shared a few vintage ones she'd purchased when inspecting collections as possible stock for her own store.

Tricia chose one of the newer tomes and began flipping through the pages of one that featured nothing but baked goods. The Bake-Off entry forms had made it clear that the ladies' charity had decided that all contestants would make cupcakes for the contest. That was fine with her, and it gave everyone a level playing field.

As she paged through the beautifully photographed luscious desserts with their accompanying recipes, Tricia wondered if she should try something exotic or play to her strength, which employed the KISS principle: Keep it simple, stupid. Of course, Angelica would work hard to impress the judges, especially Larry Andrews. So, she thought she had an in with the chef. Tricia was pretty sure not only would he not remember her, but if he did, he might disqualify her. A judge with any integrity would do so.

Tricia became so engrossed in her task that she almost forgot about lunch. When she finally looked at the clock on her kitchen wall, she saw that it was only five minutes to one, closed the book, and rushed out of her apartment.

Upon entering Booked for Lunch, which was filled with a crowd of chatty customers downing sandwiches and wraps, pop and iced tea, Tricia found her sister at her usual back table. Like Tricia, she, too, had been perusing a cookbook. In fact, she was flipping through a book by an author called the Cake Boss.

Tricia scooted into her side of the booth, but Angelica didn't even bother to look up. "Did you sign up in time?"

"Just," Tricia admitted. "And if he'd had his way, Russ wouldn't have let me enter at all."

"What a spoilsport."

"The temp told me she would safeguard my entry until it could be picked up by the Booktown Ladies Charitable Society."

"Sounds like she's too good to last long at the Chamber."

"From the sound of it, she didn't intend to return after today, either."

"Smart woman." It didn't do to talk too much about the changes at the Chamber since Angelica had retired from its presidency. In addition to undermining all Angelica's hard work, Russ had also squandered the goodwill of most of his constituents.

"Anyway, as I was about to leave, the head of the Booktown Ladies Charitable Society came in. Her name's Adelaide Newberry and she's a real character."

"In what way?"

Tricia described her meeting with the eccentric woman. "Have you ever heard of her?"

Angelica shook her head. "No." A devilish smile crossed her lips. "Do you know that some people consider *me* to be a character?"

"I can't imagine why," Tricia said drolly.

"Well, I have even better news. There's a chance Larry Andrews *might* do a signing at the Cookery."

"Even with this last-minute an invitation?"

"You were right. I should've been on this like a tick the minute I heard he was coming to town."

"I'll say."

"But I've now got Antonio working on it."

"Isn't that kind of a conflict of interest?"

"Why?"

"Because the Cookery is under the Angelica Miles umbrella, not"—Tricia lowered her voice—"Nigela Ricita Associates."

Angelica waved a hand in dismissal.

"I thought June was arranging it."

"She kept getting the runaround. They turned her down, so she just said thank you and hung up. I had to keep urging her to try again and finally just gave up. Antonio gets things done."

Tricia couldn't argue with that. "When would you hold the signing?"

"Whenever the chef can fit it into his schedule."

"How will you rally enough people to fill the store on such short notice?"

"All I have to do is put up an announcement on social media and there will be droves of women showing up on my doorstep, drooling for a signed book. I've got an emergency order in for copies of his last three books that should arrive by tomorrow morning. This could be quite the coup."

"You haven't had a signing in quite a while."

"I haven't had anybody signing-worthy show up in the area, either."

Molly, the older, buxom blonde waitress, finally arrived at the table. "What can I get you ladies?"

"The soup of the day is potato bacon," Angelica told Tricia.

"I'll have a cup of that."

"So will I." Angelica looked up at her sister. "Want to split a BLT?"

"Sounds good to me," Tricia agreed.

Molly nodded and turned to leave.

"So what's this appointment you have to go to this afternoon?" Angelica asked.

Tricia sighed. "Another fruitless discussion with the Pets-A-Plenty Animal Rescue."

"Oh, dear, you are not still chasing that impossible dream, are you? Can't you take the hint that you're not wanted?"

"I don't know why some of the members—or should I just say the director has decided to dislike me. I've never given him any reason to," Tricia said.

"If you ask me, he feels threatened because of your experience and knows that you would do an outstanding job and outshine them all."

"Now you're being facetious."

"Not at all. I speak the truth. Just remember, they are tiny fish in a small pond."

"And what am I?"

"A king salmon—or maybe just the queen." Angelica found her words funny and laughed.

Tricia was not amused.

Angelica closed the book and set it aside. "How are things at Haven't Got a Clue?"

"Just dandy," Tricia said, and managed not to roll her eyes. "If I never showed up for work again, I'm sure they'd never miss me."

Angelica scowled. "It sounds to me like someone's sulking."

"Not sulking, just feeling a little like a fifth wheel."

"There're still plenty of other things you could do to find fulfillment. Everybody keeps talking about opening a candy store. You even said so yourself that Stoneham really needs one."

"And what do I know about making candy?"

"You didn't know how to cook until you gave it a try. Like me, you would succeed at anything you attempted. If it's capital you need . . ."

"No, but thank you."

"I was only going to offer you an opportunity."

"I'll make my own opportunities," Tricia said firmly.

Angelica shrugged.

Molly arrived with a tray with two cups of soup and small plates with half a sandwich on each, along with a small mound of potato chips. "As you're the owner, I won't be charging you a plate fee for splitting your meal."

"How kind of you," Angelica said. They'd heard that line a little too often since Molly had been hired.

"Let me know if you need anything."

"Just water," Tricia said.

"Oh, sorry," she said, and backed off.

Tricia waited until Molly was out of earshot before speaking. "I miss Bev."

"You're not the only one, but Molly has more or less settled in. And, of course, you did see Bev last night on your date, didn't you?"

"Yes."

"And how *was* said date with Marshall?" Angelica asked, leaning forward.

"It wasn't a date."

"Did he pay for your drink?"

Tricia nodded.

"Then it was a date," Angelica asserted, and picked up her spoon. She sampled the soup and nodded with approval. "I suppose I shouldn't ask what happened after the social part of your evening."

"No, you shouldn't." The fact that they'd simply talked—and she'd revealed things to Marshall she hadn't told Angelica—gave Tricia another reason not to elaborate.

Angelica sighed. "I guess I'm just a little jealous. I'd like to find a Marshall of my own."

"You don't have time for a relationship."

"That's true." She shrugged. "Have you heard anything else about that Olson woman's death?" Angelica asked.

Tricia shook her head and reached for the pepper shaker. She sprinkled a layer on her soup and stirred before tasting it. It didn't disappoint. "Although I did speak to Joyce this morning."

"And?"

"She's upset—who wouldn't be? Having a death occur in your backyard has got to be earth-shattering."

"Someone died in your living room and you didn't move out."

That was true, but Tricia hadn't spent a lot of time in that room for a few weeks after that death, either.

"She'll recover," Angelica said, and took another spoonful of soup. "Are there any suspects?"

"I'm sure Grant would look to find someone other than Joyce. At least, I hope so for her sake. I really don't think she's capable of murder—especially over such a petty dispute."

"People have been killed for less," Angelica said, which was true enough.

"I wonder if I should—"

"Stay out of it," Angelica ordered.

"I was just going to ask a few questions."

"Stay out of it," Angelica said a little more forcefully. "You have more important things to do, like convince the animal rescue people to take you on."

"I thought you didn't approve of the way they've treated me."

"I don't, but if it keeps you from getting involved in situations that are none of your business, I will hope they finally come to their senses and welcome you aboard."

Tricia didn't have an opportunity to respond, as Molly finally returned with two water glasses garnished with lemon slices and set them on the table in front of them. "Drink up, ladies."

Angelica's smile was tight. "Thank you."

Tricia ate her lunch and listened as Angelica pondered tracking down Adelaide Newberry to find out when Chef Andrews would be arriving for the Bake-Off, and also wondered if her company, Nigela Ricita Associates, should offer to host a reception. Of course, since most of the village still had no clue that Angelica owned the business with her son, Antonio, there might not be a backlash. But Tricia found it hard to concentrate. Despite Angelica's warning, she had no intention of not asking whoever might be relevant about Vera Olson. It was too bad Vera's BFF and the village's former best source of gossip now languished in jail awaiting trial. There was only one other person who listened intently to gossip: Pixie.

There was only one problem. She listened, but she didn't usually repeat it.

SIX

The Pets-A-Plenty Animal Rescue was located on Mason Avenue in the next town over from Stoneham. They were fortunate to have a small facility that could accommodate a number of cats, dogs, rabbits, and ferrets, although many of their wards were in foster homes awaiting their forever families. Mr. Everett and his wife, Grace, had obtained their cats from the shelter, and their philanthropic foundation, funded by the proceeds from Mr. Everett's lottery win, had given the rescue's new building drive a generous donation after each adoption. They would need substantially more funds to build the proposed facility on a piece of land on the outskirts of town.

Tricia parked her car on the fringe of the small lot, which was nearly filled to capacity. The board consisted of seven members, and they'd been one member short since Brindle Mears had relocated to Winter Springs, Florida, after one too many New Hampshire winters. Tricia had been invited to sit in on their meetings as a tentative candidate until a permanent replacement could be found. She, too, had given generously to the rescue, which she thought might have given her an edge, but its president, Toby Kingston, had never warmed to Tricia and for some reason seemed to resent her. Tricia knew her reputation as the Stoneham Village Jinx had preceded her and wondered if that was the problem. There wasn't anything she could do to improve her standing on that account except to offer what she hoped were sound opinions and share the knowledge she'd gained when working for a big nonprofit years before in Manhattan.

As Tricia approached the squat cinder-block building, a woman emerged with a jaunty beagle on a leash. "Did you just adopt him?"

The woman looked Tricia over with what seemed like suspicion, but then she gave a faint smile. "Yes. He's on his way to his forever home."

Tricia bent down to let the dog sniff her hand before she petted it on the head. It looked at her with adoring eyes and seemed to be smiling. "I'm so happy for you, little guy. Have a happy life."

The woman gave a tug on the leash and walked away. Tricia watched as she coaxed the dog into the back of her car and closed the door. The woman hopped into the driver's side and drove away. *Another happy ending,* Tricia thought, and entered the building.

In recent months, Tricia had hoped she'd become a familiar face at the pet rescue. She said hello to several of the staff members as she headed for the conference room at the end of the hall. The door was shut, but Tricia knew she wasn't late. In fact, she had arrived several minutes before the meeting was due to start, and knocked on the door before she entered. The six members of the executive committee sat around the rectangular conference table with yellow pads of paper and water bottles before them. Most of them clutched pens that were poised to take notes.

"Oh, looks like the meeting started without me," Tricia said, disconcerted.

Bonnie Connor, who acted as the committee's secretary, looked up and over her half-glasses. "My goodness, Tricia, we thought you weren't coming this afternoon."

"Why would you think that?" she asked.

The gazes of all the members turned toward their leader. Toby Kingston frowned. "Someone left a message saying you weren't available."

Every muscle in Tricia's body tensed. "I don't know who that could've been—because it certainly wasn't me," she said, and took an empty seat at the table where there was no welcoming bottle of water. There had been no message, and by the looks on the faces of the others, they seemed to believe the same thing.

"What have I missed?" Tricia asked, struggling to keep her voice level.

"We were just going over the budget for July," Bonnie said.

"Which we finished," Kingston said. "We're ready to move on to the last item on our agenda."

"The last item?" Tricia asked, feeling confused. What time had they started the meeting?

Kingston didn't bother to comment and plunged ahead. "The date for the annual Mutt Strut is August fifth. I've allocated a hundred dollars for publicity and prizes."

"That's less than half of what we allotted last year," Rebecca Shore piped up.

"If we want that new building, we need to conserve funds," Kingston said. "However, if any one of you wants to chip in the additional money—or find the funds from other sources—we can revisit the topic."

"No one person should be making unilateral decisions. The whole board should be voting on these things," Myron Tinker said with umbrage.

"I was brought in to make the hard decisions," Kingston asserted, his expression hardening. Yes. He was the only paid member of the organization. The nonprofit depended on volunteers for the rest of its staff.

"I would be happy to make up the shortfall," Tricia said.

"Oh, Tricia," Bonnie said, "you've already been more than generous."

"My sister and her dog, Sarge, have taken part in the Mutt Strut for the last two years, and I know she and the rest of the participants would be disappointed if it was downsized."

"It's a significant source of revenue," Myron pointed out.

"If Tricia is willing to make up the shortfall, then there's no reason for further discussion," Kingston said. He looked at the clock on the wall. "Meeting adjourned at 2:10. Thanks for attending." He collected his things, stood, and then made for the door.

"Wait," Bonnie cried. "I have an additional topic we should address."

Kingston turned but made no effort to return to the table. "What is it?" he asked, sounding irritated.

"One of our most ardent volunteers passed away suddenly yesterday," Bonnie said. "I'm sure the funeral will be held before our next meeting. It would be nice if we sent flowers for the wake to show our appreciation for all her hard work on our behalf. We could take the money out of the miscellaneous fund."

"How much are we talking?" Kingston asked unsympathetically.

"Fifty or sixty dollars."

"Make it twenty-five," Kingston said, then opened the door and strode out of the conference room.

Bonnie frowned, obviously upset. "He never even asked who it was."

"Yes, who was it?" Rebecca asked.

"Vera Olson."

Tricia did a classic double take. "Vera Olson was a Pets-A-Plenty volunteer?" she managed, her mouth going dry.

Bonnie nodded. "Yes. She's been a part of the organization for more than a decade. Did you know her?"

"Uh . . . I met her just yesterday morning at one of the bookstores in Stoneham."

"Oh, dear. That must have been just before she passed." Bonnie leaned in and lowered her voice. "It appears she may have been murdered."

"Murdered?" Rebecca echoed, shocked.

Bonnie nodded. "It couldn't have been an accident."

No, Tricia thought, *it surely wasn't.*

"It seems her neighbor is under suspicion over some silly misunderstanding. At least, she's been named a person of interest," Bonnie added.

Tricia hadn't heard that, but she wasn't surprised.

Bonnie shook her head. "I can't imagine anyone not liking dear Vera."

After the performance Tricia had witnessed the day before, she certainly could.

"How did she die?" Carl Stover asked.

Bonnie lowered her voice even more. "Run through with a pitchfork."

"Why on earth would anyone have a pitchfork? That's a farm implement. Didn't Vera live in a little Cape Cod home in Stoneham?" Myron asked.

Bonnie nodded.

"Well, I think a twenty-five-dollar bouquet is going to look pretty chintzy," Phyllis Barnes said. She was the committee's treasurer and did the bookkeeping for the group. "I'm sure if we walk around the building we'll be able to collect at least another twenty dollars to get better flowers."

"I'm sure we could get that right here in this room," Carl put in, and reached for his wallet. He pulled out a ten. "Poor Vera. How will we ever replace her?"

"It seems she was well loved," Tricia said, hoping they'd tell her more about the dead woman.

"Oh, yes," Rebecca said, and shook her head. "She had allergies, so she couldn't have a pet of her own, but she was a devoted volunteer. She did a lot of clerical work for the organization."

"But if she was needed, she'd clean cages and would ferry the smaller animals to the Milford Animal Hospital, too. She often brought fresh catnip in for the cats," Bonnie added.

"Isn't it unusual for someone who's allergic to dog and cat dander to volunteer at an animal rescue?" Tricia asked.

"Vera was fine as long as she didn't actually touch them. And she loved them so—especially any beagles that came in for adoption, although she never said why—at least she never told me," Phyllis put in.

"Did she get along with everyone here?"

"Oh, yes," Rebecca answered quickly.

"Not quite," Phyllis contradicted her. Her gaze moved to the still-open door. "She wasn't fond of Toby."

"And who is?" Rebecca whispered conspiratorially.

This was the first time Tricia had heard any kind of dissent within the executive committee. It also showed that she and Vera had at least one thing in common. Tricia didn't like the man, either.

"Was there a reason Vera didn't like him?"

"She never verbalized it to me, but there seemed to be some kind of animosity between them the last time they spoke."

"And when was that?" Tricia asked.

"A week or two ago?" Bonnie asked, looking at Phyllis for confirmation.

"It may have been more. She was prickly for weeks."

"Did they argue?" Tricia asked.

"No, but they had a private conversation in Toby's office, and when Vera came out she was quite upset, but when I asked, she wouldn't say why. Toby can be a bit brusque."

A bit? Tricia begged to differ.

"I guess it doesn't matter now that she's dead," Carl said. "So who else is going to chip in for the flowers?"

The women reached for their handbags and Myron took out a money clip and extracted another ten from it, tossing it on the table. "Rest in peace, Vera."

Tricia opened her wallet, took out two fives, and then pulled out her checkbook to make good on her promise to help fund the Mutt Strut. So Vera was loved by most but only tolerated by Toby Kingston. Tricia liked to think that put them in the same camp here at the Pets-A-Plenty Animal Rescue.

One thing was sure: Tricia needed to find out a lot more about Vera Olson.

When Tricia returned to Haven't Got a Clue, she found things running smoothly . . . as usual. Pixie and Mr. Everett were helping customers, all of whom seemed to be sporting smiles and spending freely, which once again made Tricia feel like an insignificant cog in the bookstore's machinery. She gave a wave and then ventured down the steps to her basement office to work . . . or was it to brood? She had a lot to think about, and the one subject she wasn't willing to think about was her own business.

Settling into her office chair, Tricia kicked off her shoes and, using her toes, swiveled around in a lazy circle. Vera Olson had admirers among those at the Pets-A-Plenty Animal Rescue. Why would such a pet-loving person—and Tricia counted herself as such a woman—be such a witch when it came to being a neighbor?

Okay, Vera resented the fact that her good friend Frannie, who was also a cat lover, had been forcibly removed from society—but Frannie had committed more than one felony. Surely that had to have made an impression on Vera. Or did the woman feel that Frannie had gotten a raw deal? Was she willing to overlook the fact that, through her actions, Frannie had killed someone and attempted to snuff out another life, just because they both had a mutual love of animals? Or had there been more to their friendship than anyone else had observed?

Joyce had said that a number of her neighbors seemed to be on her side. Apparently, they weren't as in love with Vera as those at Pets-A-Plenty had been. What had Vera done to alienate them? Except for Toby Kingston, the rest of the Pets-A-Plenty executive committee had seemed genuinely sorry to hear of Vera's death.

No doubt about it, the woman was an enigma.

Tricia thought about the best way to find out more about the dead woman, which was to talk to the people who knew her. As she thought about it, Tricia knew what she needed was a goodwill ambassador. And the best candidate for that title weighed about eight pounds and usually sported a little blue bow attached to his collar. His name?

Sarge.

SEVEN

Angelica was not in residence when Tricia entered her sister's cookbook and gadgetry store, the Cookery. At least, that's what her new manager, June, said.

"I came to take Sarge for a walk."

June looked at her watch. "It is about time for him to go out, I suppose. It's been a couple of hours since Angelica was around to do it."

"That's why I'm here. We both need the exercise. I'll just go get him," Tricia said, as though for some reason June might have a reason to deny her access to the dog. She unlocked the door at the back of the shop and trundled up the steps to Angelica's apartment. As soon as Sarge heard footsteps, he began to bark, but he was ecstatic to see Tricia because he knew that she was good for either a couple of dog biscuits or the opportunity to take a walk—two of his favorite things in life.

As soon as Tricia reached for his leash, the dog jumped up and down in absolute ecstasy. Oh, if only life were that uncomplicated and rewarding for his human counterparts.

"Calm down!" Tricia ordered, but the little dog's joyful anticipation was positively palpable. "Yes, I'm glad to see you, too. And we are going to have the most amazing walk."

Sarge needed no further prodding. He stood before the door, his tongue hanging out, panting expectantly when Tricia scooped him up and took him down the stairs. "We'll be back soon," she told June, and took Sarge out back so that he could do his business before she steered him west toward Joyce's and Vera's neighborhood.

They started down the alley behind the main drag until they came to the walkway between the Patisserie and Joyce's Have a Heart bookstore, cutting through to Main Street. Tricia paused to look through the big display window, but it was Joyce's assistant, Lauren, who stood behind the counter waiting on a customer. Perhaps Joyce was holed up in her office. Tricia continued to the corner. When traffic allowed, she and Sarge headed west toward Pine Avenue.

Sarge knew the way. He and Tricia had traced the same trajectory literally hundreds of times. In fact, Tricia was sure she and Sarge had covered much more of Stoneham on foot than the dog had done with his actual owner. He was a delight to walk, for his first owner had trained him well. And, of course, Angelica insisted on wearing shoes known to damage one's Achilles tendons and were hardly walkworthy, so it wasn't a surprise that she and Sarge made far shorter inroads when it came to walking the streets of Stoneham.

Tricia knew that the majority of residents of Pine Avenue were retirees, so the odds were in her favor that she might encounter one or more of them on any given afternoon. So many of the residents were gardeners, often out weeding and watering, that there was a good possibility that some of them might speak to her. And because she and Sarge had become part of the scenery, she had at least a nodding acquaintance with quite a number of the street's residents.

As she turned onto Pine Avenue, Tricia was disappointed to see that there didn't appear to be anyone out tending their yards. Of course, it was afternoon and the people on the east side of the street wouldn't want to be outside with the summer sun beating down on them. Those on the west side would be in shadows. She crossed the road so that she would be closer to those who might be out, but it seemed as though in the future she might have to change tacks and take Sarge for a walk in the morning, before the heat of the day—when temperatures were better suited to taking care of lawns and gardens.

Her gaze strayed to Joyce's house. Unlike the day before, all the blinds were down and the drapes were drawn, giving the house a rather forlorn appearance. Next door, Vera's house looked as it had—curtains open and red begonias blooming, as though to look cheerful and welcoming for its owner, who had left the area in a body bag and wouldn't be returning.

Sarge tugged on the leash to remind Tricia that they were on a serious walk, not a casual stroll. She quickened her pace.

Up the street, a woman strode down her driveway, stopping in front of her mailbox. As Tricia approached, she could hear the sound of a dog barking and saw the head of some kind of terrier through the home's screen door. She'd spoken to the same woman after Carol Talbot's death but couldn't remember her name, but she was sure the woman would remember Sarge.

"Hello," Tricia called cheerfully.

The woman collected her mail and closed the box's door. "Hi." She bent down. "And hello, Sarge!" Nobody ever forgot Sarge. The woman let him sniff her hand, and then petted him. "It's been a while." Her own dog started barking furiously at his owner's betrayal.

"Oh, be quiet, Bruno!"

Why was it people with small dogs gave them such fierce names? Of course, Angelica hadn't named her dog. When she'd adopted the little guy, she'd kept the name Sarge's first owner had given him.

"Beautiful day. And this is such a quiet street. Not like Main Street, where I live," Tricia said, hoping it would be the perfect conversational opening.

"It wasn't quiet yesterday—not with all those cop cars and emergency vehicles."

"I heard what happened to Vera Olson," Tricia said, and sighed. No need to mention she'd helped find the dead woman. "I suppose the whole neighborhood will mourn her loss."

"Not exactly."

"Oh?"

"She was the neighborhood PITA."

"Pita?"

"Pain in the . . . rear end."

"Why was that?"

"She was an animal rights zealot. Mind you, I love animals. I've got Bruno, a cat, three goldfish, and I'm pet sitting my granddaughter's guinea pig while the family is on vacation. But Vera thought of herself as a member of the pet police. She berated dog owners who tied their dogs up—even if they were in the yard gardening and watching their pets, called the cops when she felt dogs barked too much—even if it was noon. She often captured cats in Havahart traps because she said they were killing the neighborhood songbirds."

"What did she do with the cats?" Tricia asked, horrified at Vera's actions and thankful her own cat was strictly an indoor pet.

"She would put up 'Lost cat' signs and take them to Pets-A-Plenty, but if no one claimed them after a week, they'd go up for adoption. I suppose Vera truly believed she was acting in the cats' best interests taking them away from careless owners."

Catching people's pets via a trap in itself was enough to make Vera the neighborhood bad guy.

Tricia looked back toward Vera's attractive house with its gardens and charming birdhouses and felt a pang of pity and regret for the woman. She obviously wanted to do the right thing by animals, both wild and tame, but she could have gone about it in a more judicious manner.

"Some people might say Vera deserved what she got," the woman continued, "but I'm nervous. There have been too many deaths on this street. We're putting the house up for sale as soon as we can get it ready."

"Where will you go?"

"Milford—or maybe Merrimack. Not too far, but away from here. I'm not leaving this part of the state and away from my grandbabies, but I don't want them coming to my house to visit anymore—not until we live somewhere safer."

Tricia nodded and felt bad that Stoneham had gained a reputation as the death capital of southern New Hampshire.

"That's too bad when there are other wonderful things about Stoneham, like the upcoming Bake-Off, the new day spa, and the Wine and Jazz Festival next month."

"That's for the tourists, and I can do without all of them." The woman bent down and petted Sarge's fluffy little head once more. "It was nice to see you again, Sarge." The dog's tail wagged so hard Tricia was afraid it might fly right off.

"It was nice speaking with you, too. Have a nice evening," Tricia said.

"You, too," the woman said, and started back up her driveway.

Tricia started down the street once more. Despite the fact that no one else was outside their home, she decided to carry on for another block so as not to cheat Sarge out of his walk, and ten minutes later they approached Stoneham's only traffic light. Sarge sat at the curb and he and Tricia waited for the signal to change. Once it did, they started across the street. Joyce must have seen them, for as they approached the other side of the street, she practically burst from the door to her shop.

"Tricia!"

"Hi, Joyce. What's up?"

"I was wondering if I could ask a favor of you."

"Sure, anything."

"Could you talk to Chief Baker on my behalf?"

Uh-oh.

"It seems he believes Vera's conversation with me yesterday morning drove me to snap. You witnessed it. Surely you can convince him that if anyone was angry enough to kill, it would have been Vera."

"Why do you think I'd have any influence over him?"

"Well, you *used* to go out with the guy. You still seem to be on friendly terms with him."

Friendly? Not so much. Civil? Of course.

"I'm not sure that would do any good. He isn't the one who makes a determination when it comes to listening to character witnesses. That's up to the district attorney."

Joyce's eyes widened in what Tricia could only interpret as fear. "But I've done nothing wrong. Just because I had an unbalanced neighbor doesn't mean I had a reason to kill her."

"I'm sure you'll be exonerated."

"Isn't DA Paul Anderson running for office again this fall? I've read enough romantic suspense novels to know what that can mean. He'll try to win a case—or at least push it as close to trial as possible—to assure his constituents he can put a suspect in jail."

"It won't come to that," Tricia said, trying to sound reassuring, but if she was honest with herself, she wasn't at all sure what Joyce feared might not come to fruition.

Tricia returned Sarge to Angelica's apartment, leaving him with a couple of dog biscuits and one of his favorite tug toys.

As she was leaving the Cookery, she ran into the Dexter twins, Stoneham's elderly identical sisters. That day, they were wearing matching cherry-striped shorts and shirts, white socks, and brown leather sandals, and clutching little red-and-white matching checked pocketbooks, with big red sunglasses settled on their noses, and red visors perched on their heads, punctuating their fluffy white coiffures.

"Tricia!" Muriel shrieked . . . or was it Midge? "We haven't seen you in ages!"

"Not since the cruise," her sister agreed.

"Hi, ladies. What have you been up to?"

"Well, after the Authors at Sea excursion, we decided to spend the rest of the winter in Florida."

"Clearwater. Love that Gulf Coast!" Midge said.

"Where we played . . ." They turned, grabbed each other's hands and squealed, "Golf!" and then laughed hysterically.

"We went to three comic book conventions, and then last summer, another two."

"There's one coming up in Vegas in a few weeks. We aren't going to miss that because"—and then the sisters chanted in unison—"what goes on in Vegas, stays in Vegas," and they laughed uproariously.

Once their giggles had subsided, Tricia asked, "What are you doing in the village today?"

"We came to see if Angelica is going to have a signing for Larry Andrews."

"I don't believe she has heard for sure if he can make it."

"Oh, that's too bad," Midge said. "We love watching him on TV—"

"Even in reruns," Muriel added, and sighed. "That man makes my heart flutter."

"Mine, too," Midge agreed.

"And we haven't got his latest cookbook, so we decided to buy a copy and try to get him to sign it for us."

"If not at the Cookery, then at the high school the day of the Bake-Off."

"We're his biggest fans," Midge put in.

"Do you ladies do a lot of cooking?" Tricia asked.

"Not a hope," Muriel said, and laughed. "But we're very good when it comes to calling for takeout."

"The best!" her sister agreed, and they both broke into giggles once again.

"I entered the amateur division of the Bake-Off just this morning," Tricia said.

"You did?" Midge asked, sounding shocked.

"But didn't you kill someone with your cooking last fall?"

"Oh, yes," Midge agreed. "We read about it in the *Stoneham Weekly News*."

Good old Russ had never run a follow-up to the story reporting on the real killer's identity and the fallout from the arrest.

"I did not kill anyone. A man had an allergic reaction to something that was added to one of my—"

"Poisoned mushrooms, wasn't it?"

"Mushroom, singular," Tricia stated, and sighed. It was best to keep any conversation with the sisters short. "Well, I don't want to hold you up."

"It was divine to see you again," Muriel said.

"Don't bake any poisoned cupcakes," Midge added.

Somehow Tricia managed to not only smile but not to throttle the old ladies. "Good-bye." She stepped aside to let the twins enter the Cookery but hesitated before entering her own store. She still had a few hours to kill before happy hour with Angelica but had no real work to do. Then again, there were always baking videos to watch on YouTube. . . . Yes, that's what she'd do.

The little bell over the door rang cheerfully as Tricia entered. Since there were no customers, Mr. Everett and Pixie sat in the reader's nook, with books open on their laps. They looked up as Tricia entered.

"Did you have a nice walk with Sarge?" Pixie asked.

"Yes. And I just ran into the Dexter twins outside the Cookery."

"That's always a joy," Pixie said sarcastically.

"And now I've got some work to do down in the office. Feel free to call me if you need me."

"Certainly," Mr. Everett said.

Tricia gave her employees a smile and, with her head held high, started for the stairs to her basement office. It wasn't until she started down the steps that her posture drooped.

Killing time. Well, it was better than killing people, and someone had killed Vera Olson. And despite her little trip around the dead woman's neighborhood, Tricia hadn't learned much that was new about the woman.

Except . . .

As Tricia settled in her chair in front of her computer she thought about what she'd seen when she'd looked at Vera's house. Something about that home was important. Now, if she could just figure out what that something was.

EIGHT

True to her word, Angelica led Tricia to the newly installed balcony when she arrived at Angelica's place for dinner that evening. At this time of day, the balcony, which overlooked the alley behind their stores, was bathed in shadows, and a light breeze caused the herbs in their colorful pots to sway.

The view wasn't as uninteresting as one might have assumed. A wooden fence that was in pretty good repair lined the east side of the alley for a good three blocks. Behind it, on the next street over, was a big stone church that dated back to Stoneham founder Hiram Stone's days. Its grounds took up the majority of the block behind Haven't Got a Clue and the Cookery and were carefully maintained by its ever-dwindling congregation.

Along with the sweating martini pitcher and glasses, Angelica had included a plate with a domed lid, under which was an assortment of crackers and what Tricia knew to be extra-sharp cheddar.

Tricia took one of the comfortable seats and stretched out her legs while Angelica poured their drinks.

"This is nice," Tricia declared, and closed her eyes in bliss. "I wish I had thought about making my balcony more entertainment-friendly."

"Well, your mistake led to my improved design," Angelica said. "Here."

Tricia opened her eyes and sat up straight, taking the glass. "Cheers."

They clinked glasses.

Today, Angelica's nails were a bright pink.

"Another manicure?" Tricia asked.

"I have to know the quality of the work of anyone I hire at the day spa."

"Still not going to tell me the name?"

"It'll be a surprise," Angelica said, and took a sip of her drink. "Besides hiring two nail techs, I've been interviewing people for the manager position, and I chose someone this afternoon. He starts tomorrow."

"He?"

"I'm an equal opportunity employer," Angelica said with conviction. "His name is Randy Ellison and he's been cutting hair for almost twenty years, has all sorts of managerial experience, and comes with excellent references."

"Why did he leave his last job?"

"His mother lives in Wilton and is in declining health, and he wants to be nearer to her."

"He sounds like a good son."

"Tomorrow morning we'll be interviewing stylists and drawing up a supply list. We're also going to have two chairs for freelancers. They might bring in nail and massage customers."

"You're hiring a masseuse?"

"But of course. And I intend to be her first customer."

Tricia sipped her martini. She should have expected anything Angelica undertook to be top-notch.

"Did anything interesting happen at your little meeting today?" Angelica asked.

Little meeting?

"You mean despite the fact that Toby Kingston pulled a fast one and changed the time without informing me?"

"That horrible man!"

"He also told the board he'd received a call that I couldn't make it."

"What is wrong with that man?"

Tricia shrugged. "I was there for the last ten minutes. I'll get a copy of the minutes via e-mail—unless old Toby told Bonnie Connor not to send them to me. Anyway, after they adjourned, I found out Vera Olson was a beloved volunteer at Pets-A-Plenty."

"Do tell."

"And that cheapskate Toby only allotted twenty-five bucks for flowers for her wake and/or funeral."

"Surely nothing's been scheduled yet."

"That may well be."

"Is that it?" Angelica asked.

"I took Sarge on a walk—"

"You mean a spy run," Angelica corrected.

Tricia ignored the remark. "And I spoke with one of Vera's neighbors. It seems Vera made a pest of herself. The woman intimated Vera acted like the neighborhood pet police, reporting on barking dogs and even catching cats that roamed the block—often putting them up for adoption at the shelter."

"But that's terrible."

"That was Vera. Anyway, as we were heading for home, Sarge and

I ran into Joyce outside her store. Or rather, she made a point to run into us."

"What for?"

"To ask me to speak to Grant on her behalf—to convince him that she's innocent of killing Vera."

"Oh, sure—like he's going to listen to *you*," Angelica said, and took another swig of her drink.

"I'm afraid I feel the same way," Tricia admitted. "And I'm a little disconcerted that she'd even ask. Innocent people don't do that . . . do they?"

"Now you're doubting her?"

"Well, I don't know how long she'd been at her house before I got there yesterday. Rigor mortis hadn't set in, so Vera hadn't been dead for too long."

"You hadn't mentioned that before."

"I guess it hadn't occurred to me until just now."

"How long does it take before a stiff goes stiff?" Angelica asked.

"Usually about two hours."

Angelica gave an involuntary shudder. "I don't like to think about it."

"Nobody does."

Angelica sipped her drink. "Let's not talk about death. We're alive, we're on my balcony drinking martinis—let's talk about something fun, like the Bake-Off."

"Sounds good to me."

"Have you lined up any sponsors yet?"

"Just Marshall."

"What are you waiting for?"

"It hasn't been my top priority," Tricia admitted—although she really ought to make it so.

Angelica leaned back in her chaise. "I wonder if we can find out who our competition is. Do we know anybody on the Booktown Ladies Charitable Society's board—or even just a member?"

Tricia shook her head. "Just Adelaide Newberry—but we're barely acquaintances. It's not an organization I ever thought about joining—although I understand they do good work."

"With all my businesses, I haven't got time for it, either, but I'm happy to support their efforts, and this Bake-Off could be wildly successful."

"Not from what the temp at the Chamber office said. Apparently, they expected a lot more applicants."

"If the Chamber had been behind it, it would have taken off," Angelica said, and shook her head.

"Even so, maybe it's better this way. I'm looking forward to seeing the high school's kitchen. I assume it'll be pretty much like that of the Brookview Inn," Tricia said.

"You've got it wrong. The Bake-Off won't take place in the school kitchen; it'll be held in the two home ec rooms. They've got four mini kitchens that were mothballed back in the nineteen nineties. Apparently, they've been using them as storerooms. Thanks to the Good Food Channel and other home-oriented networks, there's been a tremendous interest in cooking and food prep. Grace was telling me that a number of students lobbied to have cooking classes brought back to the curriculum."

"I was never offered a cooking class in high school." The truth was Tricia hadn't been interested.

"Of course, I didn't *need* classes," Angelica bragged. "I was already working my way through *Mastering the Art of French Cooking* when I was fourteen."

Tricia remembered some of the disasters from those recipes but decided not to mention them. Angelica was only allowed to cook when their grandmother was in residence—and usually, their parents were off gallivanting around the globe. Their mother, Sheila, thought the domestic arts were beneath contempt. She always had hired help, but Grandma Miles had taught the girls how to make a bed with hospital corners, the proper way to iron a skirt, dress, or blouse, and how to do laundry—tasks that had come in handy when Tricia had gone away to college and later when she'd married. But cooking skills had eluded her—mostly because she hadn't been properly motivated . . . until the last couple of years. Now she understood the joy Angelica experienced when she made people happy by feeding them food she'd taken the time to prepare.

"I've never visited any of the Stoneham schools," Angelica said thoughtfully and sipped her martini, which was nearly finished. "I'd like to know what those home ec rooms look like. I wonder if there's a way to get a peek before the competition begins."

"School's out for the summer. They're not going to let us poke around and have a look," Tricia protested.

"Why not? We're taxpayers—and believe me, with all my properties, I'm paying through the nose."

Tricia couldn't argue with that logic, but it didn't mean it would get them anywhere. "Maybe you could bluff and say you'd give a cooking scholarship or something."

Angelica looked thoughtful. "That's a great idea—except for the bluffing part. I really *would* give a scholarship to some budding chef wannabe to go to a great school like the Culinary Institute of America. But who would we make the offer to? I don't know anybody on the school board."

Tricia didn't, either—but she could find out. "It seems to me that Mr. Everett told me he was once on the school board—this was back when he owned his grocery store."

"Then maybe he can get us an in."

"I'll ask," Tricia said. "Maybe we could dig up some dirt on Vera

Olson while we're there. I understand she was on the school board for ten years."

"Yes, but that was more than five years ago."

"Somebody at the school might remember her. I mean—once you met her, she wasn't easy to forget," Angelica said. Tricia nodded. She lifted the dome on the cheese and crackers and assembled a snack. "So, if Mr. E poops out, who do we know that can get us into the school? This is where Frannie would have been helpful."

"You can visit her in jail and ask, but I'm pretty sure she wouldn't want to assist you in your quest."

Angelica frowned and took another sip of her drink. She glanced at the crackers and cheese and then looked away. "I think I've lost my appetite."

"Have another drink. I'm sure it will come back," Tricia said, and polished off the rest of her own.

Angelica stood.

"But before you go, I've got a question. I ran into the Dexter twins outside of the Cookery. They were wondering if you've set up a signing with Larry Andrews and—"

"Still no word. I really don't want to get stuck with several dozen of his cookbooks if Antonio can't make this happen."

"Just return them for credit."

"No," Angelica said vehemently. "I know from personal experience how devastating that can be to an author's royalty statement. I'll eat the cost even if I have to give them all away as Christmas presents."

Tricia was sure she wouldn't welcome several copies of the same book as a gift. Well, perhaps if they were all by vintage and esteemed mystery authors and had different dust jackets from various editions she could make an exception.

Angelica collected their glasses, deposited them on the tray, and went back inside to prepare another round, leaving the cheese and crackers. Tricia lifted the dome and made herself a snack. As she nibbled, she pondered what she'd relayed to her sister.

Vera had not been dead long before she'd been found. Joyce would have had the opportunity—but not necessarily a motive—to kill her. And she certainly wouldn't have killed Vera knowing Tricia was about to arrive. She'd have at least tried to dump the body back in Vera's yard. Joyce wasn't a big woman, but if she'd been able to maneuver Vera's body onto a wheelbarrow, she could have moved it. Or would that have left a track across the grass and through the gate into Vera's yard?

Tricia didn't want to speculate further. She wanted to believe in her friend's innocence. And yet, Joyce wasn't really a friend. They spoke to each other on the street and, in the past, at Chamber of Commerce meetings. But they'd never gone out to lunch or shared confidences about their lives. They were acquaintances, nothing more.

And yet, that didn't mean Tricia wanted to believe that Joyce was capable of murder, either.

Still, Tricia was sure she'd seen something amiss in Joyce's yard. Too bad she couldn't identify what that something was.

NINE

Since it was part of Pixie's new responsibilities to open and close Haven't Got a Clue, Tricia found herself taking her early brisk morning walk, returning home, showering, and then lazing around until just after ten, when she would make an appearance. But that morning she decided to try another cupcake recipe. Inspired by one of the videos she'd watched the day before, she searched for and found a recipe online that called for cold coffee and decided to make mocha-chocolate delights. As she measured out the cake flour, she noted that she would soon need to make a trip to the grocery store to replenish her supplies.

The cupcakes had cooked and cooled and were frosted just before it was time for Pixie and Mr. Everett to start their workday, so Tricia put them on a pretty plate, took them down to the shop, and had made the coffee just prior to their arrival.

Pixie was the first inside the door. "Coffee, coffee, coffee!" she called with what sounded like gratitude. "It smells wonderful. And more cupcakes. Another experiment?"

"Yes. And I want an honest review after you've tasted one."

"I haven't lied to you yet. They've all been great."

The door opened, the bell tinkling cheerfully once again, and Mr. Everett entered. "Good morning, ladies. Ah, more cupcakes. And what flavor have we today?" he asked as he headed for the back of the shop to retrieve his hunter green apron.

"Chocolate mocha."

Pixie was already pouring the coffee into their personalized mugs. "Sounds heavenly."

When Mr. Everett returned, the three of them took their cups, cupcakes, and napkins to the reader's nook, where Miss Marple joined them.

"You know you don't like cupcakes," Tricia told her cat.

Miss Marple protested with a strident *"Yow!"*

The humans settled back to enjoy their treat. Pixie took a huge bite and wiped the icing from around her mouth. She swallowed. "Good grief, that's fantastic. Is this the recipe you're using in the Bake-Off?"

"I was kind of shying away from chocolate. I figure everybody else will choose that."

"Not necessarily," Mr. Everett said. "They may feel the same as you, and then the judges wouldn't have any chocolate."

"He's got a point," Pixie said, and took another bite.

Tricia nodded and bit into her cupcake. It really was *good*!

"I take it the frosting is a buttercream derivative," Mr. Everett said, holding up his cupcake and scrutinizing it.

"Yes. I love the fact that the buttery goodness isn't overshadowed by the chocolate and coffee flavors."

"Do you prefer it over a cream-cheese-based icing?"

Tricia shook her head. "I like them equally well."

"Me, too," Pixie agreed, and took another bite of her cupcake.

Tricia was more interested in talking about a different subject. "Mr. Everett, do you know anybody on the current school board?"

Mr. Everett took another bite of his cupcake, chewed, and looked thoughtful. "I can't say as I do. It's been many years since I was a member."

Tricia let out a weary breath and nodded.

"But Grace does," he said helpfully. "Our foundation gave a substantial donation to the school district for improvements to their library. She worked with several people and oversaw the installation of new computers and software for their media center, as well as other areas that needed upgrades."

"That was very generous of you."

Mr. Everett shrugged. Tricia believed he must be the humblest man she'd ever met.

"I'll give Grace a call and see what I can do about introducing you to someone."

"Thank you. I really appreciate it."

"May I use your office phone to make the call?"

"Of course."

Mr. Everett nodded, wiped his mouth with a napkin, and rose, then headed for the back of the shop and the stairs to the basement.

"So what's with the school board?" Pixie asked.

"It seems Vera Olson was a member some years back."

"Ha! You're sleuthing again."

"I'm just worried about Joyce," Tricia said. "If I could find out anything that can help her, of course I want to do so." And then a flush of guilt ran through her. That didn't necessarily mean going to Chief Baker as a character witness and pleading Joyce's case. Not without some kind of evidence at least. All the more reason to talk to people who knew Vera well.

Tricia and Pixie had finished their cupcakes and were enjoying a second cup of coffee before the hoped-for onslaught of book buyers arrived, when Mr. Everett reappeared. "Good news, Ms. Miles. Grace is having lunch today at the Brookview Inn with a Ms. Blake, a former school board member who served along with the late Vera Olson."

Tricia tensed. Had she been that transparent about her motives?

"I'm assuming you wanted to speak with someone about her," Mr. Everett said as though sensing her sudden apprehension.

"Well, yes. But it's only because—"

Mr. Everett shook his head. "It's understandable that you'd be curious about the woman. You did, after all, find her body."

That sounded a lot better than being called nosy.

"That's very kind of Grace to invite me, but—"

"It was she who initiated the invitation. I am merely the bearer of news."

Tricia thought about it. Yup, *nosy* about covered it.

"What time am I to meet her?"

"Noon."

"I'll give Grace a call to let her know I'll be coming."

"No need. I already assured her you would."

"Thank you, Mr. Everett."

The three of them looked at one another. "Time to get to work," Pixie said, sounding like the store's manager. That was fine for her and Mr. Everett. Tricia didn't have a damn thing to do.

Returning to her apartment, Tricia texted Angelica, telling her she was having lunch with Grace, and received a text in return.

Not to worry. Having lunch with my new manager, Randy. Dinner at my place tonight.

That was a given.

When lunchtime approached, Tricia changed into a pretty summery dress and brought along a white sweater. The air-conditioning at the Brookview Inn was very efficient and she wasn't in the mood to catch a chill.

She arrived a few minutes early and paused at the entrance to the inn's dining room, giving it a once-over. Grace sat alone at a table near the window and had obviously been on the lookout for one of her tablemates. She waved, gesturing for Tricia to join her.

Tricia crossed the expansive room and paused to give Grace a quick hug before she sat down, setting her purse on the floor beside her. "It was awfully sweet of you to invite me to join you and your friend for lunch."

"She's not really a friend," Grace admitted. "More an acquaintance. We'll be discussing foundation business. But when William mentioned Vera Olson, I figured you might like to speak with Elizabeth."

"I hope you don't think I was angling for any kind of—"

"Of course not, dear. You're just as curious as a cat. But unlike inquisitive felines, I don't want you to allow yourself to fall into harm's way. I do so worry about you when you undertake these little adventures."

Adventures? Tricia had never thought of her sleuthing forays as adventures.

Grace looked up and signaled one of the waiters. "Would you like to start with something to drink, my dear?"

"Oh, I—"

"I'm going to have one. As you know, dear William is a bit of a teetotaler. He doesn't begrudge me a sherry now and then, but he's not into spirits."

"Well . . ."

The waiter arrived. "Ladies, what can I get you?"

Grace nodded in Tricia's direction.

"A dry gin martini. Up, with olives."

"And you?" he asked Grace.

"The same."

Tricia blinked in surprise.

The waiter nodded. "I'll be right back."

"I must admit I'm a little startled by your choice."

Grace smiled and shook her head wistfully. "So many times I've seen you and Angelica enjoy your martinis and longed for one myself."

"The secret life of Grace Harris-Everett?" Tricia asked.

"No one is an open book," Grace said, and smiled.

Tricia nodded. "Should we have waited for Elizabeth?"

"She only drinks coffee." Grace looked up. "Ah, and here she is now."

Tricia turned to see a handsome woman of about sixty, wearing a white linen suit and pumps. What was startling about her was her jet-black hair in a long pageboy cut. But it wasn't the style Tricia found startling so much as the thick layer of lacquer that seemed to form a kind of helmet around her head. Tricia was sure even hurricane winds wouldn't muss that do. Elizabeth carried a dark briefcase, which was in stark contrast to the rest of her ensemble.

"Hello, Grace. And who have we here?" Elizabeth asked as she took the seat to Tricia's right.

"Elizabeth Blake, this is my dear friend Tricia Miles."

Elizabeth offered her hand. "My pleasure."

Tricia shook and nodded.

"Elizabeth is vice president of Intervention, an organization that helps children who age out of the foster care system."

"It's very important work," Elizabeth said sincerely. "These young adults are often given a little spot of cash and a good-bye wave, with little to no resources, and no skills to help them navigate in the adult world."

"That's very sad," Tricia agreed.

"The Everett Foundation has been very generous to our organization in the past, and we hope it will support us again this year."

Elizabeth made to open her briefcase, but Grace patted the air over the table to forestall a presentation. "I'd prefer to read your report at my leisure. But I can assure you that William and I both believe in the work you do and will, of course, support your efforts for another year."

"You're very generous."

Grace ducked her head modestly.

The waiter arrived with a tray and two large martini glasses. He set them on the table before Grace and Tricia. "May I get you something?" he asked Elizabeth.

"Coffee, thank you."

Grace gave Tricia a conspiratorial smile as though to say, *"I told you so."*

The waiter nodded and again took off.

Grace picked up her glass and sampled her drink. "Quite nice."

Tricia did likewise. Quite nice indeed.

"Elizabeth was a member of the Stoneham School Board for almost a decade," Grace said conversationally.

"That's where my interest was piqued about children in the foster care system. When the opportunity came to work for Intervention, I jumped at the chance."

"Tricia once worked for a nonprofit as well."

"That was a long time ago," Tricia said modestly. "I understand you were on the school board at the same time as Vera Olson."

"Yes," Elizabeth said gravely.

"Did you hear about her untimely death?" Grace asked. Coming from her, the question sounded more like a concerned query rather than the opening for salacious gossip.

Elizabeth looked troubled. "Yes." It seemed like she wanted to say more but appeared to be biting her tongue.

"I only met her once," Tricia said casually. "In fact, it was the day she died. She came to the Have a Heart bookstore when I was there and practically laid out the owner in lavender—if you'll pardon that expression—for cutting a branch from one of her trees that hung over Vera's neighbor's house and yard."

"Vera was never one to keep her feelings hidden," Elizabeth said tactfully. "She was passionate about many things, but animal abuse was her major pet peeve."

"We feel the same way, don't we, Tricia?" Grace asked.

"Indeed."

"We have cats," Grace said as though to answer Elizabeth's unasked question. "Did Vera have any family?"

Elizabeth nodded. "I believe so, although she never much spoke about them. She had no children. I don't believe she ever married. She was pragmatic, with strong opinions, and wasn't above rattling a few cages, if you'll pardon the animal pun, but I can't imagine she'd provoke someone to murder."

Could Tricia get away with more questions pertaining to Vera's personality, or should she concentrate on the other topic she had in mind?

The waiter returned with Elizabeth's coffee and she immediately picked up her menu to order. She probably had other meetings to attend with prospective donors. Tricia and Grace ordered, too.

"You must have seen a lot of changes to the school system during your tenure," Tricia said, to steer Elizabeth onto a new topic.

"I keep up with what's going on."

"Were the high school's home economics classrooms mothballed while you were on the board?"

Elizabeth nodded. "Not many students were interested in the domestic arts. When Mrs. Gilchrist, the home ec teacher, retired, they suspended the classes due to dwindling enrollment."

"I understand those rooms are being resurrected for the upcoming Great Booktown Bake-Off," Tricia said innocently.

"Yes," Elizabeth said. "Thanks to a grant from the Everett Foundation, and a nice donation from the Good Food Channel, come September they'll be offering several courses for students who are interested in careers in the food industry. They've been renamed the culinary rooms."

"I'm so glad we were able to be a part of its restoration," Grace said, and sipped her martini.

"For too long we've been trying to steer all of our students toward a college education. There's nothing wrong with aspiring to higher education, but student debt can be crushing, and many industries are looking for skilled workers in the manual arts. That's another reason why Intervention has consulted with the board to revive classes to prepare students for construction apprenticeships, plumbing, and metalworking. Those jobs pay well and there's a national shortage of workers."

Tricia nodded. She knew about such shortages. Contractors seemed to be few and far between these days, and finding good ones was even harder. "And those students interested in the culinary arts?" she asked.

"Starting in the upcoming school year, we can now accommodate them."

"And that's thanks in part to the Bake-Off?" Grace asked.

"Yes. They'd already had student input, and when the opportunity arose earlier this year to pursue the Bake-Off—they leapt at the chance," Elizabeth admitted.

All of which sounded like a win-win situation not only for the students interested in careers in food service but as a great public relations opportunity to trumpet Stoneham to the world at large. Unfortunately, it seemed that Russ Smith had missed the boat when it came to the Chamber of Commerce endorsing the competition. Angelica—and Tricia, had she won the last Chamber election—would have jumped at the chance to herald the positives when it came to investing in the continuing rejuvenation of the once dying village. With Russ's tepid interest in his job as Chamber president, the community at large would have to take up the task.

"It sounds like you know a lot about the Bake-Off," Tricia said.

Elizabeth blushed. "As it happens, I was to be one of the judges as a representative of the Booktown Ladies Charitable Society."

"You were?" Grace said, sounding surprised.

Elizabeth nodded sadly. "My sister is having knee replacement surgery that day and asked me to be there for her. The head of the society, Adelaide Newberry, will be taking my place."

"My sister and I have both signed up to be contestants," Tricia confided. "Do you know how many others we'll be competing against?"

"Less than we anticipated. Only eight—which means we've had to cancel the second session on the day of the amateur competition."

Tricia's mood took a definite upswing. Eight! She was a novice; she'd been worried about how she was going to compare to more experienced bakers. Her chances of winning had just risen exponentially.

"I would dearly love to see the rooms before the competition," Tricia said wistfully. "Just to get the lay of the land."

"I'd be happy to arrange it with Principal Randall," Elizabeth said.

"Oh, Elizabeth—that would be too kind of you."

"Not at all. I can imagine how stressful it will be the day of the contest. If you know how things are laid out, it might ease your anxiety before the Bake-Off."

"Thank you so much."

"If you give me your number, I'll give you a call later this afternoon."

Tricia reached for her purse and withdrew one of her business cards and handed it to Elizabeth, just as the waiter returned with their lunch orders.

Elizabeth looked at her watch.

"Are you in a hurry to get back to work?" Grace asked.

"I'm afraid so. I may have to take a few days off work when my sister gets out of the hospital. And I'm so sorry I'll have to miss this once-in-a-lifetime event."

Once in a lifetime?

Vera Olson had just missed it. Her life was over—and not from natural causes.

TEN

Tricia arrived back at Haven't Got a Clue to find the store devoid of customers and Pixie and Mr. Everett once again reading in the comfortable chairs of the nook. Miss Marple lay sprawled across the coffee table, her head resting on a pile of old *Suspense Magazines*, looking utterly exhausted from yet another hard day of napping.

"Looks like a quiet afternoon," Tricia commented, taking the third seat.

"The day's not over and we've done well today," Pixie assured her.

"Haven't Got a Clue is always in good hands with you at its helm," Tricia said, and smiled, but her favorite day of the week was now Sunday because that was Pixie's day off—the day *she* was in charge of the store, when *she* got to interact with the customers, when Haven't Got a Clue was hers alone once more.

Tricia caught sight of Pixie's reassuring smile and felt guilty.

She had encouraged her protégée to excel and now she felt jealous because it no longer felt like her beloved vintage bookstore was her own.

Pixie frowned, her gaze fixed on Tricia's face. "Is everything okay?"

Tricia shook herself. "Of course. Why do you ask?"

"Because you seem . . . sad."

Tricia forced a smile. "I guess I'm preoccupied. I've got to choose a recipe for the Bake-Off and perfect it, and I only have a week to do so."

"Whatever you make will be terrific, won't it, Mr. E?"

"Just like those cupcakes you made this morning," he agreed.

"But there's something else on your mind," Pixie said, her gaze intensifying.

"You're right," Tricia admitted. "Vera Olson's death hasn't been far from my thoughts since the moment Joyce Widman and I found her."

"You poor little thing," Pixie sympathized. "You're much braver than I am when it comes to dealing with . . ." She let the sentence hang. Had she meant to say *stiffs*? *Dead bodies? Corpses? The unalive?*

Tricia shuddered and was determined to steer the conversation in another direction. "I'm expecting a call from Elizabeth Blake, who I met at lunch today with Grace. She's going to try to get me in to see the rooms the Bake-Off will take place in."

"Oh?" Mr. Everett asked.

Tricia nodded. "Angelica *and* me."

"Won't that give you an edge the other competitors won't have?" Pixie asked.

"I don't see how. We all still have to pull our recipes together, bake our entries, and decorate them in ninety minutes. Knowing what the room looks like can't really change that. I just want to see it. To get a feel for it."

The phone rang. All three of their heads turned in the direction of the vintage black rotary phone that sat on the glass display case that doubled as a cash desk. Tricia jumped to her feet. "I'll get it." She hurried across the room and picked up the heavy receiver. "Haven't Got a Clue. This is Tricia."

"Tricia? It's Elizabeth Blake."

"Thank you for getting back to me so soon."

"I've spoken to Principal Randall and she'll see you tomorrow morning at nine o'clock. Is the timing all right for you?"

"It's perfect. Thank you so much."

"It was my pleasure. And I wish you well in the competition. I'm sorry I won't get a chance to taste your entry."

"Thank you."

"Until we meet again . . ."

"Good-bye."

Tricia replaced the receiver, a smile tugging at her lips. And yet when she turned to face her employees, neither of them looked very happy. Their expressions were of . . . disappointment?

Inspecting the home ec rooms would not give her an unfair advantage. What she hoped it would do was inspire her to pursue victory.

No. Tricia would not have an advantage except to see her workspace, which probably wasn't nearly as nice or as large as her own kitchen on the floor above. She expected the workspace to be dated and cramped, but perhaps charming in its own way. Still, that wasn't going to give her an edge when it came to the judges' rulings. To win, her cupcake would have to not only taste wonderful but be beautiful as well.

To win, she needed to practice, practice, practice, until she was sure her entry would be the very best she could make. And she only had a week to ensure it.

* * *

Tricia spent the first part of the afternoon sitting at her kitchen island, surrounded by cookbooks filled with decadent recipes, and then in front of her laptop watching yet more YouTube videos in an effort to teach herself the basics of cake decoration. Sadly, her efforts had not been encouraging. She had the tools, but she didn't have the ability to use them. She had an awful lot to learn if she was going to present the Bake-Off judges with the most beautiful cupcake they'd ever seen.

It was just after six when, once again, Tricia locked and left her store. She let herself into the Cookery, then headed up the stairs to Angelica's apartment above. Sarge started barking hysterically, and once inside, she tossed him a couple of dog biscuits to shut him up.

"I've asked you not to give him more than one treat," Angelica admonished her for at least the hundredth time.

"I know, but he enjoys them. And how can I resist that hopeful little face?"

Angelica was not convinced.

"Are we sitting out on the balcony again tonight?" Tricia asked. "It's not too hot."

"I hadn't planned on it, but it was pleasant out there last night, wasn't it?"

"I feel like I've been cooped up all day and need as much fresh air as I can get—although I do have a bit of a surprise for you."

"A good one or a bad one?" Angelica asked suspiciously.

"Good."

"Oh, then why don't you take this plate of deviled eggs out and I'll bring the pitcher and glasses."

Deviled eggs meant leftovers from Booked for Lunch, but Tricia didn't mind. Tommy was an excellent short-order cook, although sometimes Angelica would help out in the kitchen if he allowed it and she was in the mood, but with getting the day spa ready to open, she doubted her sister had the time that week. Tricia grabbed the plate and a few paper napkins.

A light breeze blew through the alley as Tricia settled on the comfortably padded chair and Angelica once again took the chaise. She poured the drinks and handed a glass to Tricia. They raised their glasses in salute and took their first sips.

"So what's the big surprise?" Angelica asked.

"As I mentioned in my text, I had lunch with Grace."

"How is she?"

"Just fine. What made it interesting is she introduced me to a woman named Elizabeth Blake, who not only served on the Stoneham School Board but did so with Vera Olson."

"This sounds interesting. Go on."

"She didn't really say much about Vera, except to confirm what I already knew, but she was very helpful in another respect."

"Stop dragging it out and get to the point," Angelica urged.

"Guess where we're going tomorrow morning at nine o'clock?"

"You didn't!"

Tricia grinned. "I did."

"You little minx."

"We're scheduled for a personal tour of Stoneham High School's home ec rooms."

Angelica positively giggled in delight. "Who's going to give it? The woman you met at lunch?"

Tricia shook her head. "The school's principal. A Mrs. Randall. I hope this isn't going to interfere with whatever you need to do at the spa."

"I've got a manager now, remember? He's already got the keys; he can meet with the computer guy to set up the point-of-sale software and the router. It's the same setup I have at the Cookery, so there won't be a learning curve for me. I can take the whole morning off if I like."

Tricia certainly had nothing to do back at her store and wished she felt so carefree about it.

"What do you think the rooms will look like?" Angelica asked.

"I want to be surprised, so I'm not going to think about it until tomorrow."

"You Scarlett O'Hara, you."

"What happened with you and your new manager, Randy? Do you like him?"

"He's such a card. We laughed all day. I met his husband, Dave. He seems like a sweetheart, too. He took us to lunch. Well, *took us* is a misnomer. We had a hot dog and Coke from the Eat Lunch food truck in the park—just like a picnic. What did you have for lunch?"

"A chef's salad."

"Boring! Have another deviled egg."

Tricia did—or at least she was about to when her ringtone sounded. She retrieved her phone from her pocket and looked at the caller ID. "Oh, dear. It's Joyce."

"Why would she be calling you after hours?"

"I'll bet to see if I've spoken to Grant on her behalf."

Beethoven's "Pastoral" continued to play.

"You ought to change that ringtone," Angelica advised. "You've had it since day one."

"Yes, and when I hear it I know it's *my* phone and not fifty other people's phones."

The music stopped and Tricia set the phone on the glass-topped table between them.

"I take it you're not going to return her call."

"I'm going to pretend I missed it."

"For how long?"

"Forever?"

"I don't think she's going to let you."

"She probably left a message. I'll text her later."

"Do you think she's going to become a problem?"

Tricia shrugged. "Maybe. Although if I had a possible murder charge hanging over me, I'd be worried, too."

"Then maybe you ought to have a little more compassion for the poor woman."

"Do you think I should talk to Grant on her behalf? And tell him what? 'Joyce is my good buddy. I don't really know her all that well, but I'm sure she didn't kill her next-door neighbor'? I can't say that because I don't know it."

"Did she seem terribly shocked at finding Vera?"

"Well, yes."

"Then that's the least you could tell Grant."

"I suppose." Tricia picked up her egg half and took a bite, chewing thoughtfully. "I'm rather surprised he hasn't called me in for yet another mini interrogation."

"They took your report right at the scene, didn't they? Perhaps he thought that was good enough."

Tricia thought about her conversation with Marshall two evenings before and the things they'd discussed. Things she hadn't mentioned to Grant or Angelica. Then she wondered why she hadn't heard from Marshall. He was probably busy. He was still new to accommodating the tourist trade and forging his connections with Milford Travel. As she considered that fact, she realized that now that she had a full-time manager, she could do some traveling herself. Perhaps go to other cities, attend auctions for rare vintage mysteries. The possibilities intrigued her.

"What's going on in that head of yours?" Angelica asked.

"Nothing much."

"Uh-huh." Angelica lifted the frill pick from her drink and plucked one of the olives from it.

"Maybe I will give Grant a call, but not tonight. I'll wait until he's on duty tomorrow. The man deserves a few hours off from the job."

Angelica nodded and returned the pick with its remaining olive to her empty glass. "Looks like we're ready for a refill. And when I get back, we can toast tomorrow's tour of the school."

"Sounds good to me."

Angelica went inside, pulling the sliding glass door shut behind her.

Tricia leaned back in her chair and took in the quiet churchyard beyond. She needed another reason besides Joyce's defense to call Baker. As she studied the solemn tombstones decorating the lawn beyond, she had it. She'd ask if he had information on what was to happen to Vera's remains. Was someone planning a service? Elizabeth had said the woman did have some family in the area. Surely someone would be taking care of it.

Tricia picked up her phone and listened to Joyce's message.

"Tricia? It's me. Have you had an opportunity to talk to Chief Baker? He called me twice today. Why doesn't he leave me alone and try to find Vera's actual killer? Call me, will you?"

The call ended.

No, Tricia would not call. She'd do as she'd told Angelica and text her later in the evening. Much later.

ELEVEN

It was just after eight the following morning when Tricia found herself ready for the school tour, and with almost an hour to spare. She picked up her cell phone to call Chief Baker but instead decided to text Marshall.

Where've you been?

Seconds later he replied. *Busy. Drink tonight around 8:30 at TD-EP?*

See you there.

Satisfied at the prospect of seeing her current lover, Tricia turned her attention to her ex. She decided to avoid official channels and call Baker on his personal number. She had no desire to fence with his annoying receptionist, Polly, who seemed to find great pleasure in denying Tricia access to her onetime paramour.

Baker answered on the second ring. "Yes, Tricia." He sounded bored.

"Good morning, Grant. I thought I'd give you a quick call to—"

"To squeeze me for information on Vera Olson's death."

"Well, kind of. I've had a few days to think about what I saw that day and wasn't sure if I'd mentioned everything to you."

"Go on."

She told him everything she'd told Marshall days before. She still hadn't figured out what had bothered her about the crime scene. Well, it would eventually come to her. She hoped.

"Thank you, Tricia. You're a good citizen."

If she were a dog, he might have patted her on the head.

"Was there anything else?"

"I was just wondering if Vera's next of kin had arranged for a funeral or some kind of memorial service."

"The body was released to a funeral home in Merrimack. That's all I know."

Funeral homes in southern New Hampshire weren't on every corner. Tricia would do an online search to see if any of the homes had posted an obituary.

"Thank you."

"You're welcome. And what about the rest?"

"The rest?" Tricia asked innocently.

"Yeah. Isn't about now when you make a heartfelt plea on your friend's behalf?"

"Joyce Widman?"

"Yes."

Tricia hesitated. "Joyce and I aren't really friends. More acquaintances," she said, which was the absolute truth.

"Then what were you doing at her home at the time when Vera Olson's body was found?"

"As I told you, I went to her store to buy some books—"

"You don't read romance novels," he stated.

"I do read romantic suspense. I cut my reading teeth on them." Well, sort of. During her teenage years, she'd ripped through them as fast as she could take them out of the local library, even if she was more interested in the suspense and skipped a lot of the romance. "Anyway, she invited me to go and see her garden and give me some veggies, as well as a few pointers."

"Why would you need pointers? You've never shown an interest in gardening."

Tricia sighed. They'd already been over this. "Now that I'm cooking on a regular basis, I'm interested in growing my own herbs."

"Uh-huh."

The silence lingered. Tricia wasn't about to get into an argument with the man.

"By the way, I heard you were going to participate in the Bake-Off," Baker said.

"I am. Why'd you mention it?"

"It so happens I've been asked to be a judge in both the professional and amateur divisions," he said, sounding just a little smug.

"You have?"

"Don't sound so surprised. I'm always on the lookout for community outreach opportunities. Our PR rep said this would be a great example. Besides, I know a good cupcake when I taste one."

"I'm sure you do," Tricia said, trying to sound a little happier about the idea—even if she didn't feel that way. She wanted to win and it wouldn't hurt if the judges were on her side. She wasn't sure she could count on Baker in that respect.

Then again, was she just channeling her sister, who thought Good Food Channel Chef Andrews might look upon her baking efforts more kindly because of a supposed "relationship"? If anything, Tricia's relationship with Grant Baker remained strained—even if they'd both moved on. An air of tension always seemed to surround them when they spoke—even when it wasn't in face-to-face conversations. If there was any unfinished business on his end, he should have voiced it a long time ago.

But she wasn't about to go there now.

"I hope my entry will please all the judges," she said neutrally.

"We'll see."

There didn't seem to be anything else to say.

"I'd better get going. I have an appointment within the hour. Thanks for taking my call."

"Don't I always?"

Yes, and maybe that should have surprised her more than it did.

A cement cornerstone at the edge of the big brick building testified that Stoneham High School had been built in 1952, just about the time that prosperity in the village had started its steep decline. And while a lot of money had been poured into the building, it still looked like a midcentury relic. New security measures had been instituted, so there was no way just anyone could enter the building during the academic year. But the school had let out for the summer, and Tricia was pleased when she was able to open one of the big plate-glass doors. The lights were out in the main hall as they entered the quiet building, but they took note of a sign that said OFFICE with an arrow pointing right and headed down the hall.

"Gosh, I haven't been inside a school since *I* was in school," Angelica whispered. "And never a *public* school." The only other sound was the tap of the heels of her stilettos echoing off the metal locker doors.

"Didn't you ever visit any of Antonio's schools in Italy?"

"I *paid* for him to go to them. I never actually *saw* any of them," she muttered.

They continued down the cool, empty hall until they passed another darkened side corridor.

"What do you think is down there?" Angelica asked.

"I have no idea."

"Let's take a look."

"Whatever for?"

"Because we may never get the opportunity again."

Tricia shook her head but found herself following Angelica's lead. Closed double doors to the left proved to be one of the two entrances from that corridor to the gymnasium.

"Remember those horrible little yellow outfits they used to make us wear at Groveland Academy for PE?" Angelica asked.

Tricia's gym uniform had been too big for her thin frame, and a group of nasty girls had made sure Tricia was aware of just how unflattering it looked on her—for every single PE class during her four years at the school. It was a relief to go off to college to be spared that biweekly bullying.

"The pool can't be far away. I wonder how big it is," Angelica asked, and started off down the hall once more.

"You're going to get us in trouble," Tricia said in a harsh whisper.

"What are they going to do? Give us detention?" Angelica stopped at a big white door with a blue-painted sign that said POOL ENTRANCE. Tricia was surprised when Angelica yanked on the handle and the door actually opened. Angelica marched right in and Tricia dutifully followed. The sign on the door to the right said BOYS' LOCKER ROOM. Angelica walked right past it to another big steel door with a thin vertical window and yanked that open.

Tricia had been expecting to be assailed with the stench of

chlorine, but there was no hint of it in the air—and she soon found out why.

"I wonder why the pool has no water," Angelica said, and walked toward the large empty expanse. According to the numbers painted on the side of the far end, it was twelve feet deep when filled.

Tricia shrugged. "Maybe they don't want to have to maintain it for three months while school's out. They could save a lot on chemicals."

"Yeah. I read somewhere that an Olympic-sized swimming pool takes something like six hundred thousand gallons of water."

"And this pool is nowhere near that size. Still, I wouldn't want to have to fill it by the teaspoon," Tricia commented. "Maybe it's closed for repairs. I mean, school just ended last week. They had to be using it right up until then."

"I guess." Angelica sighed. "I wish I still had a pool—and a pool boy."

"You had a pool boy?"

"Well, sort of. He came to clean the pool twice a week." She smiled. "That was back when I could wear a bikini. I'd slather myself in suntan oil and lie there on my chaise listening to the water lap as he scraped the bottom of the pool for stray leaves and dead critters."

"Critters?"

"Of course. The thing was a death pit for insects, the odd mouse, and sometimes a bird. Oh, and frogs. They can swim, but eventually they get tired and end up in the skimmers, and that's why you need a pool boy, because no way was I going to deal with dead critters."

Well, that was more information than Tricia needed. She looked at her watch. "We ought to get to the principal's office. We're going to be late one minute from now."

Angelica did an about-face and led the way back to the corridor, where they retraced their steps until they were once again in the main hall. Another hundred feet or so and they arrived at the school's main office. A casually dressed woman sat at a steel-and-Formica desk before a computer screen. "Can I help you?"

"Hello, I'm Angelica Miles, and this is my sister, Tricia. We have an appointment to see Principal Randall."

"Yes, I saw it on her calendar. I'll let her know you're here." She picked up the phone on her desk and made a call. "Mrs. Randall will be out in a moment. Please have a seat."

The sisters glanced at the uncomfortable-looking plastic-and-metal chairs, which were probably devised to make recalcitrant teens feel as uncomfortable as possible while waiting for an audience with the principal.

"No, thanks. I think I'll stand," Tricia said.

Angelica wore three-inch heels. She sat.

The secretary began tapping on her computer keyboard and Tricia wandered over to a bulletin board, with its calendar of the upcoming school year, posters for a fund-raiser at a chain restaurant up on the highway, and coupons from L.L.Bean for sweatshirts with the school's logo. High school seemed to have happened eons ago for Tricia.

Finally, the office door to the right opened and Mrs. Randall entered. Her dark hair streaked with gray, the school's principal looked stereotypically stern, and Tricia instantly felt guilty, remembering the looks Pixie and Mr. Everett had given her the day before when she'd told them of her plans to visit the school before the Bake-Off. "Ms. Miles?" the woman asked. Even her voice sounded grim.

"Yes," the sisters said in unison.

Angelica practically jumped to her feet. "I'm Angelica Miles, and this is my sister, Tricia."

Mrs. Randall offered her hand to both of them. "I was surprised to hear from Elizabeth Blake on your behalf," she told Tricia, and her tone implied she wasn't happy at receiving the call. Tricia gave what she hoped was a sincere smile, but Mrs. Randall's steely gray principal's eyes seemed to pierce right through her. "Please step into my office," the woman said gravely. Tricia had never been called into a principal's office before and found she'd broken out in a cold sweat.

Once seated in the same uncomfortable chairs before Mrs. Randall's tidy desk, Angelica became all business.

"As you probably already know, I own Booked for Lunch, the little retro café in the village, as well as my bookstore, the Cookery. I'm very interested in your culinary program and the possibility of offering a scholarship to your students."

"That's very generous of you," Principal Randall said, but her tone said otherwise.

"I'm happy I was allowed to accompany my sister on a tour of your facilities."

Mrs. Randall looked skeptical. "Are you participating in the Bake-Off, too?"

"Why, yes," Angelica said.

The principal's eyes narrowed. "Are you trying to get a leg up on your competition, as well?"

Angelica straightened in her chair, a look of utter horror crossing her features. "Mrs. Randall, I certainly hope you're not accusing my sister and me of trying anything underhanded. Yes, we bake, but we have just as much of a chance of winning as our competition, and I don't see how seeing the home economics room could possibly give us an edge."

"I beg your pardon, Ms. Miles, but in the last couple of days, I've been contacted by all but one of the competitors—from both the amateur and professional ranks. I must say you are the only one who has tried to bribe the school."

Tricia gasped and Angelica's eyes grew so wide Tricia worried they might pop out.

"I assure you, Mrs. Randall, that I have every intention of establishing the scholarship. I have dedicated my life to cookery—as evidenced by my bookshop, my restaurant, and the bed-and-breakfast I co-own, and I'm offended that you've intimated a lack of character and untoward motives on my behalf."

Mrs. Randall merely shrugged. No doubt she'd heard enough tall tales from teens to write a book. "I promised Ms. Blake you'd get your tour—she called in a favor—so let's get on with it."

Mrs. Randall rose and the sisters unhappily followed the principal down the long hallway, up a flight of stairs, and down another corridor, finally pausing in front of a large wooden door. Mrs. Randall took out a key and unlocked it. She turned the handle and opened it inward. "Be my guest," she said, and held out a hand, allowing Tricia and Angelica to enter the darkened room.

They stepped inside and saw cabinets in the shadows. Mrs. Randall reached out and flipped a series of switches until the room was bathed in light.

"Wow," Tricia said, a little unnerved. "This is like stepping back into the nineteen fifties."

The room was divided into an instruction area with desks and a chalkboard and two kitchenettes painted a sickly green and equipped with older white appliances. Tricia noted that the stoves were all electric—Angelica was not going to like that—but the room did possess a certain retro charm. Tricia could picture girls dressed in poodle skirts with saddle shoes giggling as they mixed cake batter, pouring it into prepared pans, sliding the pans into the oven, and then, after they were baked, pulling them out to cool and decorate. For some girls, this would be the only cooking instruction they'd receive. Tricia knew the feeling. Until recently, she hadn't had any interest in cooking; she left that to her sister, who had excelled at it. Thanks to their grandmother, who taught Angelica everything she knew about cookery, Ange had proved to be a natural.

"Well, what do you think?" Tricia asked her sister.

Angelica forced a smile. "It's just darling," she said. "I wish we'd had something like this at our high school when we were growing up. Nobody I knew even cared about cooking. When I mentioned how much I liked to bake, my best friend, Mary Jane, looked at me as if I'd grown another head."

"But the stoves," Tricia said. "They're electric."

Angelica sported a sly smile. "Nothing I can't handle. How about you?"

Tricia smiled. "Anything you can do, I can do better."

"Well," Angelica said, "at least you didn't burst into song."

Mrs. Randall looked at them, her expression not unlike Angelica's friend Mary Jane's. "I assure you, every contestant will have the same restraints."

"Do you mind if we look through the drawers and cabinets to familiarize ourselves with the equipment?" Tricia asked.

"It won't do you any good. The room will be thoroughly cleaned and rearranged before the Bake-Off. Each contestant will have an opportunity to familiarize themselves with their work area before the competition begins."

That sounded reasonable.

Angelica's stilettos clicked as she walked around one of the kitchenettes. Her fingers brushed across the worn Formica counter. "I wonder what this kitchenette could tell us if only it could speak."

"Hopefully, 'good luck,'" Tricia said.

"That's not what I meant," Angelica said. "Think of all the young women who passed through here. Doesn't it make you wonder what happened to them? Where did they end up? What did they do? How did their lives play out?"

"I guess there's a reason you're the writer in the family instead of me," Tricia said.

Principal Randall continued to look at them with what could only be described as boredom. No doubt she had better things to do than to watch them snoop around. As if to prove it, she looked at the big clock near one of the cabinets. "Have you seen enough?"

Angelica sighed. "Yes, thank you for taking the time to see us and let us have a peek at our workspaces."

Mrs. Randall's smile was anything but authentic. "It was no trouble at all."

They followed the principal back to the first floor, where Mrs. Randall paused at the school's main entrance. She gestured toward the door. "Ladies."

"Whom should I contact about establishing the scholarship?" Angelica asked.

"Then you were actually serious about it?"

"Of course."

"If you'll leave me your card, I'll set something up and then call you."

Angelica withdrew a business card from her purse and handed it to the woman. They said their good-byes and the sisters left the building and headed south down Main Street.

"Well?" Tricia asked.

"I didn't like that woman. I have a mind to double my scholarship—just to show her how authentic my offer is."

"You go, girl!"

"I mean it."

"I know you do." They looked both ways at the corner and crossed the side street.

"What are you going to do now?" Angelica asked.

Tricia shrugged. "Go home and make another practice batch of cupcakes."

"I wish I could, but I have to get back to the day spa. Then again, I really don't need the practice. After all, I've been making cupcakes for almost as long as you've been alive."

Tricia ignored the dig.

She'd show Angelica.

Now, if she just could find the perfect recipe.

TWELVE

Tricia arrived at Haven't Got a Clue just as Pixie was about to unlock the door. "Another beautiful day in Stoneham," Pixie called. She had to be the happiest woman alive. And why not? She had a job she loved, a new home, and a husband who cooked for her. Tricia had no reason to feel anything but happiness for her friend and co-worker, but instead, she felt depressed. But then, with Vera Olson's death and the Bake-Off hanging over her, maybe she was just feeling a little overwhelmed.

"It is," Tricia agreed.

"Any plans for the day?" Pixie asked as she stowed her purse behind the cash desk.

"Just trying out another recipe for the Bake-Off. I hope you won't mind taste testing yet again."

"Not a chance." Pixie looked over at the beverage station. "I'll get the coffee going. You get up those stairs and start making those cupcakes."

"Will do," Tricia said, and headed to the back of the store for the stairs to her apartment above.

An hour later, Tricia looked at the finished cupcakes before her. She'd gone for a plain yellow sponge with an almond-flavored frosting, garnished with toasted sliced almonds. They smelled pretty good but looked . . . boring. Despite the dozen or so decorating videos she'd watched, Tricia's efforts at embellishment were not inspiring. Just swirling frosting on the top of a cupcake wasn't going to win the Bake-Off prize money for Tricia's charity, not with cutthroat competition like Angelica. What Tricia needed was a ringer. Maybe that wasn't quite right; what she needed was to *be* a ringer.

Angelica wasn't the only woman on earth who knew how to make a rose out of frosting or fondant, but where could Tricia find someone to teach her? There was only so much you could learn from a book or watching YouTube videos. What she needed was some hands-on experience.

The only professional bakers in town were Nikki Brimfield-Smith, Alexa Kozlov from the Coffee Bean, Tommy, the short-order cook at Booked for Lunch, and of course the pastry chef at the Brookview Inn, Joann Gibson. All of them had entered the competition in the professional category; they weren't about to help Tricia learn to decorate so she could win in her division. But there had to be other people who were skilled in that capacity. She just had to find one of them.

But before she even faced that hurdle, she needed to hit the grocery store and stock up on cake flour, eggs, and butter—lots of butter. So, after dropping off the cupcakes in her store for her employees and customers, off to Milford she went.

It was only a ten-minute drive, and Tricia soon arrived at the parking lot of the biggest supermarket in the area. As she approached the store, she saw a woman who looked vaguely familiar exiting. She stood in the middle of the aisle just staring until a car horn blasted her from her reverie, jostling her memory. She scooted out of the way of the offensive driver and called, "Officer Pearson?"

The blonde woman looked up. Without the bulky navy uniform and cap, Officer Pearson looked a lot more feminine in jeans, a pink tank top, and sandals than she did when on the job. She carried two plastic grocery bags but no sign of a purse.

"Can I help you?" she called.

Tricia hurried over to intercept the officer. "It's Tricia Miles. I was in Joyce Widman's store when Vera Olson arrived and tried to start an argument on Monday."

"Oh, yeah," Officer Pearson said, and seemed distinctly uncomfortable at the reminder. "You found the body at Ms. Widman's home, too."

"Joyce and I found it. I was wondering if there were any new developments in the case."

"I'm not authorized to talk about such things outside of the department."

Probably true, but something about her tone and body language made it seem like no matter what Tricia asked, her answers would be evasive.

"I'm worried about my friend. I don't think she's capable of committing a murder—and especially over such a petty argument."

"That's been her reputation," Pearson said succinctly. "I'm sorry. I really need to get going. I'm working second shift tonight and have other errands to run this morning."

"I'm sorry. It was nice speaking with you."

Pearson nodded and headed for her car once again. Tricia crossed the tarmac and paused to watch the officer steer her late-model white Kia toward the lot's exit; then she shrugged and entered the store.

Grabbing a small cart, Tricia headed straight for the produce section, where she selected several lemons and limes and a pint of strawberries, figuring any of them would make a great-tasting cupcake or frosting. She considered stopping at the deli but decided against it and instead figured she'd just get a loaf of bread in the bakery department.

Bakery?

Good grief! Why hadn't she thought of that before? She pushed her cart with greater speed and practically skidded to a stop in front of one of the glass display cases. Beyond it, a gum-cracking woman of about fifty, with bleached blonde hair, dressed in baker's whites, wielded a large pastry bag filled with pink icing and was piping a scroll design on the edge of half a white-frosted sheet cake.

Tricia stood there, mesmerized, just staring at the woman's hands as she worked, the evident ease she possessed, and her speed.

When she'd finished with the scrolls, the woman looked up. "Can I help you?"

"I hope so. I'd like—"

"The book of designs is over there." She pointed. "Pick out what you want and let me know."

"I was hoping I could convince you to teach me to do what you do."

The woman grabbed another pastry bag, this one filled with icing a pale lilac in color. She began to make roses, filling the first corner. "Teach you to do what?"

"Make roses and scrolls with frosting."

"What for?"

Tricia bit her bottom lip. Should she admit it? "Well, I'm participating in the Great Booktown Bake-Off and—"

"Oh, yeah, I heard about that."

"Have you entered?"

The woman shook her head. "Nah, I can't bake for sh—" She didn't finish the sentence. "Cake and cupcakes just aren't my thing."

"But you work in the bakery?"

"Yeah, and before that, I was a waitress. They trained me to do this. The cakes come already baked. We just do the personalization. This one is for a kid's eighth birthday party. The pink and purple together look sucky, if you ask me, but it's going to make some little girl pretty darn happy."

It probably would, and for a moment Tricia remembered her fifth birthday cake and the slice she'd never gotten to eat. She shook herself back to the present.

"Could you teach me?"

"When? And what's it pay?"

"Double what you make here an hour."

The woman looked thoughtful. "This competition is in a few days, isn't it?"

Tricia nodded. "Next week."

"I work here from noon to four every day."

"Could you come to my home in Stoneham in the morning and give me some pointers?"

"I've got to drop my granddaughter off at daycare, but I could be there around nine. It should only take a few hours to teach you the basics."

"That's all I need."

"Okay. By the way, I'm Donna."

"And I'm Tricia. Glad to meet you."

Tricia gave Donna her business card and scribbled her cell phone number on the back. "See you tomorrow, then."

"I'll be there." And with a sigh, Donna went back to the little girl's dream cake.

She might have felt resigned, but Tricia felt energized.

Maybe she'd have a chance to win the Bake-Off after all.

* * *

Since Tricia was already in Milford, she decided to swing by the Pets-A-Plenty animal shelter. As she entered the building, she heard a lot of barking—much more than usual, but there was a distinct lack of humans to be seen at the usually busy rescue.

Tricia strode up to the reception desk, where a harried volunteer clasped a phone in one hand and held the index finger of her other hand in her other ear.

"I'm sorry, but you have to sign paperwork and come to the shelter in person. We don't just drive pets to your house to see if you'd like to adopt them. Yes, yes, I understand, but those are our rules. Yes. Yes. Good-bye." She hung up the phone. "Some people," she muttered, then seemed to realize Tricia stood on the other side of the counter. "I'm sorry," she said, sounding embarrassed. "Can I help you?"

Tricia had to raise her voice to be heard over the din. "Are any of the Pets-A-Plenty board members in today?"

"No, ma'am."

"Not even Toby Kingston?"

"He has meetings off-site all day."

"Oh." Did the man ever show up for work? Again Tricia noted the loud barking from the kennels behind the door beyond the desk. "Is everything all right?"

"No. We're seriously short-handed today. Most of the animals haven't eaten or had their cages cleaned."

Miss Marple had been fed at her usual time. The strays and abandoned cats and dogs were probably confused and apprehensive, in addition to being hungry.

"Can I do anything to help?"

"Uh, no."

"For what it's worth, I've been nominated as a possible replacement on the Pets-A-Plenty Board of Directors. If someone will give me some direction, I'd be glad to step in and do whatever I can to help out."

The woman eyed Tricia's attire. "You might get dirty."

"As a longtime pet owner, I'm well acquainted with cleaning up after cats and dogs." Okay, she'd never owned a dog, but she had been walking Sarge on a regular basis—and that meant picking up after him, too.

The woman scrutinized Tricia once again. "Well, I guess so. Come on." She lifted the counter and beckoned Tricia to follow her to the kennels beyond.

The barking was almost deafening inside the kennels where anxious dogs jumped up against the chain link as though to garner even more attention from the humans who walked along the aisle.

"Cori?" the woman called.

An older, gray-haired woman popped her head out of a doorway at the far end of the corridor.

"What?"

"I've got a warm body who wants to give you a hand."

"I'll take whatever I can get."

The receptionist waved a hand in the direction of her colleague and then abandoned Tricia to return to the shelter's lobby.

"Hi, I'm Tricia Miles."

"Cori Haskell," the beleaguered woman said. In front of her were at least twenty bowls filled with kibble and another set with water. "Those poor puppies haven't eaten since last night. We had two volunteer cancellations this morning. I wasn't supposed to come in until four, but they called me half an hour ago."

"Just tell me what to do, and I'll do it," Tricia said.

Half an hour later, all the dogs and cats had been fed and watered. It was then that the cage cleaning began.

Nobody wants to clean up cat and doggy doo, but Tricia didn't mind, and she got to make friends with so many of the shelter's residents, which was heartening and heartbreaking at the same time.

"Thanks for stopping by," Cori said after Tricia had told the woman about her own cat and her sister's dog. "It's really hard to keep the place staffed. Volunteers come when they can—and we try to schedule them—but . . . life happens. If your kid is suddenly sick, your volunteer job goes out the window. It seems like it's harder to staff the place in the summer when kids are home from school and vacations happen."

Tricia could understand that.

"How long have you been volunteering for the shelter?"

"Two months."

"Really?" Cori seemed so well versed in the tasks that needed to be accomplished, Tricia would have guessed she'd been a volunteer a lot longer.

"Yeah. I got pissed off when Monterey Bioresources came to New Hampshire, and I felt I needed to do something to promote animal welfare. They've got a compound just outside of Concord."

"Monterey Bioresources?" Tricia asked.

"They're a company that works for Big Pharma and the cosmetics industry. They test products on dogs, cats, and bunnies. Terrible experiments like squirting hairspray in their eyes and injecting them with drugs to see how they react—which is sometimes lethal."

"I never heard of them before."

"And it's not likely you ever would—except for me telling you. The whole operation is low-key. You can't even see the buildings from the road. They've got a long driveway and very little in the way of signage.

They don't *want* you to know they're there or what they do because any person who gives a damn about animals would be appalled."

Tricia was already appalled. Of course, she knew that the medical and pharmaceutical industries heavily relied on animal experimentation, but she also knew that a lot of their supposed research could now be done by computer modeling based on past results. Was it really necessary to subject innocent animals to that kind of torture? And yet she had heard that some agencies that professed to be animal activists were just as cruel, saying they wanted to help protect animals when their agenda was just as detrimental to the lesser species they pretended to advocate for.

Tricia decided right then and there that when she got back to her computer she would do some research on Monterey Bioresources to find out just what their reach was in her adopted state.

"I get all that, and I'm in your court," Tricia said. "But I'm not sure what that has to do with Pets-A-Plenty."

Cori seemed to shrink into herself and lowered her voice. "Because there're rumors that some of the animals that are supposedly adopted from here are being sold to Monterey Bioresources."

Tricia's mouth dropped in horror. "Surely you're wrong."

Cori shook her head. "I wouldn't have told you what I suspect—know—if you hadn't said you might become part of the board. I'm not sure everyone who currently serves on it is really out to protect the animals."

"How do you know?"

Again, Cori looked almost frightened. "The volunteers talk among ourselves. There have been some funny adoptions. Sometimes we'll have six or seven guinea pigs and ferrets, and then they'll all go at once. Same with some dogs. Somebody in charge might know what's going on and is trying to cover it up—but you didn't hear that from me."

Which meant that if push came to shove, Cori might not be willing to testify about it. And who could blame her?

Tricia looked down the aisle, catching sight of so many dogs that sat before the chain link looking pathetic and longing to be loved like she and Angelica loved Sarge. The sadness that enveloped her was like a ten-ton weight on her soul. Pets-A-Plenty was a no-kill shelter. But did they do enough due diligence when it came to vetting the people who adopted the animals?

She really didn't know.

THIRTEEN

After her troubling conversation with Cori, Tricia decided she needed a bit of a pick-me-up and stopped at Granny's Garden, a nursery just outside the Stoneham village line. As she got out of her car, she saw a large outdoor display of birdbaths, concrete and resin statuary, metal and white-plastic arbors, flower-filled urns, and clay planters.

She took the time to go through the entire display before turning to the greenhouses, which were filled with a vast variety of annual flowers and vegetables ranging from tomatoes to peppers, zucchini, broccoli, summer squash, and Brussels sprouts. Tempted as she was, Tricia pushed her cart and stopped to collect two varieties of bite-sized tomatoes in plastic planters (as the clay ones were far too heavy for her to maneuver on her own), a pot of thyme, and another of cilantro, and again lamented the fact that she hadn't better thought out the design of her far-too-small balcony on the east side of her home. Maybe she'd repurpose it in a year or two, but for now, she was stuck with what she had. She also bought two flower boxes and the metal hangers to fit over her balcony rail, along with several six-packs of pansies and begonias. One of the nursery employees suggested she buy a couple of spikes to give her arrangement a little height, which seemed like a good idea.

Tricia was about to check out when the cashier suggested she buy a twenty-pound bag of soil in which to plant her flowers. While waiting for someone to fetch the dirt, Tricia realized she had no gardening gloves, nor a trowel, and two more items were added to her purchases.

Tricia parked her Lexus in the alley behind Haven't Got a Clue and unloaded her car, thankful her home included a dumbwaiter. No way did she want to haul a heavy sack of dirt up a flight of stairs. Still, everything needed to be brought into the store first—and that still meant steps. After parking everything on the landing behind the shop, she moved her car to the municipal parking lot and hoofed it back to Haven't Got a Clue.

Tricia unlocked the back door and began to haul everything into the shop, and soon Mr. Everett showed up. "Let me give you a hand with that, Ms. Miles."

"Oh, thank you, Mr. Everett."

"Getting into gardening?"

"I thought it would look nice to have some flowers to spruce up my balcony—and I bought a few herbs for cooking, too."

Pixie appeared as they were hauling in the last of the supplies. "Holy cow—did you rob a nursery?"

"I've offered to help Ms. Miles with her purchases. Would that be all right?" Mr. Everett asked Pixie.

"Sure. I can hold the fort. Holler if you need me."

It took four trips in the dumbwaiter before everything had safely landed on the second floor, and Mr. Everett climbed the stairs to join Tricia to move everything to the balcony.

"Would you like some help planting the flowers?" Mr. Everett asked.

"Oh, no. I don't want Pixie to think I'm monopolizing your time."

A small smile crossed the old man's lips. "Ms. Miles, it is you who are paying me, and I would be pleased to help."

"Thank you. But I only have one pair of gardening gloves."

"Afterward, I will avail myself of soap and water."

Tricia laughed. "I guess you're right—I just don't like the thought of dirt under my fingernails."

"Perhaps when you have more gardening experience, you won't even notice it."

Again Tricia laughed. "I'll bet you're right."

They started right to work, and soon the flower boxes were installed and filled with potting soil, and then they started to plant, with the spikes going in first.

"What made you decide to start a new hobby now?" Mr. Everett inquired.

"I guess it was visiting Joyce Widman's garden on Monday." Tricia paused, staring down at the peach-colored pansy she held in one hand. "They say gardening is a metaphor for life. Vera Olson's death keeps preying on my mind. I guess . . . I needed a little ray of happiness." She proffered the little flower, which seemed to sport a face. "I'm going to enjoy taking care of these little guys for the next few months."

Mr. Everett nodded. "Ms. Olson's death was unfortunate."

Tricia really wasn't interested in going through it all again and decided to change the subject. "I stopped at the Pets-A-Plenty shelter earlier. They were terribly short-handed and I helped them out for an hour or so."

Mr. Everett patted the dirt around one of the purple pansies. "They will need to bolster their ranks if they are to build the new, much bigger facility."

Tricia nodded. "What's your opinion of the place?"

Mr. Everett shrugged. "We found them very helpful when we adopted our cats."

"Did you notice anything . . . funny?"

"Funny as in unusual?" he asked.

Tricia nodded.

Mr. Everett shook his head. "I must admit we limited ourselves to the cat house, as we were only interested in adopting felines. Why do you ask?"

"I had a conversation with one of the volunteers." Tricia didn't want to go into details. "As a potential board member, she wanted me to be aware of some things she thought were a little abnormal."

Mr. Everett's brows furrowed. "Is it something you feel you should pursue?"

"If they accept me as a board member, I certainly would."

He nodded. "With your extensive work experience in guiding such an endeavor, you would be a tremendous asset to the charity."

"I like to think so. But I'm afraid it doesn't look good."

"And why is that?"

Tricia shrugged and went back to her planting. "The director has taken a dislike to me. I'm not sure I can overcome that hurdle."

"They would be very foolish not to take you on."

Tricia managed a smile. "Thank you."

Tricia's ringtone sounded and she quickly peeled off her gloves to answer the call. "All hands on deck," Pixie said excitedly. "A couple of buses just rolled down Main Street."

"We'll be right down." Tricia tapped the end-call icon. "We're about to be hit with customers."

"And we've finished just in time," Mr. Everett said, patting the dirt around the last of the begonias.

While Tricia quickly watered her new flowers, Mr. Everett washed his hands in the kitchen sink and then they headed down the stairs to greet their customers.

Tricia was practically giddy to jump in and run the register for the next two hours, which seemed to speed by incredibly fast. All too soon the last of the book buyers walked out the door, bags filled with tomes, and Tricia and her employees sat down in the nook to take a breather.

"Look at the time," Pixie said, her gaze moving from the clock to Tricia. It was already after five. Less than an hour to go before the store closed for the day. "And didn't that feel good?"

"I thank heaven above for every bus that brings us customers," Tricia said.

"They sure scarfed up the coffee and goodies we had, too."

"Well, that's what it's there for. Hopefully, it makes them happy enough to buy more books."

"They sure bought a lot today. You need to start thinking about finding some new stock," Pixie said.

"I did look at what we have on hand and came to the same conclusion. I'll make some calls and go online to see what I can come up with. We want to have plenty of books available for the rest of the summer." Pixie nodded. "What's your take on stocking more Nancy Drew mysteries?" Tricia asked.

"Definitely. We've got older ladies who want to revisit the series and try to collect every book—and not only that but introduce the series to their grandkids. We can definitely move them, the Hardy Boys books, and Trixie Belden, too."

"Great idea."

Pixie got up. "I'll start cleaning up the beverage station if you want to scoop up the cash and receipts and get it ready for tomorrow's bank deposit."

Tricia stood, too. "Good idea."

With most of the day's receipts in hand, Tricia went down to her basement office and got everything ready for the bank and then locked the zippered bank bag in the back of her desk. She glanced at the clock and decided she had enough time to do a quick Google search on Monterey Bioresources.

The website she turned up was tidy and easy to navigate. Bully for them. At the top of the site was a slideshow of happy pets—a Labrador retriever with a ball in its mouth, guinea pigs, ferrets, pink pigs, all happy and healthy. But as Tricia dug into the site she found that Cori at the shelter had been wrong about the company. They didn't do direct experimentation on animals; they just raised them *to be* experimented on by any company that would pay the price. One of their featured canines was beagles—Vera Olson's favorite dogs.

Tricia paged through the company's mission statement, their history, and the benefits of animal research—not convinced.

Companies within the medical and pharmaceutical industries had strong words of praise for Monterey Bioresources, but the whole idea of raising puppies and piglets for research sickened her.

But then, didn't it also make her a hypocrite to feel that way? The agricultural industry raised pigs, cows, and chickens for slaughter—and unless she instantly became a vegetarian, she had no right to condemn a company whose products might help find cures for cancer and other diseases.

A glance at the time listed at the bottom of her computer screen reminded Tricia she had better get back to her store, for it was just about time to close.

Mr. Everett dusted the shelves while Pixie stood behind the cash desk, the yellowed pages of an open book in front of her. "We didn't have any more customers."

"And we're not likely to. Why don't you two head on home? I've got a martini waiting for me next door."

"I wouldn't want to keep you from it," Pixie said, and laced a bookmark between the pages before closing her current read. Mr. Everett divested himself of his apron and Pixie grabbed her purse while Tricia withdrew her keys from her slacks pocket and closed the blinds on the big display window, turned off the lights, and turned the OPEN sign to CLOSED.

"Good night, Ms. Miles," Mr. Everett said.

"Thank you for helping me plant my flowers."

"You're very welcome."

"See you tomorrow," Pixie called, and the two employees headed out the door and off toward the municipal parking lot.

Tricia locked up and walked over to the Cookery, where she found Angelica cleaning out the cash drawer while June gathered her purse, getting ready to leave.

"Hello," Angelica greeted her sister. "We had a wonderful sales day. How about you?"

"I'm not complaining. Sorry I didn't call to cancel our lunch."

"Don't worry—I was too busy to eat, too. Why don't you head on upstairs? Everything's ready. I'm just going to lock up and then I'll come and join you."

"Righto. Good night, June."

"And to you, too."

Tricia headed for the stairs and Angelica's apartment above. As usual, Sarge was in seventh heaven to see his Auntie Tricia and nearly did a backflip in anticipation of the biscuits he knew were to come. "Calm down already!"

As Angelica had said, their martinis and glasses were chilling in the fridge, along with a plate filled with what looked like melba rounds, cream cheese, plump pink shrimp, and some kind of jam wrapped in plastic. She got them out, too. She was just about to pour the martinis when Angelica made an appearance.

"What a day. I am *so* ready for that drink." Angelica stashed the bank bag with cash in a drawer and washed her hands. "Want to sit outside again?"

"Yes. I might even kick off my shoes, too."

"Well, let's not waste time." Angelica grabbed the tray with the drinks and Tricia carried the plate of goodies as they made their way onto the balcony. Once outside, Angelica set the tray down and looked in Tricia's direction—then did a double take. "Hey, there are flowers on your balcony."

"Aren't they pretty? I stopped at the garden center and bought them, and then Mr. Everett helped me plant them."

"He's such an angel."

They took their seats and Tricia pointed to the plate of appetizers. "What are these things?"

"Shrimp pepper poppers, and they couldn't be easier to make, either," Angelica said. "Take a melba round, toss on a little cream cheese—you can use the reduced-fat kind if you're so inclined; I wasn't—put on a boiled shrimp and a little dab of that wonderful pepper jam I sell in the shop, and voilà! Easiest appetizer in the world and it actually tastes good."

"I'll have to remember that," Tricia said, taking her seat. She gazed out over the fence in the alley. The world seemed at peace, and she did kick off her shoes while Angelica poured the drinks, handing one to her. "Cheers."

They took their first sips.

"So how was your day?" Angelica asked.

Tricia looked at Sarge, who sat by her chair looking hopeful, and then remembered the pictures of beagles on the Monterey Bioresources web pages and decided she wasn't going to mention it to Angelica. "Uh—not bad. I ran into that new lady cop, Officer Pearson, at the grocery store this morning."

"And?" Angelica asked.

"She wasn't exactly happy to see me."

"What do you mean?"

"I don't know how to describe it. She seemed uncomfortable that I called to her and then about the subject of our brief conversation."

"Seeing you out of context probably made her feel like a fish out of water."

"*She* was the one out of context. She was dressed in civvies and it took me a few moments to remember where I'd seen her and who she was."

"And what did you talk about?"

"Joyce, of course. Or rather—she *wouldn't* talk about Joyce's situation."

"That's not really surprising, is it?"

"No. But it seemed odd that she seemed to feel uncomfortable about it."

"If she patronizes Joyce's store, that's really not all that surprising, is it? On the reverse side, I know I would hate to think any of my customers could be up to no good."

"Yeah," Tricia agreed. "But something wasn't right about the encounter."

"Like what?"

Tricia sighed. "I don't know. I can't put my finger on it."

"How long has she been with the police department anyway?"

"Two or three months."

"Does Grant ever do anything for his new hires?"

"Like what?"

"I don't know. Take them around to introduce them to the merchants along Main Street?"

"Not that I know of."

"Unlike today, I'm so rarely at the Cookery anymore that I wouldn't know. But I would think it would be a good idea to have a cop on the beat—if only for PR value."

"The force is too small to waste manpower for that."

"I don't know. They say that cops on the beat—who know the locals—could stop crime before it happened. I wonder if that should be mentioned at the next Board of Selectmen meeting."

"I'll let you be the one to introduce the subject."

"Maybe I will."

"What's going on with the day spa?"

"I do wish you'd come over and see all the changes I've made. After all, you'll be using their services, too."

"You assume."

"Oh, come on. Why drive to another town when you can just walk down the street to get your roots done or have a manicure. You'll be in and out in an hour instead of wasting all that time traveling."

"I suppose," Tricia said neutrally.

"What else is new?"

"Pixie has informed me that we're running low on stock."

"You mean you hadn't noticed yourself?"

"I did, but with all this baking I've been doing, I haven't had a chance to pursue it. I'd better make it my business to do so pretty quick."

"You need to diversify. I mean, there are only so many copies of vintage mysteries out there."

"And the old pulp paperbacks crumble so easily," Tricia agreed.

"The truth is, my stock of vintage cookbooks is running low, too. I hate to admit it, but sometimes I actually miss Frannie. She used to stop at yard sales and find all sorts of interesting books, cookie cutters, and bowls we could sell in the shop for a tidy markup."

Tricia knew that was the only reason her sister would miss her former store manager.

"I've got a lot of time on my hands these days. I may even start going to yard sales to see what I can find."

"I'd love to go with you, but I'm so busy," Angelica lamented.

"You put in a seven-day workweek. I'm sure you could take a couple of hours off every Saturday—at least for the rest of the summer. We should make a plan to go thrifting. I'm sure Pixie could give us some helpful pointers."

"Great idea."

"Two pairs of eyes are better when searching for older mysteries and cookbooks, too. We both have a pretty good idea of what the other sells."

"You're right." Angelica drained the last of her martini and popped one olive into her mouth and chewed. Sarge gave a little *woof!* "Darling boy, your mommy hasn't forgotten you. Come inside and she'll give you a nice treat before she makes another pitcher of drinks." She got up and turned to Tricia. "Did you want more pepper poppers?"

Tricia shook her head, gazing down at Sarge and seeing the look of absolute adoration he gave his mistress, and then again thought about the dogs raised at Monterey Bioresources for a miserable life in a metal cage with no hope for love and companionship. The thought made her cringe. She stood, too. "Can I help you make those drinks?"

"Sure, why not?"

So the three of them—two women and a dog—went inside to continue happy hour.

But how bitter a thought it was to know that the dogs raised for experimentation would never know what it meant to walk in the sunshine or feel real grass beneath their paws.

FOURTEEN

Donna showed up exactly at nine o'clock the next morning, and Tricia led her to the kitchen in her apartment above Haven't Got a Clue. She'd prepared by baking a dozen cupcakes and two eight-inch yellow cake layers and by purchasing an array of tubs of commercially prepared frosting. She also had a bag of confectioners' sugar on hand in case the prepared stuff proved too soft to pipe. In addition, she made sure she had every tip available for cake decorating, plus a gross of disposable piping bags, too. A fresh pot of coffee was brewing, and she had set out her teapot with an assortment of tea bags—plus two different kinds of colas in the fridge in case Donna had a preference.

"Wow. You're ready for anything," Donna said, taking in the supplies cluttering the kitchen island.

Tricia managed a weak laugh. "I just wanted to be prepared. Would you like coffee or tea or a soda?"

Donna shook her head. "Nope. Let's get to work."

Donna didn't have the finesse of the cake decorators on YouTube videos, but she could make a nice-looking rose, and by the time they'd finished their first lesson, Tricia could, too. That, at least, gave her hope. As she stood over her cake and cupcakes with variously tinted ornamentation, she couldn't help but smile.

"Thanks so much for coming over," Tricia said as she handed Donna a check.

"Thank you." Donna waved the piece of paper. "Every little bit helps me get closer to my dream."

"And what's that?"

"Opening my own candy shop."

Tricia smiled. "Funny you should say that. So many people around here have told me they think Stoneham needs a candy store."

"I wasn't thinking of locating it here. I thought about opening one in Merrimack."

"Why there?"

"Rents are lower than in Stoneham or Nashua. There's a spot in a strip mall that I've had my eye on for a while."

"We've got great foot traffic for almost eight months of the year. I think there'd be enough local support to keep you open during the slow months."

"I don't think so."

"What if I knew someone who might give you a break on a lease here in Stoneham?"

Donna shrugged. "I'd have to see the agreement, but it would be closer. I live just outside of Milford. And I know my candy sells here."

"What do you mean?"

"I have a contract with the Coffee Bean. The candy featured in one of their display cases is all mine."

"Really?" The Coffee Bean did indeed carry some decadent-looking chocolates, but it was a very small selection and Tricia had never indulged in them.

Donna nodded. "As a matter of fact, I just bought a new candy mold the other day—of little opened books."

Tricia's eyes widened. "You haven't yet made them for the Coffee Bean, have you?"

Donna shook her head. "I haven't had a chance to try it out. I was thinking I'd make the pages with white chocolate, and then fill in the rest with milk or dark chocolate. They'd be awfully cute, and they'd probably be quite popular in a place known as Booktown."

They would indeed.

"Would you mind holding off offering them to the Coffee Bean—just until after the Bake-Off?"

Donna positively grinned. "You want to top your cupcake with one of those little books."

"It would look adorable—and might just give me the edge I need to win, or at least final. It would really help my charity. I'd be willing to make it worth your while."

"As I understand it, you have to make everything that goes on the cupcake, save for sprinkles, et cetera, and right at the competition."

Tricia nodded. It sounded like Donna had looked into the rules of the Bake-Off since they'd first spoken. "Pouring melted chocolate into a mold doesn't sound all that hard."

"It's not as easy as you think, at least depending on the quality of the chocolate you want to present. The way I do it has many steps, like tempering the chocolate. But if you only want something the quality of those commercial sampler boxes of chocolate, you can use candy melts, but you won't be a chocolatier. That takes time and a lot of experience. I've been taking classes for years, and I even have a degree in it."

This woman was really serious about her chocolates.

"I just want to be able to produce a piece of candy that looks cute and will taste good enough to get by. They're judging the cupcake, hopefully not just the decoration. Would you help me—please?"

Donna looked thoughtful, then shrugged. "Yeah, I guess I can teach you enough to get through the contest, and I can loan you the mold. But only if you promise to give it back right after the Bake-Off."

"You have my word."

"Okay. I've got time to come over tomorrow morning."

"Fine, just tell me what ingredients I need to get and I'll be ready."

After showing Donna out, Tricia returned to her apartment and sent the domed cake plates down the dumbwaiter to her store. The customers never complained when there were free goodies available, although Pixie had mentioned finding a few paperbacks with sticky covers.

Once downstairs, Tricia transferred the cupcakes to the beverage station, setting out a thick wad of paper napkins.

"Yet more practice goodies?" Pixie asked.

"Yes."

She took a gander. "Whoa! You're learning to decorate?"

"Just in time for the Bake-Off. What do you think?"

Pixie grinned, her gold canine tooth flashing. "That they look good enough to eat."

"Help yourself."

"Don't mind if I do—but my skirt might have something to say about it. With all this baking you've been doing, I've had to let a couple of them out."

"Don't be silly. You look fantastic."

Pixie looked down at her vintage pink suit and the chunky white beads that hung around her neck. "I do, don't I?"

Tricia laughed. "Now you're beginning to sound like Angelica."

"I'll take that as a compliment," Pixie said, and reached for the glass dome. She set it aside and picked up one of the cupcakes, setting it on a napkin.

"They're not anything spectacular; just yellow cake, I'm afraid—I'm still trying to decide what recipe I'll use for the Bake-Off."

"There are lots of things you could do to make them look even prettier."

"Like what?"

"Edible sparkles, maybe airbrushing them with different color glazes."

"You sound like you've been boning up on decorating, too."

Pixie waved a hand in dismissal. "Nah, I just watch too many cooking shows on TV." She laughed. "Fred says I should stop watching them and get in the kitchen and actually cook for a change."

"So why don't you?"

"It would cut into my reading time."

Which seemed a perfectly reasonable explanation—at least to Tricia.

"I have a quick errand to run. I'll be back in a few minutes," Tricia said.

"I'll be here all day," Pixie promised.

Tricia left the store, waited for traffic, and then crossed the street, heading for the Coffee Bean. If she was going to ask Angelica about rental space for a candy store, she figured she'd better have a taste of Donna's product. Apparently, anybody could melt chocolate bits, but making a delectable product was something else. From the sound of it, Donna had the knowledge and the experience. Now to taste test the results.

Only one other person waited to be served when Tricia arrived at the coffee shop, which gave her time to study the chocolates on offer. Each shiny morsel sat in a little brown glassine candy cup. As she'd observed before, there were only eight different kinds of dipped chocolates, half made of milk chocolate and the rest of dark. She'd try them all—or at least buy one of each and share them with Angelica.

It was Alexa herself who was behind the counter that morning. Tricia always enjoyed hearing her Russian accent and thought of her as a friend.

"Tricia, velcome. Vhat can I do for you today?"

"I'd like to buy a box of your chocolates."

"I vish I could take credit for them. They're wery nice."

"I met the woman who said she makes them for you."

"Yes. Donna North."

"That's her."

"Ve been carrying them for almost a year now."

"But they don't sell well?" Tricia guessed.

"Oh, they do. But more people vant cupcakes, brownies, and scones. I vill give her a bigger order closer to the holidays. How many do you vant?"

"One of each, please."

Alexa donned plastic gloves, withdrew a flattened box, and popped it into its upright position before opening the back of the display case and selecting the chocolates with a piece of baker's tissue. "I heard you found another one," she muttered.

"Yes," Tricia admitted with a sigh. There was no mistaking what Alexa had meant.

"I heard she vas mean to Joyce the day she died."

"Vera was certainly angry with her on Monday," Tricia said.

"Joyce could be in serious trouble," Alexa said, then set the box on top of the counter and tucked in the tabs, closing it. She sealed it shut with a foil sticker that said SWEET AS CAN BE CANDIES. Was that what Donna hoped to call her future shop?

"Wera alvays seemed nice to me. She vanted me to bake doggie treats in bulk. She vent to the Patisserie first; Nikki vas insulted—so Wera came to me before the holidays last year."

"Did you bake them for her?"

"But of course. Catering is part of our service—people, dogs—who cares? Money is money. She decorated them herself to make them pretty for the pooches at the animal rescue place vhere she wolunteered."

"I heard about that—I mean, that she volunteered for Pets-A-Plenty. I guess she was well liked there—by most."

"The director did not like her. They never got along." Alexa shook her head.

"Oh?"

Alexa nodded knowingly.

"Sounds like you knew Vera quite well."

"She vas a regular customer. I am wery sorry she has died. It's newer good to lose a repeat customer."

Tricia could second that. "How much do I owe you?"

Alexa rang up the sale and Tricia paid. "Are you looking forward to the Bake-Off?"

"I vould like to vin—if only so that I could show off the framed certificate and deprive Nikki of the pleasure."

No love lost between those competitors.

"I wish you all the luck in the world," Tricia said.

"It vill be stiff competition, but I am hopeful."

"See you at the Bake-Off—if not before."

"Good-bye," Alexa called.

As she crossed the street, Tricia wondered if she should share the chocolate bounty she'd bought with Pixie and Mr. Everett, but she decided to wait until after Angelica had had an opportunity to sample the chocolates. She had a discerning palate and would be the best judge of its quality. Tricia would buy more if they were as delectable as they looked.

But when she entered Haven't Got a Clue, Pixie picked up on her purchase thanks to the bag with the store's logo prominently displayed. "Hey, been over to the Coffee Bean? Checking out the competition?"

"Excuse me?"

"Cupcakes."

"Uh, no. Chocolates," Tricia admitted. "They're made by a local candy maker. I wanted to see if they were good enough for . . ."

"Are you going to invest in a shop?" Pixie asked hopefully.

"Not exactly, but I wanted to get Angelica's input on the product."

Pixie nodded. Tricia wasn't sure if her employee knew about Angelica's secret life as Nigela Ricita, but if she did—and the same with Mr. Everett and Grace—they never said a word or hinted they suspected the truth. Tricia preferred to keep it that way.

Tricia's ringtone sounded and she pulled her phone from her pocket, checked the number, and smiled.

"Hello, Beauty," Marshall said.

"Then you must be the Beast."

"Only in bed," he said with a laugh.

"Ha-ha. What's up?"

"Are you free for lunch?"

"I could be. What did you have in mind?"

"It's been ages since I had anything even approximating ethnic food. Care for some Mexican or Chinese?"

"Chinese sounds wonderful."

"I'll pick you up in ten minutes?"

"I'll be ready."

"See ya."

Tricia hit the end-call icon and smiled.

"Someone's got a date," Pixie sang.

"Yeah, and I'd better let Angelica know I won't be showing up for lunch." Tricia quickly sent a text.

Not to worry. Will ask Randy to join me. We can talk more about the spa. See you tonight at my place.

Tricia shook her head. "She's already replaced me with the spa's new manager."

"Angelica's already got a manager?" Pixie asked, sounding surprised.

Tricia nodded. "He sounds extremely competent. They may actually do a soft opening before their official date. They've been interviewing nail techs, too. Angelica comes home with a different color polish every day."

Pixie nodded, looking thoughtful.

"I'd better go grab my purse. I don't want to keep Marshall waiting once he gets here."

Tricia found herself smiling as she headed up the stairs to her apartment. A lunch invitation out of the blue was just the thing to perk up her day.

And she wondered if Marshall might have another reason for suggesting a lunch date, too.

FIFTEEN

Marshall's car appeared right outside Haven't Got a Clue's door on time, and Tricia practically hopped in. "So, where are we going?"

"I thought that little place in Merrimack would do," he said as the car eased away from the curb.

"Oh, yes. I've been there before with Angelica."

"In addition to the regular menu, they have a secret one for authentic Chinese food."

"I've heard some places do that. I guess I've never had the real thing."

"Once you've been to China and eaten what the regular person eats, you can't stomach the Americanized crap anymore, but you're free to peruse that menu if you wish."

Tricia glanced askance at her date. "That sounds like a challenge."

Marshall merely smiled.

The restaurant was located in a mundane strip mall, and Tricia wondered if one of the empty storefronts might have been where Donna had originally anticipated locating her candy operation. They walked through the entrance and were greeted by a giant, gold, smiling Buddha. A young Asian woman led them to their table at the far side of the restaurant. As Tricia sat down, she looked to her left to take in the big saltwater fish tank she remembered from her last visit. The fish swam back and forth and she felt sorry for them. They may have been born in the endless sea, only to end up in what for them was a tiny tank—man's inhumanity to fish on full display. It reminded her of the beagles in those terrible metal cages at Monterey Bioresources.

"We won't be needing the menus," Marshall told the hostess. "We're going to order something a little more authentic. But we would like to start off with some tea."

No two-martini lunch for Tricia.

The woman smiled. "Very good. Can I recommend the chicken feet?"

Tricia couldn't help the involuntary grimace that passed over her features.

"Fantastic. Thanks."

"Your server will be right back with your tea." The hostess turned and walked away.

"Chicken feet?" Tricia asked uncertainly.

"Oh, yeah. They're delicious. They cook them for half of forever so that they're almost gelatinous. They're served with a ginger black bean sauce that's out of this world."

"I'll take your word for it," Tricia said, chagrined.

"Really? You're not going to try them?"

"Why don't we order two dishes and we can share," she suggested.

"And what were you thinking of getting?"

"Something vegetable based." Definitely.

"Do you like bok choy?"

"I do, actually."

"That's acceptable," he said in a rather condescending tone.

Oh, really?

The waitress arrived with their tea and some crispy noodles with sides of the usual duck sauce and Chinese mustard. At least Tricia was familiar with those items. Not that she was nervous about trying something unique. Marshall had never steered her wrong when it came to tempting her with new-to-her foods.

Marshall ordered for them, including stir-fried bok choy. Once the waitress had departed, he launched into another subject.

"I had another meeting with Milford Travel this morning. They're going to let me tag along on one of their guided tours as an unpaid assistant. If I like it, we'll negotiate some kind of longer-term association."

"Who's going to take care of the Armchair Tourist while you're gone?" Tricia asked.

"I didn't get a chance to tell you before now, but I've decided to hire an assistant manager. I'm going to interview a third candidate today. What do you think?"

"Pixie's a wonder. I don't know what I would do without her." But Tricia could remember when Pixie was just an assistant—and not the assistant *manager* of her store. Oh, how she missed those days. "If you travel, where will you be going?"

"Ireland. They want to stick to English-speaking countries, at least at first. I would have preferred something a little less pedestrian, but there will be a learning curve, so it makes sense."

"Uh-huh."

Tricia listened politely, alternately dipping noodles into the sauce or mustard and sipping her tea while Marshall gave her an in-depth report on his meeting. His enthusiasm made her smile, and she wished she felt that same zeal.

Their entrées arrived with a bowl of brown rice and Tricia looked at the fried chicken feet, tried not to grimace, and wondered where the rest of the chickens had gone. Sweet-and-sour chicken? Sesame chicken? Chicken egg foo yung—or maybe all of them?

"It smells good," she said truthfully if not enthusiastically. But was she actually going to be able to eat a chicken's foot?

"Why don't you just try one? I won't ask you to eat any more."

"Well, okay."

Tricia took the serving spoon and fished out one of the uninviting feet, putting it on her plate. Marshall took a much bigger helping, along with some of the stir-fry. "Well, dig in," he said.

Screwing up her courage, Tricia picked up her fork and cut off a tiny piece of the meat and put it in her mouth. The taste was actually pretty good. She took another larger bite. Not bad at all. Picking up the serving spoon, she helped herself to two more of the feet, a scoop of the stir-fry, and a little rice.

Marshall seemed pleased by her acceptance and dug into his meal, continuing his recitation right where he'd left off.

By the time Tricia had had her fill, she leaned back in the booth. "I have to admit, that was superb."

"Not bad," Marshall agreed. "I tried making the chicken feet myself, but it's just too time-consuming. It's much easier to come here when I get the urge for them."

Tricia was about to laugh when she looked up and saw Joyce Widman enter the restaurant. She was about to wave her over to say hello when Joyce was joined by someone else: Officer Cindy Pearson, who was not in uniform. Tricia instinctively ducked down as the hostess took the couple to a booth on the opposite side of the room, and Tricia was pretty sure they hadn't seen her.

"That's odd," she whispered.

"Yeah, it isn't often my date tries to take a powder," Marshall said in his best Bogie impersonation.

"No. Joyce Widman and Officer Pearson just came in together."

"What's so odd about two people coming to a restaurant to eat?"

"Because Cindy Pearson is a cop. The one who took Joyce in for questioning the day of Vera Olson's murder."

"So? Didn't you tell me that this officer was also a customer at the romance store?"

"Yes."

"So, maybe they've struck up a friendship. I've done that myself."

"Or maybe they were friends *before* the murder," Tricia said.

"Why would that be a problem?"

"As far as I know, neither of them mentioned it to Chief Baker."

"That you know of," Marshall pointed out. He shook his head. "My dear Tricia, you've read far too many mysteries. You can't help yourself from trying to find criminal intent where there is none."

"I'm not looking for criminal intent. I just think it's a little unusual."

She didn't have a chance to elaborate, for the waitress arrived with the check. "Can I get you anything else?"

"Do you want the leftovers?" Marshall asked.

Tricia shook her head.

"Could I have a take-home box?"

The waitress nodded. "I'll be right back."

Tricia's mind was still whirling with possibilities as Marshall dipped into his wallet and extracted a number of bills, leaving them on the table.

The waitress arrived with the box and Marshall filled it and then placed it in the plastic bag that had accompanied it. "Tonight's supper is taken care of."

They got up to leave. As Tricia passed the second aisle of booths, she glanced over to the table where Joyce and Officer Pearson sat.

For some reason, she wasn't surprised to see that their eyes were locked and they were holding hands.

SIXTEEN

The ride back to Stoneham was quiet—at least on Tricia's end. She barely listened as Marshall talked about the possibilities of an alliance with Milford Travel, and Tricia didn't confide her suspicions about a possible relationship between Joyce and Cindy Pearson.

When Joyce had arrived in Stoneham six or so years before, she said she'd been fresh off a divorce. She'd never given Tricia any details about why she and her former spouse had parted, but Tricia was sure Joyce had been married to a man. Could the reason for their enforced separation have been that Joyce had fallen in love with another woman? And if Joyce was now interested in women, why did she sell, and presumably read, romance novels that dealt with male-female relationships?

Of course, Tricia was aware that sometimes women who'd had bad experiences with men called it quits on the opposite sex. One of her former female co-workers who had partnered with another woman had once confided to her that while she was in love with her new companion, she wasn't all that thrilled with the sexual side of the relationship. There was more to life than just sex, she'd opined.

Then again, maybe Joyce was bisexual.

And what were the ramifications of a relationship between a possible murder suspect and someone in the police department who was investigating the crime? Sure, there was a serious conflict of interest on Cindy Pearson's part. The fact that the women were meeting in a town outside of Stoneham meant they hadn't wanted to be seen by friends or colleagues. Had all their trysts been away from prying eyes—and wagging tongues—in Stoneham?

Tricia was so preoccupied, she didn't notice that the car had stopped and the engine had been turned off until Marshall touched her arm. "Hey, are you okay?"

It was then Tricia realized they had returned to the Stoneham municipal parking lot.

"I'm sorry. I was lost in thought."

"I'll say. Is there anything you want to talk about?"

Not to him. What preoccupied Tricia's mind was something that required girl talk. Or more precisely, sister talk.

"Not right now."

Marshall shrugged, picked up his container of leftovers, and opened the driver's-side door. Tricia got out and the two of them started toward the main drag's sidewalk. Along the way, Marshall reached for Tricia's hand. It soon became sticky with perspiration, but she didn't let go and neither did Marshall, that is, until they stopped in front of her store's door.

"Thank you for lunch. It was . . . illuminating." And in more ways than one.

"I'm happy you were so open to trying something new. Next time, I hope you'll give the snake soup a chance."

Tricia wrinkled her nose. "Maybe not."

Marshall laughed, leaned forward, and kissed the tip of Tricia's nose.

"What are your plans for the rest of the day?"

"I need to get ready for the Bake-Off."

"So no drink at the Dog-Eared Page and . . ." He raised an eyebrow and let the sentence trail off.

"I didn't say that."

"Good. Then I'll see you around eight?"

She smiled. "I wouldn't miss it."

This time he gave her a proper but not a passionate kiss. Tricia didn't want tongues wagging about her, either.

"Hey, Tricia," Pixie called cheerfully as Tricia came through the door of Haven't Got a Clue. "What's new?"

"Have you ever had Chinese chicken feet?"

"Oh, yeah. They're de-lish! Me and Fred order 'em all the time from this little dive in Merrimack."

Did everybody know about the secret Chinese menu except Tricia? "Yes, so I discovered."

"Good for you! What else is new?"

Tricia knew Pixie meant in the romance department, but that wasn't a subject she was likely to get into—and neither was what she'd seen when leaving the restaurant. "Not much. But the day is still young."

"You got it."

"I'm going down to the office to do a little work. Call me if you need me."

"Will do."

Pixie's gaze dipped back to the open book on the counter and

Tricia headed for the stairs to the basement. Settling in her office chair, she awakened her computer and did a quick Google search on Officer Cynthia Pearson of the Stoneham Police Department. As she'd assumed she would, all she found was a brief mention from a press release that had been posted on the Stoneham PD website. But she not only picked up a middle initial but that the officer was originally from the Boston area, which helped her in her next search. Then again, the only entry that popped up was from a Classmates.com yearbook entry. Apparently, Officer Pearson had once been a track-and-field star at Brookline High School in Massachusetts. Her senior picture didn't look all that different from what she looked like today. Tricia frowned.

On impulse, Tricia decided to Google herself and found more than twenty entries that harked back to her years at the nonprofit in Manhattan, as well as pictures and short articles on Haven't Got a Clue. Unfortunately, there were too many newspaper and TV entries that mentioned her in conjunction with some of the deaths that had occurred in Stoneham.

She clicked the little *x* in the corner of her screen. She didn't need to be reminded of those occasions.

Tricia leaned back in her chair. A fat lot of good her search for Officer Pearson had been. What had she really learned? The woman's middle initial, that she used to run fast (or did she jump high?), and that she wasn't a local.

If Cindy Pearson was new to the village, probably not that many people knew her. This is where the long tentacles of Frannie Armstrong's spy network would have been useful. Pixie listened to gossip, but she didn't often repeat what she heard. Still, was it really gossip to ask a question about the woman? Tricia decided to find out and headed back up the stairs to the shop.

Pixie was speaking with a customer, giving a bit of a speech about author Dashiell Hammett's most famous sleuth, Sam Spade. Pixie really did have a flair for the dramatic, and, of course, she was dressed as though she could have been a dame the famed detective might have been attracted to. She would have made a wonderful docent in some kind of a mystery-oriented museum.

Tricia waited behind the register, and when the woman came up with her purchases, she rang up the sale while Pixie continued to chat. Since there were no other customers in the store, this took another ten minutes, since neither Pixie nor the customer seemed to be in a hurry to end the conversation. At last, the woman left the store.

"That was a pretty good sale," Pixie commented, sounding pleased.

"You have a way of getting people to part with their credit cards."

"All in a good cause," she said, grinning. Then she scrutinized Tricia's face. "What's on your mind?"

"My mind?"

"Yeah."

Not much got past Pixie.

"I've been thinking about the new lady cop in town."

"Officer Pearson?"

Tricia nodded.

Pixie scowled. "I try to stay away from cops—probably from being arrested so many times. But I think it's good they hired at least one woman. Course, they can be just as mean as men, and some of them can rough you up just as bad."

Oh, dear. Tricia hadn't considered how the subject of the new policewoman might affect Pixie.

Pixie seemed to notice Tricia's hesitation. "You were saying?"

"Uh, I've met her a few times."

"And?"

Tricia shrugged. "She seems . . . nice."

Pixie nodded and seemed to be considering her next question. "You miss Frannie, don't you?"

"The woman tried to kill me," Tricia said gravely.

"Yeah, but she sure knew what was going on here in Stoneham at every minute of the day."

"Yeah," Tricia ruefully admitted.

Pixie's mouth drooped. "I thought she and I were friends. We went to tag sales together, remember?"

Tricia nodded.

"I was horrified when she changed, and especially when I found out she was trying to hurt you and Angelica. And threatening Antonio and Ginny's daughter Sofia was just deplorable." Pixie shook her head, her eyes filling with tears, and for long moments there was only silence in the shop. Finally, Pixie spoke again. "I'm not Frannie. I'm not like her at all."

"No, you're not," Tricia said, giving her employee—and more important, her friend—a sincere smile.

SEVENTEEN

After she'd locked her own store, Tricia walked ten steps north, took out her keys, and unlocked the door to the Cookery. Locking it behind her, she headed up to Angelica's apartment—knowing she'd be greeted with a wagging tail and happy barking. She wasn't disappointed.

"Good evening," Angelica said as Tricia gave Sarge his treat and then set the bag from the Coffee Bean on the island. The accouterments for martinis sat on the counter, but Angelica hadn't yet started to make them. "Shall we go outside again?"

"Maybe for our second drink," Tricia suggested.

Angelica's eyes widened. "Oooh. You want to talk secrets."

"Maybe not secrets—but subjects not intended for eavesdroppers."

"Well, I'm all ears," Angelica said, and took the chilled glasses from the freezer and the pitcher of martinis from the fridge, and poured their drinks. That night, she also had a plate with cucumber pinwheels. Just four—two each—and just enough.

"Here or the living room?"

"Here is fine," Tricia said, pushed the bag aside, and sat down on the closest stool at the kitchen island.

Angelica handed her a glass. "Cheers."

They drank and Angelica took another stool. "So, how was your lunch with Marshall?"

"Exactly what I wanted to talk about." Tricia took a sip of her drink to fortify herself. "We went to that little Chinese restaurant in Merrimack. He ordered chicken feet."

"Really? How were they?"

"Surprisingly good. Next time he threatened me with snake soup."

"Oh, I don't think I'd like that." Angelica sipped her drink and looked thoughtful. "Then again, maybe I would."

Tricia gave an involuntary shudder. "But that wasn't the only interesting thing that happened."

"Do tell."

"As we were finishing our meal, Joyce Widman walked into the restaurant . . . with a date."

"Oh? I didn't know she was involved. Anyone I know?"

"Know of—yes. Know personally? No."

"Well, don't keep me in suspense."

"Joyce came in with Officer Cindy Pearson."

Angelica frowned. "That's not a date. That's girls having lunch."

"You and I have had lunch hundreds of times, and we have never sat at a table holding hands and gazing into each other's eyes."

"Oh. That does sound like a date." Angelica took another sip of her drink.

"I wonder if Chief Baker knows about it."

"Are you going to ask?" Angelica asked with incredulity.

"I don't know. I mean . . . Cindy Pearson could get into a lot of trouble—maybe even lose her job over it."

"Which is why they were in Merrimack instead of Stoneham."

"I think so. But let's face it, Merrimack isn't all that far from Stoneham, and plenty of people just like me go there to shop, eat, or play golf. If they are dating, it's not going to be a secret for very long."

"But why would a woman who sells romance novels that feature men and women want to date a woman?"

Tricia told Angelica about her former co-worker.

"Not my cup of tea, but I can understand why it would happen. What did Marshall have to say about it?"

"He didn't see them—and I didn't tell him about it. I don't want to be responsible for spreading rumors—not that I think he would repeat it to anyone. But I'd also like to know who else knows about them. This is where having Frannie around would be helpful."

"Gone but not forgotten," Angelica said. "Maybe you should just keep this information under wraps until or unless it becomes relevant."

"What if it's already relevant?"

"That's not for you to decide."

Tricia shrugged. "I guess you're right," she said, and polished off the last of her drink, which had gone down much too quickly. "Getting back to secrets . . . have you decided on a recipe yet?"

"Maybe," Angelica hedged. "How about you?"

"I've narrowed it down," Tricia said evasively. That wasn't exactly true, but she was seriously considering a recipe containing lemon zest.

"Has Nigela Ricita Realty rented out the old Chamber building yet?" Tricia asked casually.

"The apartment upstairs has a tenant, but the office space is, unfortunately, still empty. Why?"

"I was wondering if it might be available for a retail space."

"Such as?"

"A candy store—or rather a chocolate shop."

"Are you going to open one?" Angelica asked, her eyes widening with pleasure.

Tricia shook her head. "But this morning I ran into a woman who makes hand-dipped chocolates. In fact, she sells some of them at the Coffee Bean. I bought a selection for us to try."

"So that's what's in the bag you brought with you. I never turn down chocolate."

Tricia retrieved the paper bag, withdrew the box, and broke the seal. She proffered it to her sister.

"What flavors are they?"

"We won't know until we bite into them."

"Chocolate really doesn't go with a martini," Angelica said.

"No, but it does go well with a nice blended whiskey, which I happen to know you've got in your liquor cabinet."

"I do. I assume you want it with ice and soda?"

"Yes, please."

Angelica cleared away their stemmed glasses and made fresh drinks while Tricia studied the shiny chocolates in the box.

Angelica returned with two old-fashioned glasses with whiskey and soda on ice. "Cheers."

They clinked glasses and sipped, and then Tricia again proffered the box. Angelica chose one at random and so did Tricia. "Down the hatch," she said, and bit into the chocolate.

Tricia did likewise and was impressed by the pronounced snap as the chocolate shell broke, its silky texture, and the explosion of pure maple goodness that blessed her taste buds. "Oh, my goodness, that's fantastic," she said after swallowing.

"What did you get?" Angelica asked.

"Maple cream. How about you?"

"Pistachio—which is ironic because . . ." But then she didn't finish the sentence. "It's absolutely divine." She polished off the other half of her chocolate, practically swooning. "Where did you say you met this woman?"

"I didn't, but it was actually at the bakery at Shaw's in Milford. Her name is Donna North."

"What were you doing there?" Angelica asked with suspicion.

"Getting a loaf of bread," Tricia fibbed, because she'd actually forgotten to buy one. "We got to talking and she mentioned she supplied the gourmet chocolates for the Coffee Bean. More than once you and I have talked about the need for a chocolatier here in Stoneham. She might just be the one."

"Oh. Well. I think I'd better taste test another one of those goodies to make sure."

Again, Tricia held out the box. "Be my guest."

They both tried another, Tricia getting an orange cream while Angelica's turned out to be salted caramel, both delivering the same sensational taste.

"Tell me more about this very talented woman," Angelica said.

Tricia gave her a brief rundown. "Unfortunately, Donna's thinking of opening her store in Merrimack in a strip mall."

"Oh, no. Chocolate this good deserves a beautiful home in a charming setting. I'll give Karen Johnson"—the woman who managed Angelica's realty company—"a call later. She's good at recruiting businesses to locate to the village. We must add Donna North to our roster of talented businesspeople. Good show, Tricia."

It never ceased to please Tricia when her sister gave her praise. For too many years it had been absent from their conversations.

"Besides finding some of the best chocolate in the state, how was the rest of your day?" Angelica asked, and sipped her drink.

"Relatively quiet." Tricia sampled her drink once more. The whiskey, with its sweet caramel aftertaste, was an enjoyable change from a martini. "How about you?"

"Work on the spa continues. Randy has some great ideas for decorating the place."

"When am I going to meet this wonderful man?"

"As soon as you walk down the street and enter the building."

"You know I want to wait for the grand opening," Tricia said.

"Yes. And speaking of which, just this morning we started taking appointments."

"Really?"

"Yes. Unlike you, some residents and merchants here in Stoneham are actually *eager* for us to open. I gave four tours today. My potential customers were pleased to learn we'd have a complimentary coffee bar with snacks, and that although we'll carry several lines of beauty products, Randy suggested we don't do a hard sell like some of the national chains. Customers don't like it."

"Another plus," Tricia agreed. She raised her glass. "Let's drink a toast to your new spa . . . whatever it's called."

"Yes, here's to my day spa." Angelica looked at her glass, which contained just shards of ice. "One more for the road?"

Tricia shook her head. "We'd better start making supper. I'm meeting Marshall in a couple of hours and I don't want to be blotto."

"Oh, well. Then again, someone might get lucky tonight," Angelica said with just a touch of salaciousness.

Lucky?

Maybe. But it might be another emotion that drew Tricia to connect with her friend with benefits. Something she did not want to acknowledge: a sense of desperation.

As usual, the Dog-Eared Page was hopping when Tricia arrived, with a boisterous game of darts going on in the back of the pub, while joyous Celtic tunes played from the sound system overhead. Tricia spied Marshall at the bar, looking far better than a dozen decorated cupcakes.

He looked up, saw Tricia, and then spoke to the bartender, Hoshi Tanaka, probably ordering their drinks. Hoshi grabbed a stemmed glass and filled it with ice to chill, as Marshall approached.

"Hey there, beautiful."

"Hey there yourself, handsome."

They gave each other a light kiss on the lips, and then Marshall led them to one of the few empty tables, as all of the booths were full. "Why don't we go outside instead? It's a lovely evening," Tricia suggested.

"Okay. I'll just tell Hoshi and meet you out there."

Tricia exited the bar by the side door. Fairy lights lit the area that had once housed the History Repeats Itself bookstore. The brick patio was dotted with a number of bistro tables and chairs, and Tricia took one near the back, away from the other patrons. The music was piped outside but wasn't nearly as loud as it had been inside the bar. She sat down to wait for Marshall, who appeared in less than a minute. He took the seat opposite her.

"How was the rest of your day?" she asked.

"Good." He gave her a toothy grin.

"Tell me all about it."

He nodded. "Remember I mentioned I was interviewing someone this afternoon for the assistant manager's position? Well, I may have found her."

Her? A frisson of anxiety coursed through Tricia. "Do tell."

"Her name is Ava Campbell and she's in her midtwenties."

Was the second-most important characteristic about the woman her age?

"What are her qualifications?" Tricia asked politely.

"She's worked in retail before, but get this—she's also traveled all over the world."

"How does someone that age become a world traveler?"

"Army brat."

Tricia nodded.

"She speaks three languages—not that I expect she'd get to use them at the Armchair Tourist, but you never know."

"Of course," Tricia agreed, trying to keep her voice light. She hadn't yet gotten over the fact that the young woman was almost half her age. Was she pretty, too?

Tricia gave herself a mental headshake. Pettiness didn't suit her.

"I'm hoping Ava works out because"—Marshall dragged out the last word—"the Ireland trip I was telling you about at lunch is definitely on."

"When would you be going away?"

"September. That gives me plenty of time to train Ava." He leaned closer. "Now that Haven't Got a Clue is running like a well-oiled machine, thanks to Pixie, I thought exploring the world might be something we could do together."

Tricia blinked. "Oh?"

"I can't think of a better traveling companion than you."

Tricia smiled. "Where do you want to go—besides Ireland?"

Marshall's eyes widened in anticipation. "Tokyo. Mumbai. Brisbane. Maybe even back to China. There's an awful lot of that country I haven't seen."

And Tricia had *never* seen. "I thought the travel agency hosted mostly cruises."

"They're going to be looking at more exotic ports of call—they're just gauging interest right now, but who knows." His voice practically vibrated with expectation. "What do you think?"

Tricia forced a laugh. "I don't know what to think. It sounds appealing." But what about Miss Marple? If Tricia went on extended trips, how would her cat feel about being abandoned? Oh, sure. Pixie and Mr. Everett could feed her and clean her litter box, but the poor cat would be left alone for sixteen hours a day and sleep alone at night.

Would Marshall expect Tricia to join him on his first trip? He hadn't mentioned it and she wasn't sure she wanted to ask. It might not be much fun if he was helping tour members with lost luggage or finding people to fix plugged sinks in their hotel rooms or cabins while she sat in a room all alone twiddling her thumbs.

Don't be such a spoilsport, Tricia chided herself.

Bev arrived with their drinks and a small bowl of potato chips. "Isn't it a gorgeous evening?" she asked as she set down cocktail napkins, their glasses, and the bowl.

"Thanks," Tricia said, and Marshall gave the waitress a nod of approval.

"Give me a holler if you need anything else," Bev said, and went to check on the guests at the other outside tables.

Tricia picked up her glass and gazed at the olives skewered by a bamboo pick with a knot at the top. She wasn't sure what she was feeling—besides unsettled. As it was, these days she didn't spend nearly enough time in her store. To leave her home and cat for weeks at a time . . . not to mention Angelica, their family dinners, and her walks with Sarge, made her heart constrict. Was she willing to give that up for companionship with a man she wasn't likely to fully bond with?

Friends with benefits. She sometimes wondered if it was the friendship or the benefits she valued most.

Marshall hoisted his glass. "Let's drink to the future—and may it be filled with lots of travel to mysterious locales."

They clinked glasses, and this time Tricia gave Marshall a more sincere smile, somehow heartened by his enthusiasm. Maybe what she needed *was* an opportunity to get away from Booktown for a while. Maybe she could look at it as an opportunity to find vintage mysteries in other countries. Considering she'd lived a fairly affluent life, she hadn't traveled much outside the US. Oh, she'd been to London, Paris, and Rome with her ex-husband, but they weren't what you could call adventurous vacations. They'd stayed in ritzy hotels and visited museums and churches. She had a feeling Marshall would be a far more exciting travel companion.

Tricia placed an elbow on the table, rested her chin in her hand, gazed into Marshall's eyes, and found she was intrigued.

"Why don't you tell me more about your plans?"

EIGHTEEN

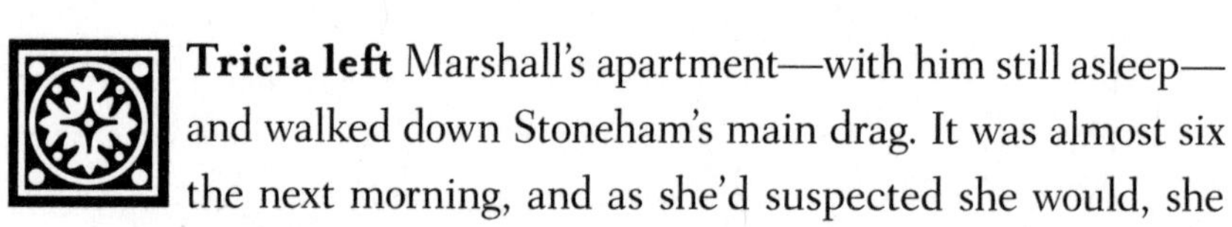

Tricia left Marshall's apartment—with him still asleep—and walked down Stoneham's main drag. It was almost six the next morning, and as she'd suspected she would, she received a stern scolding from Miss Marple. If Tricia took Marshall up on his offer to travel, maybe Miss Marple could stay with Grace and Mr. Everett, although she'd been a solitary cat for most of her life. She might not take well to sharing the affection of two of her favorite humans with other felines.

After feeding her cat, Tricia took an abbreviated walk, showered and changed, and was on the road at just after eight. She found all the ingredients she needed to make chocolates at the grocery store in Milford, anticipating the work—and the fun—that would be involved in making her first molded candies. One thing was for sure—she wasn't going to tell Angelica about it, not so she could steal Tricia's thunder at the Bake-Off.

Everything was set up when Donna arrived at 8:50. Donna had

brought not only the book mold but other tools of her trade, including a six-inch scraper, which she said would be necessary to wipe away the excess chocolate. It wasn't a tool Tricia would need per se, but Donna was a professional and she couldn't help acting like one. Once she explained what they were going to do, they immediately started to work.

Donna had been right. Tricia thought she'd melt chocolate and then slap it into a plastic mold, but Donna explained how the molds needed to be clean—really clean—without so much as a drop of water or the grease from a fingerprint, which could mar the chocolate shell. The book mold was made of a soft plastic—but not silicone—which Donna explained meant it had more detail than one made of harder plastic. Sure enough, there were actually little squiggles across the pages to mimic text. Silicone molds, she warned, were a bear to clean.

Tricia had cleared a shelf in her refrigerator so that they could chill the chocolate in between pours, even though, as Donna explained, the temperature wasn't ideal—just a little too cool. But then Tricia wasn't making a confection for the International Chocolate Awards committee.

While they waited for the chocolate to chill, Tricia introduced a new subject.

"I had an opportunity to speak to someone at Nigela Ricita Realty about a possible location for a candy store here in the village."

"And?" Donna asked cautiously.

"Do you know where the Stoneham Chamber of Commerce used to be located on Main Street?"

Donna nodded. "It's the newest storefront in the village."

Tricia nodded. "The back could be converted into a commercial kitchen without too much of a hassle. They'd like to talk to you about it. It seems Ms. Ricita herself is interested in seeing such a store open in the village. She'd like for you to talk to Karen Johnson about it—that's the Realtor in charge of leasing it."

Donna frowned and let out a breath. "This is starting to sound scary."

"I thought it was your dream to open a store."

"Yeah, but there's a lot to think about. I'm worried I might not be ready."

"It is scary opening your own business," Tricia agreed. "For many years, I had a dream to open a vintage bookstore and collected inventory for almost a decade," Tricia admitted. "When the opportunity arose to relocate here in Stoneham, I jumped at the chance."

Donna's gaze remained fixed on the counter.

"Is it a matter of money?" Tricia asked, hoping the question wasn't too unbecoming.

"Well, not really," Donna said, a note of despondency entering her tone. "I mean, right now it would be. But as it happens, I'm about to come into an inheritance. Or I will after probate."

"Oh, my. I'm so sorry for your loss. Is it recent?"

Donna nodded. "My aunt and I weren't all that close, but it turns out she left half of her estate to me and half to the Pets-A-Plenty Animal Rescue."

A shiver ran down Tricia's back. "What was your aunt's name?"

"Vera Olson."

Tricia blinked, her mouth going dry. "Vera Olson?"

"Did you know her?" Donna asked.

"Uh . . . I met her—just the one time. In fact, it was the morning of the day she died."

Donna's eyes widened.

"She visited the Have a Heart bookstore and was a little upset. I sort of witnessed the disagreement between her and the store's owner."

Donna didn't seem surprised. "Chief Baker told me a little about their tiff. I find it hard to believe my aunt would cause a scene. She was only really passionate about one thing—animal welfare—which was why she wasn't as close to our family as she once was. Some of them thought Aunt Vera carried her love of all things furry to an extreme." Donna eyed Tricia. "What was my aunt so upset about?"

"Her neighbor—who also owns the romance bookstore—had a limb cut from your aunt's tree."

Donna frowned, nodding. "I went and inspected the house and the property the other day. I saw the raw cut on that old maple. If it had been my tree, I guess I would have been just as upset if I hadn't been consulted about something like that. It was a sloppy job. But I guess without permission, they couldn't have come into my aunt's yard and cut the limb closer to the tree trunk to shape it up."

"I'm afraid Joyce, the neighbor, didn't ask your aunt."

"That was really rude of her."

Tricia thought so, too.

"I suppose she'll be happy not to have my aunt for a neighbor anymore. Although from the sound of it, she seems to be the top suspect in my aunt's murder."

The only one, as far as Tricia knew.

"Do you know this woman? Is she capable of murder?" Donna asked.

"I wouldn't have thought so."

"Does that mean you've changed your mind?"

"No. I like Joyce and I certainly wouldn't want her to be responsible for your aunt's death. But I also know that Vera didn't get along with everyone at the Pets-A-Plenty animal shelter." Toby Kingston in particular. Had Chief Baker looked into that dynamic, too? Tricia would have to find out—but maybe keep silent about what she'd seen at the Chinese restaurant the day before.

Then again, Toby Kingston wasn't a ball of personality, either. He'd taken an instant dislike to Tricia as well, not giving her much of a chance to prove herself in spite of the generous donations she'd made in the past, plus her experience working for a nonprofit with a budget that eclipsed Pets-A-Plenty's by a factor of ten or more.

"The chocolate should have hardened by now," Donna said, and turned for the fridge. She'd spread a dishcloth onto the granite counter, then took out the mold and held it in her right hand, gently whacking it on her left to dislodge the candy. "We'll let it sit on the cloth for a few minutes to let any condensation evaporate."

Next, it was time to wash the mold. "A soft cloth, a little dish soap, and then letting it air-dry will extend the life of the mold. Whatever you do, don't put it in the dishwasher. The harsh detergent can scratch it—and the extreme heat of the dry cycle is bad for the plastic, too."

Tricia nodded. She was grateful Donna was willing to trust her with the mold, and she wanted to return it in excellent shape.

Tricia stared at the little chocolate books. "They're incredibly cute."

"Try one," Donna said, and picked up one.

Tricia did likewise, feeling a little guilty, but she needed to test the candy to see if it would pass muster. No doubt about it, the little books were not the same quality chocolate as what Donna sold to the Coffee Bean. There was no pronounced snap of tempered chocolate, and in fact the chocolate melted at her touch, but they weren't any worse than an everyday chocolate bar, either. They would look cute and be an acceptable addition to her cupcake.

Now she just had to make a final decision on what flavor cupcake to bake.

Tricia walked Donna to the door and told her she'd call after the Bake-Off.

"Good luck," Donna said as she passed Pixie on the sidewalk.

"Isn't that Donna from Shaw's bakery department?" Pixie asked as she headed for the back of the sales counter to stash her purse.

"Um, yes. It was. We're . . . friends."

Pixie's eyes widened, but she said nothing.

Tricia moved to stand on the other side of the counter. "You're a woman with many talents," she began.

"Ha! You make me blush," Pixie said.

"Have you ever made chocolates?"

Tricia could almost read Pixie's thoughts. *So that's what you're up to!*

"I'm not really into cooking, but when Christmas rolls around, I've been known to don an apron and make something totally fattening. My friend Claire, she did some craft shows between stints in the joint. I helped her make some little chocolate pumpkins on a stick and wrap them in cellophane."

"Did you use a mold?"

"Oh, sure. And it was so easy. We put candy melt wafers in a glass bowl in the microwave for like thirty seconds, then stirred them until they were all melty. We used a baby spoon to fill each mold, then shoved them in the fridge for fifteen or so minutes, which gave us time for a coffee break; then we turned them out on a piece of parchment paper. Done!"

Perhaps Tricia could have just consulted Pixie for candy-making tips and saved a few bucks.

"Are you making candy?" Pixie inquired.

"Well . . . sort of. I'm really getting into the whole dessert thing and considering my options for the Bake-Off."

Pixie nodded but made no comment in that regard. "What's on tap for today?"

Tricia shrugged. "I'm still bothered by Vera Olson's murder. I need an excuse to go back to Pets-A-Plenty and ask more questions about her. It might be that her fellow volunteers knew her best."

"Here's an idea; why don't you hit up some of the board members to sponsor you for the Bake-Off?" Pixie suggested. "You said you didn't have many of them."

Tricia's eyes widened in anticipation. "That's a great idea. Why didn't I think of it?"

"Maybe you've been preoccupied."

Was it that noticeable?

"I think I'll grab my purse and go right now. That is, if you don't mind."

"That's what I'm here for."

And at that moment, Tricia was entirely grateful.

NINETEEN

In no time at all, Tricia had arrived in Milford, parked her car, and headed up the walk into the Pets-A-Plenty shelter. The door opened and a vaguely familiar woman stepped outside with a beagle on a leash. She looked past Tricia and strode right by her.

"Wait!" Tricia called.

The woman stopped but didn't turn.

Tricia walked over to join her, and the little dog sniffed the grass before squatting.

"Didn't you just adopt a dog last week?"

The woman forced a smile. "Why, yes."

"And now you're getting another one?"

"No. I'm taking Jasper here for a walk. I'm a volunteer at the shelter." She wore a T-shirt with the Pets-A-Plenty logo on it but didn't sport a name badge. "We often take the dogs out for walks. It helps in our evaluations to make sure they're fully socialized and ready for their forever homes."

Jasper pulled at the leash. It was obvious the young dog hadn't had any kind of obedience training. Perhaps the rescue left that up to the new owners.

"Do you like volunteering here at the shelter?" Tricia asked.

The woman looked perturbed. "Of course. I wouldn't be here if I didn't find the work satisfying."

"Sorry." Tricia bent down to give the dog a pat on the head. His tail wagged in ferocious little circles as he lapped up the attention.

"I'd better get going," the woman said, gave the leash a tug, and started dragging the puppy forward.

Tricia watched them head down the sidewalk, remembering what volunteer Cori had told her about Monterey Bioresources and the missing animals. Still feeling uncomfortable, she pivoted and started back for the shelter. Inside, the place felt strangely empty. Tricia walked up to the reception counter, where an unfamiliar woman stared intently at a computer screen.

"Excuse me." The woman looked up. "I'm Tricia Miles. I'm a replacement candidate for the board of directors. Are any of them on the premises?"

The woman behind the counter shook her head. The name tag on the polo shirt emblazoned with the Pets-A-Plenty logo said DOREEN. "Sorry, I'm the only one in the building. Everyone else is out to lunch."

At eleven thirty? "When will they be back?"

"After one."

Tricia nodded, disappointed. "Then I guess I'll come back later this afternoon."

"Suit yourself."

Tricia turned and headed for the door, feeling vaguely disconcerted. On all her other visits to the shelter, she'd found the volunteers to be extremely friendly and outgoing. Now she'd met two in the space of five minutes who seemed not only standoffish, but tight-lipped as well.

As Tricia walked toward her car, she looked up to see the woman with the beagle puppy down the street a ways putting the dog into a crate in the back of a black SUV. She watched as the woman got into the vehicle and took off, heading toward the highway.

On impulse, Tricia retraced her steps and entered the shelter once more. "Excuse me," she called, and Doreen the receptionist reappeared from behind the employees-only back room.

"I met a woman outside who said she was walking one of your dogs, but I just saw her get into a car with the puppy and drive off."

"She's taking him to the vet."

"But she just told me she was taking Jasper for a walk."

"She did that, too. It's not at all unusual," Doreen said blandly.

Tricia nodded.

Doreen stood there, looking bored. "I'm sorry, but I really need to get some work done."

"Sure," Tricia said, unsettled that she'd been so bluntly dismissed. She gave the woman a halfhearted smile and retraced her steps to her car. As she pulled out of the empty lot, she looked back and saw Doreen standing at the shelter's front door, watching her.

With no immediate goal and an hour and more to kill, Tricia found herself heading for the Wadleigh Memorial Library on Nashua Street. As it turned out, they were having a book sale. Since the stock was getting low at Haven't Got a Clue, Tricia took her time perusing the titles, scoring several copies of Agatha Christie reprints and a couple of older cookbooks for the Cookery. After that, she ended up at a small café and bought herself a cup of coffee, taking time to go through one of the old cookbooks, which had probably been a donation, as there were no filing numbers attached to the spine.

Since she'd taken an interest in cooking, Tricia had come to enjoy leafing through old cookbooks like the ones her grandmother had owned and was sorry she hadn't shown an interest in food prep until recently. How she would have loved to have quizzed her Grandma Miles on how to make those featherlight biscuits she used to prepare on Saturday mornings or the crusts that topped the from-scratch fruit pies she made during the summer. Angelica had memories of those times, and Tricia vowed she would ask her sister to share some of those stories.

It was then Tricia remembered her standing lunch date with Angelica at Booked for Lunch. She probably wouldn't make it if she hoped to talk to some of the board members. Pulling out her phone, she texted Angelica. *Sorry to stand you up two days in a row.*

Not a problem. Will get a quick bite and keep working at the day spa. See you tonight.

Tricia ordered a half BLT sandwich and a cup of vegetable soup and ate them at a leisurely pace. After all, she didn't have an appointment and wanted to make sure someone from the board would have returned to the shelter. She didn't want to be disappointed again.

It was 1:10 when Tricia returned to the Pets-A-Plenty site and once again strode up to the reception desk. This time, another younger woman was on duty. She wore the same polo shirt and her name tag said AUDREY. "Hi, can I help you?" she asked brightly, much more friendly than Doreen had been.

"I was told earlier that one or more of the board members might be available to see me this afternoon. I'm Tricia Miles, one of the candidates for the open board seat."

"Oh, yeah. I've heard your name being mentioned. You own a bookstore in Stoneham."

"Yes."

"Ms. Shore is in the main office. Let me ask if she has time to visit with you."

The woman disappeared and soon came back. "She said come on back." Tricia followed the woman past the employees-only door.

The shelter's main office was really just a large room with several desks with computers sitting on them. Rebecca Shore sat behind one of them with a smattering of printed spreadsheets scattered across the desk.

"Hey, Rebecca," Tricia called.

"Tricia, what a nice surprise. Please, have a seat. What brings you here on a non-meeting day?"

Tricia settled on the brown-painted metal folding chair beside Rebecca's desk. "I'm participating in the Great Booktown Bake-Off next week and Pets-A-Plenty is my designated charity. I was hoping I might get one or more of the shelter directors to sponsor me."

Rebecca grinned. "Talk about a small world. I'm signed up for the Bake-Off, too—as is Toby Kingston."

"Toby is a cupcake baker?"

"Among his other charms," Rebecca said sarcastically. "I'm afraid we've got the whole place sewn up when it comes to sponsors. In fact, some of the volunteers have sponsored both of us."

"Oh, dear." Tricia looked around the room, finding it unusual that the only paid employee—Toby—wasn't on the premises. She would have liked to have spoken to him about her earlier encounter with the staff. As he wasn't all that interested in talking to her during meetings, perhaps it would be better to just confide in Rebecca. But first, she had another question.

"About Toby . . . Do you know why he's taken such a dislike to me?"

Rebecca's gaze dipped and she shrugged. She knew something, but she wasn't about to tell. "I'm sorry you feel that way. But I think that's a subject you should take up with him."

Tricia nodded. "How did he feel about Vera Olson?"

"You didn't hear it from me," she said, leaning forward and speaking confidentially, "but he thought she had an inflated ego and believed that only she knew how the shelter should be run. On more than one occasion he reminded her—and in front of other staff—that she was only a volunteer and if she continued to be insubordinate, she could be replaced. We lost a few of our helpers because of that."

Which helped explain the lack of volunteers two days before. "Did the board call him on it?"

"We should have," Rebecca said guiltily. "But then he's just as likely to take a swipe at one of us. After all, we're only volunteers, too."

"But surely your charter gives you the right to overrule him if he doesn't act in the best interest of the organization."

"We'd be hard-pressed to prove that. Donations are up thirty-four percent since Toby came on board. Our costs have dropped by ten percent, too. It's hard to argue with those kinds of results."

Yes, it was.

"Did Toby and Vera ever have shouting matches?"

"A few times, but for the past couple of weeks Vera seemed subdued—and it was *after* she'd had a private conversation with Toby."

What could Toby have said that would have cowed Vera? Was there something fishy going on within the shelter?

"How often did Vera volunteer?"

"We have a schedule. Our volunteers sign up and we try to accommodate them, but Vera was like a piece of the furniture. She was here most days of the week—and often came in to feed the animals and clean cages on holidays, too."

Tricia frowned. Hadn't someone said that touching the cats and dogs gave Vera an allergic reaction? Maybe she didn't actually touch them when feeding or cleaning up after them.

"Is something wrong?" Rebecca asked.

"I was just thinking. Which reminds me, I was here during the lunch hour, and something kind of odd happened. I ran into a volunteer who said she was taking a puppy for a walk, but then she loaded the dog into an SUV and drove away with it."

"There's nothing odd about that at all," Rebecca said flippantly. "We want to make sure all the pets we home are socialized. The puppy went to the Milford Animal Hospital for shots. It's just standard procedure."

"That's what the woman at the desk said."

Rebecca nodded, smiling faintly. "Doreen mentioned your concerns. She said Cheryl was taking the dog to the vet for its shots."

"Do you know this woman, Cheryl?"

Rebecca looked thoughtful. "I don't think so. We have a lot of volunteers—over a hundred, in fact. I'm in and out of here throughout the week, and some of our helpers are only here a couple of hours a month. I'm sure I haven't met everyone. I'm looking forward to the Mutt Strut as an opportunity to meet not only with the people who've given our dogs forever homes but also with members of the staff who are participating, too. You should come with your sister. It's a lot of fun."

Tricia nodded. "Maybe I will." She stood. "Thanks for taking the time to see me, Rebecca."

"You're welcome here, anytime. And good luck at the Bake-Off—but not too much. I want to win, too."

Tricia couldn't help but smile. "May the best baker win."

TWENTY

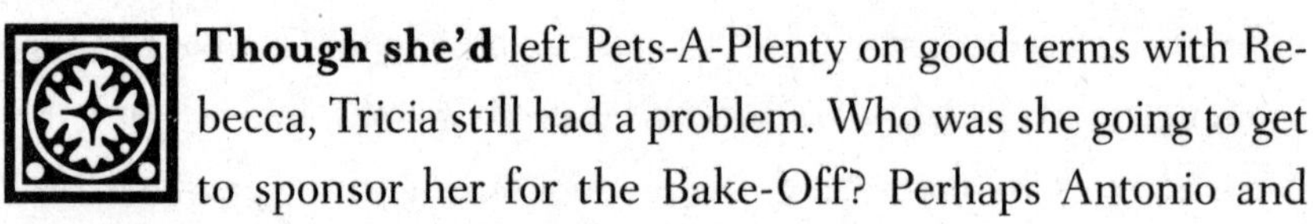

Though she'd left Pets-A-Plenty on good terms with Rebecca, Tricia still had a problem. Who was she going to get to sponsor her for the Bake-Off? Perhaps Antonio and Ginny would be willing, but then, they'd probably already sponsored Angelica. Would they be open to sponsoring her as well? She'd give Ginny a call later. And she wondered if the Everett Foundation might be willing to sponsor her, too. She could always ask Grace.

Angelica probably had asked all the people in her employ to sponsor her—and who was going to say no to her? Not that their jobs would be in jeopardy, but Angelica had a way of finagling everything she wanted.

Tricia was still pondering the problem of sponsorship when she parked her car in the municipal lot, retrieved the books she'd purchased at the sale, transferring them to a canvas bag that she kept in her trunk for just such purposes, and started back for her shop. Lost in thought, she was startled when the door to the Patisserie burst open and Nikki Brimfield-Smith popped out in a frosting-stained chef's jacket.

"I understand you've entered the Bake-Off," she said contemptuously.

"Uh, yes. I was the last contestant to sign up."

Nikki scowled. "What makes you think you've got the chops to run up against a trained pâtissier like me?"

"I'm not competing against you. Just other talented amateurs."

Apparently, that reply hadn't satisfied Nikki, whose scowl only deepened. "You think you're so special—that you can accomplish anything."

Tricia wasn't sure to how to respond to that remark, so she stood there, just staring at the woman.

"Cat got your tongue?" Nikki taunted.

"What is your problem? If you're still smarting about your breakup with Russ, don't blame me for your marital problems." He was the last man on the planet she'd want to be with—and even Russ understood that.

"He was never in love with you. He only wanted you because you rejected him."

Tricia shook her head sadly. "I wonder what your mother would say about your snide attitude and the terrible things you've said to me in the last year or so."

Nikki's eyes blazed. It was Tricia who had engineered a reunion between Nikki and her estranged mother some five years before. Tricia had last seen Fiona Sample eighteen months ago during and after the Authors at Sea cruise, and she couldn't have been nicer. Nikki had decided to feel bitter toward Tricia despite there being no reason other than pure spite.

"You won't win the Bake-Off," Nikki tried again.

"You're probably right, but that doesn't mean I can't have fun during the competition. I doubt you will," she said, and turned on her heel.

"Well, you won't have any fun at Pets-A-Plenty, either," Nikki called after her.

Tricia stopped and pivoted, puzzled by the remark. "What do you mean?"

"Just that the only way you could get on their board was to try and buy your way in."

Tricia frowned. "I don't know what you're talking about."

"Why don't you ask Mr. Everett? People in the village are talking about how his charitable foundation has offered Pets-A-Plenty a hefty donation—but *only* if they take you on."

This was news to Tricia. She practically had to bite her tongue to keep from asking for more details. She wasn't about to give Nikki the satisfaction.

And who else was talking about it?

Tricia said nothing and turned, starting off for her store once more, leaving Nikki to laugh derisively in her wake. She passed by the Have a Heart romance bookstore but didn't dare look in the window. She wasn't in the mood to talk to Joyce, either, and quickened her pace.

Tricia was still feeling shaky as she entered Haven't Got a Clue. Inside, Pixie and Mr. Everett were standing by the cash desk, sharing a laugh. It was so seldom the older man chuckled that Tricia felt even more disconcerted. They looked up at her entrance.

"Are you all right?" Pixie asked, her humor pivoting to anxiety.

"Why?"

"You're white as a sheet."

"I just heard something that kind of shook me."

Pixie moved from behind the cash desk and grabbed the canvas bag in one hand and Tricia's arm in the other, leading her to the reader's nook. "Sit down before you fall down."

"I'm okay," Tricia protested, but Pixie insisted. She and Mr. Everett took the other seats.

"Now, what's wrong?" Pixie asked.

For a moment, Tricia thought she might cry. She had to swallow a couple of times before she could speak. She looked at her employee—her friend—her surrogate father.

"Is it true that the Everett Foundation made the promise of a substantial contribution to the Pets-A-Plenty Animal Rescue on the condition that they appoint me to their board?"

Mr. Everett's eyes widened and then he quickly looked away. "I—I have very little to do with the actual distribution of funds through the foundation," he hedged.

"That doesn't answer my question," Tricia said.

"I'm afraid you'll have to speak to Grace about that."

That was just as evasive an answer. Tricia wasn't sure how she felt about the situation. Did Grace think she couldn't get the job on her own? Obviously, yes, because she *hadn't* been able to get the job on her own, at least not so far.

"Please, Ms. Miles. I know Grace has the utmost respect for you and your abilities. She wouldn't have done it to hurt you in any way. I believe she only wanted to help you achieve something you wanted to do and would be very good at. She knows how much Miss Marple and Sarge mean to you, and that we wouldn't have Mikey and Penny if you hadn't allowed us to care for Miss Marple last year."

Tricia still wasn't sure how she was supposed to feel. Hurt, yes, but she understood the reasoning behind Grace's actions—kindness—and Tricia wouldn't fault her for that.

"I understand," she said simply. But Tricia also knew that if Toby Kingston didn't like her and merely tolerated her presence, not only would it be detrimental to the shelter, but the tension could impact everyone at the rescue operation. Toby had already made it unpleasant for her. Might he grow even more resentful if she was a permanent member of the board?

Now that she knew, Tricia saw no other course but to ask Grace to withdraw her name from consideration. She also knew it was a discussion that had best be made in person.

"Ms. Miles," Mr. Everett began once again. "We know how much you wanted to make a difference for poor kitties and dogs that need homes. I assure you that Grace has only your best interests at heart—as do I."

Tricia tried to smile. "I know that. It's just . . ." But she couldn't finish the sentence. Instead, she stood.

"If you'd like to speak to Grace, she's working in her office today."

On a Saturday?

As though sensing her unspoken question, Mr. Everett answered, "It seems Grace's secretary needs a day off next week, so they decided to put in a full day today."

"Then I think I'd better go see Grace right now and straighten this out." Again, Tricia looked at her employees. "Please don't call her before I can speak to her." She waited until both Pixie and Mr. Everett had given her their promises, then she headed out the door. Less than a minute later, Tricia entered the second-floor office of the Everett Foundation. As usual, the secretary, Linda, sat behind a computer screen at her desk. "Tricia. This is a welcome surprise. What brings you here today?"

"Is Grace available? I really need to speak to her."

"As a matter of fact, she is. But she's with someone right now. Can you wait a few minutes?"

Tricia considered her options: flee and never speak of what she'd learned—which was ridiculous; she'd already spoken to Grace's husband about it—or put on her big girl panties and let Grace know that her actions were not only out of line, but insulting.

No, she couldn't be that rude. She knew it was kindness, and probably love, that had caused Grace to intervene on her behalf. But that didn't mean she had to like it.

Tricia sat in one of the upholstered chairs covered in a nondescript gray fabric. The foundation meant for its funds to go to worthy causes—not fancy offices with expensive art and splendid furnishings.

Still feeling shell-shocked, Tricia sat there, trying to come up with the right wording to express everything she felt, and in a nonjudgmental way, when the door to Grace's office opened and a man in a rather shabby suit walked out. Grace followed.

"Thank you for seeing me and considering my request," the man said as he headed for the exit.

"Good-bye," Grace said, and then noticed Tricia's presence. "Tricia, dear. What are you doing here?" Grace asked, her tone one of delight.

Tricia rose from her seat. "Linda thought you might have a few minutes to spare so we could chat."

"Of course. Come right in."

Grace ushered Tricia in and then closed the door to the outer office. Tricia took a seat in front of Grace's desk, identical to the one she'd just sat on in the reception room. It was just as uncomfortable.

Grace took her seat and leaned forward, her hands folded on the desktop, looking cheerful. "Now, what can I do for you?"

Tricia took a deep breath. "It's about my being considered a candidate for the Pets-A-Plenty board of directors."

The sparkle in Grace's eyes seemed to wane. "Oh."

"I heard, via the grapevine, that the Everett Foundation promised a big donation if the shelter were to take me on."

Grace let out a weary sigh. "I'm sorry you heard about that."

"No more than me," Tricia said truthfully. "But I guess it's better that I did. I'd like you to withdraw my name."

"I wouldn't have suggested the idea if I didn't think you would be fantastic in the job."

"I know, Grace, but I feel sure that if my presence was forced upon them that I'd never have the respect of the board. Heck, I don't have Toby Kingston's respect right now—and I suspect it's because of my being inflicted upon the organization."

"Have the others treated you badly?"

"No, but then I'm not sure they know why I was even suggested for the open seat."

The two women were silent for several long, awkward moments, and Tricia could see that it was hard for Grace to look her in the eye.

Finally, Grace spoke. "I'll speak to Toby."

"And remove my name from consideration?"

"Only if he says he hasn't found you qualified for the job."

"Grace—"

"I believe in you, Tricia. I think you would be a sensational asset to the shelter."

"Thank you, Grace."

"Is there some way I can make this up to you?" the older woman asked sincerely.

Tricia thought about it for a moment. "Well, you could sponsor me in the Great Booktown Bake-Off."

"Consider it done. And what's your charity?"

"Pets-A-Plenty."

Grace nodded. "We've donated to them on a number of occasions. They were very helpful when we adopted Charlie, Mikey, and Penny."

"Did you ever meet Vera Olson there?" Tricia asked.

"I don't believe so. Of course, I knew of her when she was on the school board, but that's about all."

Tricia nodded and rose. "I guess I'd better—" She was about to say "get back to work," but that wasn't true. "Head back home," she said instead. She stood and so did Grace.

"My dear, I hope this little misunderstanding won't stand in the way of our friendship."

Tricia managed a smile. "Not a chance." She stepped forward and gave Grace a hug. Though she was nothing like her beloved grandmother, Grace had easily followed in Grandma Miles's footsteps when it came to dispensing unconditional love.

Grace pulled back. "And I'll see you at our family dinner tomorrow?"

"Of course," Tricia said, giving her friend a smile. "Until tomorrow."

Tricia exited the office and headed for the door.

"Nice to see you again," Linda called, and Tricia gave her a halfhearted wave.

Tricia hadn't gone more than three steps down when her ringtone sounded. She decided to answer it in the stairwell rather than face the noise out on the street. She didn't recognize the number, but it was local. "Hello?"

"Hi, Tricia, it's Donna North."

"Hi, Donna. What can I do for you?"

"It's what I might be able to do for you. I ran into my lawyer at the liquor store this afternoon and we had a little chat. He said it could take up to a year to settle my aunt's estate. But he also gave me the okay to start disposing of her possessions. I can't sell the house, but I can sell the contents as long as I put the money in an estate account."

"Oh." Tricia wasn't sure what else to say.

"I can't touch that money, but if I'm going to open a candy store, I need to get as much of this stuff done before I'm spending fifteen or sixteen hours a day on my business."

"I see," Tricia said, although she wasn't sure she did.

"My aunt had a lot of books. Besides being an advocate for animals, she was also big on reading. I wondered if you could come and look at what she had and maybe buy some and give me some advice on how to unload the rest."

"Did she read mysteries?"

"Yes—and romances, and she also had a lot of cookbooks."

Tricia needed no more persuasion. "I'd be glad to. How about tomorrow? Are you free?"

"That would be great. Could you come to her house around ten?"

"Sure. My sister owns the Cookery, which sells vintage cookbooks and kitchen gadgets. Can I bring her along, too?"

"The more the merrier."

"Fine. We'll see you tomorrow."

Tricia ended the call. Talk about a golden opportunity. Not only could visiting Vera Olson's home help solve the problem of her dwindling stock, but she might just learn something that could point toward her killer.

Maybe—maybe not. She'd have to wait until the next day to find out.

TWENTY-ONE

When Tricia reentered Haven't Got a Clue, she could see that Pixie was practically bursting at the seams to know what had gone on during Tricia's conversation with Grace, but she didn't ask and Tricia didn't volunteer the information, either. As Tricia had suspected he would, Mr. Everett made himself scarce and had retreated behind one of the bookshelves so as not to have to deal with what could be an unpleasant situation. He needn't have worried. As though to avert attention, Pixie asked about the contents of the canvas bag Tricia had brought in earlier.

"The Milford Library had a sale. I picked out the best of what they had in mystery and cooking. Those books are for Angelica."

"We'll need more than that to get through the month."

"I've got an appointment tomorrow to look at the books from an estate that will be coming on the market soon." She decided not to mention to whom the books had belonged.

"That's good."

"Would you like me to take the books down to the storeroom, Ms. Miles?" Mr. Everett asked.

She shook her head. "There are only a few. I'll leave the cookbooks up here and take them over to Angelica after we close."

The door opened and a man and woman entered the store, and Pixie went to help them, while Mr. Everett moved to stand behind the register.

Tricia removed the mysteries from the bag and stowed the bag behind the cash desk, then headed for her office-storeroom. Next, Tricia made herself busy by adding the books to her spreadsheet and printing out an inventory sheet. She shelved the books and checked the list against the stock in the basement. Pixie was right. The shelves down in her storeroom were approaching bare.

Tricia thought about all she had learned that day, and one thing stuck out: No matter what happened with Pets-A-Plenty, she at least owed it to the organization to find more people to sponsor her for the Bake-Off.

She sat down at her desk, pulled out her phone, signed in, and was about to tap her contacts button when she paused. Ginny was gearing up for the second annual Stoneham Wine and Jazz Festival. She'd done a splendid job the year before, but she'd found herself working twelve and fourteen hours a day. She often worked Saturdays, too. Tricia could wait a day and ask her at their family dinner but decided it might be harder for Ginny to say no in person if she was so inclined.

Tapping Ginny's name, Tricia waited as the phone rang.

"Hi, Tricia. What's up?" Ginny asked brightly.

"Am I calling at a bad time?"

"No. Sofia is down for a nap and I'm sitting on my butt and relaxing for the first time today. All week, really," she said, and laughed.

"I'm so missing our Thursday lunches. I can't wait until the festival is over and we can resume them once again."

"I miss our one-on-one chats, too."

"But that's not why you called."

"I have a tremendously selfish favor to ask."

"You—selfish? I don't believe it. You're the least selfish person I know. You and Angelica," she added.

"I left it rather late to ask people to sponsor me for next week's Bake-Off—"

"Consider it done. It's got to be either you or Angelica who wins—at least that's who I'll be rooting for."

"Thanks, Ginny, you're a doll."

"Naturally," she said, and laughed again. "So what else is going on with you?"

"Not much." And suddenly Tricia felt a tremendous urge to unburden her troubles. "Well, I did kind of . . . find a body on Monday."

"Oh, yeah," Ginny said, suddenly sobering. "I heard about that. I meant to call you, but—"

"Don't worry about it. Since then, I've learned some disturbing things about the Pets-A-Plenty pet rescue and just this afternoon something almost equally unsettling."

"Like what?"

"Like . . . Grace tried to bribe the shelter to give me a position on their board."

"Oh, Tricia—no! I'm sure you've got that wrong."

"I've spoken to Grace about it and it's true."

"Oh, Tricia . . . You had to know Grace is one hundred percent behind you. She would never—"

"I know—I know. But I have to admit it kind of hit me hard."

"What did Angelica say?"

"I haven't told her yet. I'll save it for later when we have dinner."

"What happens now?"

"I've asked Grace to withdraw my name from consideration. It's only decent."

"I understand how you feel. I'm sorry. I know how much you wanted to be of help to them and all the cats and dogs needing homes."

And ferrets and guinea pigs, too.

"I've got plenty of other things to do."

"Like win that Bake-Off," Ginny said encouragingly.

Tricia smiled. "Yeah."

A cry sounded in the background. "It looks like Sofia is awake."

"You'd better see to her. And we can talk more tomorrow."

"I can't tell you how much I look forward to our Sunday family dinners."

"Me, too."

Sofia wailed for her mama.

"Talk to you tomorrow," Tricia said, and they ended the call.

Tricia set her phone down on the desk. She felt a little better about the whole Pets-A-Plenty mess and decided to dedicate the next few hours to trying to run down upcoming estate sales. She'd missed the boat by not heading out to look for tag sales that morning, so she checked eBay and Craigslist and made a few calls from tips she'd gotten via e-mail, but she wasn't much further ahead when it came to finding more inventory. Haven't Got a Clue's new assistant manager was doing far *too* good a job at selling the store's stock. Tricia would just have to hope Vera Olson's book collection could help her out of this jam.

She winced. Estate sales always made her feel a bit ghoulish—pawing through the possessions of the recently departed. Tricia didn't even know if Vera had been laid to rest. She should have asked Donna when she'd found out the two women were related.

Meanwhile, Tricia tried not to let her thoughts wander back to Vera Olson's death, the mess with Pets-A-Plenty, and her fractured relationship with Grace. It was a fact that fractures mended, and she felt sure that this hiccup in their relationship would soon pass.

By the time she finished her busywork, it was just about closing time and Tricia was only too happy to bid her employees good night and head to Angelica's apartment for happy hour.

"See you on Monday," Pixie called.

"And I'll see you tomorrow at noon," Mr. Everett said.

"Good night."

Tricia grabbed the bag of cookbooks, turned the OPEN sign to CLOSED, and locked up. Never had she wanted a martini as badly as she did that evening.

As usual, Sarge was ecstatic to see his favorite auntie, and she tossed him two biscuits—enough to make him happy and not enough to get her in trouble with Angelica. She didn't need any more strife.

"Hello!" Angelica called, sounding annoyingly bubbly.

"Hi," Tricia groused.

Angelica scrutinized her sister's face. "Bad day?"

"In more ways than one."

"Then I'd better hurry and pour the drinks. Do you want to sit outside again?"

It was a beautiful summer evening, but Tricia wasn't sure she wanted to discuss what was on her mind in front of a potential audience, should someone be walking their dog or taking a cut through the back alley on a bike.

"Inside is fine."

"Let's sit in the living room. It doesn't get used nearly enough. Besides, I have a surprise for you."

"I'm not sure I'm up for another one."

"Oh, dear. That doesn't sound good. Go and sit down. I'll be right with you."

Feeling downtrodden, Tricia wandered into Angelica's living room, placed the canvas bag on the big coffee table, and flopped down on the couch, feeling as though her bones might no longer be able to support her weight for another minute.

Angelica brought a polished silver tray with the martini pitcher, two glasses, a small plate of cocktail wieners wrapped in puff pastry, napkins, and toothpicks. Tricia had been so distracted, she hadn't even caught the aroma when she'd arrived. But Sarge had and had abandoned his biscuits for something he figured was much tastier.

"Oh, no, you don't," Angelica admonished her dog. "They're not healthy for you."

"They're not healthy for humans, either—but we eat them anyway."

Angelica frowned. "I suppose you're right." She addressed Sarge. "Okay, but just one."

Sarge's wagging tail went into overdrive.

Angelica fed her dog the treat and then ordered him back to his bed so that he didn't bug them for more. Nothing like having a well-trained dog. She then poured their drinks, handing one to Tricia. "Here's to tomorrow being a better day. In fact, here's to the surprise I spoke of—and I hope that it *makes* your day."

Tricia raised her glass. She could use some cheering up. She took a hearty sip. Damn fine.

Angelica took a sip of her drink and then put down her glass. "You look so down. What happened?"

Tricia explained how Grace had tried to fix her appointment to the Pets-A-Plenty Board of Directors.

"Oh, dear."

Tricia nodded. "Nothing says loving like a little touch of nepotism."

"But you know she did it out of love and caring."

"I know, but I would much rather have earned it."

"And who says you still can't?" Angelica asked.

"Toby Kingston has made his feelings clear. And after Grace speaks to him, I'm sure I won't be invited to return for their next meeting."

"Well, then it's their loss. You have years of experience running a nonprofit. They'd be fools not to snap you up and exploit your expertise."

"One would think."

"I'm so sorry, Tricia. I know you really wanted to help them."

"There are plenty of other things I can do with my time." It was just unfortunate that she hadn't found many of them during the past six months, when she'd had far too much time on her hands.

"So what's your big surprise?" Tricia asked.

Angelica's eyes lit up. "Well, as you know, the day spa is nearing completion. Since Randy came on board, we're actually a little ahead of schedule. The sign went up today. Did you happen to see it?"

Tricia shook her head and took a sip of her martini. "I passed the shop, but I guess I had other things on my mind and didn't notice."

"I took a picture." Angelica retrieved her cell phone, tapped the photo gallery icon, and swiped through a number of images before enlarging the picture to fill the screen and handing the device to her sister.

Tricia gave it a bare glance and was about to politely say, "How nice," when she actually read the wording. Her eyes bulged and her mouth dropped open in horror. "You named it Haven't Got a Care?" Tricia cried.

"Yes, isn't it brilliant?" Angelica said with delight.

"Brilliant?" Tricia practically squealed in distress.

Angelica frowned. "I thought you'd be pleased."

"Why would I be pleased? It's going to prove very confusing to my customers. They'll walk into your day spa expecting to find vintage mysteries and come out upset and annoyed, not to mention walking into my store and expecting a makeover."

"Or they might get a manicure or facial and feel really good about themselves," Angelica asserted.

"Why on earth would you think a similar name would be good for *my* business?" Tricia demanded.

Angelica shrugged. "I sure wouldn't mind if it was mine."

"Well, I mind," Tricia said, and threw back the rest of her drink, nearly choking on it.

Angelica looked despondent. "I'm sorry, Trish. I thought you'd be flattered. I . . . I don't think it can be changed before the grand opening. I'll have to go back to square one. Get a new DBA, file for a new LLC—or at least see if I can amend it . . ."

"Forget it," Tricia said, even if she wasn't in a forgiving mood. To keep from having a total meltdown, she asked, "What can you tell me about the lease for the candy store?"

"I didn't ask for all the fine details. That's up to Karen to work out with Donna. But we are willing to offer her a hell of a deal. And we'll prorate the lease so that she has an opportunity to get on her feet. One year at fifty percent, then six months at seventy-five, and after that the full market value."

"That's very generous of you."

"It is," Angelica said with no hint of hubris. "The first year is the hardest for anyone going into business. I believe in her product and I want that chocolate shop to succeed."

And she hadn't even met Donna North.

Now to hope Donna didn't talk herself out of such a great opportunity.

"Speaking of Donna, she's invited me to her aunt's house to evaluate and possibly buy parts of her book collection."

Angelica sat just that much straighter. "Really?"

"She says there are cookbooks, too, and that I can bring you along . . . if you want to go."

"I would," Angelica said. Then she frowned. "You're being awfully nice to me considering how angry you were just a few minutes ago."

Tricia sighed. "You're my sister."

Angelica nodded. That seemed to be a good enough answer for her.

"And now it's time for my gift for you, or at least the Cookery," Tricia said, and reached for the canvas bag. She withdrew the vintage cookbooks and, much to Angelica's delight, handed them to her.

"Where did you get these?"

"The Milford Library had a sale."

"And you picked these up for me?"

"If you want them. Otherwise, feel free to sell them. They didn't cost much."

"It's the thought that counts."

"I was looking at them while I ate my lunch and they reminded me of the cookbooks Grandma Miles had. I wish I'd paid more attention to the things she cooked—and taught you how to make."

"She had a lot of patience," Angelica said, leafing through one of the books.

"Do you have any good cooking stories about her?"

Angelica's smile was sweet with remembrance. "Do I ever!"

"Well, why don't you pour us another drink and tell me a few. I would sure love to hear them."

"I'm going to make sure Sofia knows about her Great-Grandma Miles and I've already started thinking about writing a children's book with the tales," Angelica said, and poured their drinks from the sweating glass pitcher.

"Oh, yeah?"

"I've already got the beginning memorized. It goes like this . . . 'Once upon a time, there was a granny who loved her little granddaughters so much, she baked them magical treats. . . .'"

TWENTY-TWO

By the time Tricia left her sister's home several hours later, her heart felt lighter. And then she returned to her dark apartment and the veil of depression threatened to fall once again. Marshall hadn't called or texted, so Tricia found herself alone on a Saturday night with her cat. Not unexpected but just a little sad.

As melancholy overwhelmed her, she had a little pity party and sat at her kitchen island and ate one of her luscious cupcakes accompanied by a mug of steaming cocoa, then spent way too much time trying to figure out the calorie count before she decided the hell with it and ate a second one, something she would have never dreamed of doing a year or two before.

She went to bed early with *Look to the Lady* by Margery Allingham, one of her favorite Campion mysteries, and read it until the wee hours before falling into an exhausted sleep.

Not surprisingly, Tricia woke up late the next morning, feeling downhearted until she remembered that she and Angelica were going to check out Vera Olson's library. The thrill of the hunt gave her something to get out of bed for.

Since Angelica's car had the bigger trunk, they decided that she would drive to Vera Olson's home. Minutes after leaving Stoneham's municipal lot, she pulled into the driveway behind a little red Hyundai, which must have belonged to Donna.

"Cute house," Angelica said upon exiting the car and inspecting the front of the home with its many painted birdhouses hanging from the limbs of the ornamental trees. "You said she was an animal freak?"

Tricia nodded. "Apparently she liked birds, too."

"I'll say."

They approached the house and were immediately scolded by a purple finch, which sat on one of the euonymus shrubs that flanked the front door. "It's okay; we're not going to hurt you," Angelica said.

"There must be a nest nearby," Tricia observed. She pressed the doorbell. Seconds later, Donna opened the door.

"Hi. Come on in."

Tricia stepped inside the house with Angelica on her heels. The entryway was small, with a colorful stone floor and a closet. Two steps farther and she was in the living room, which was set up like a mini library, complete with a large worktable, a reading nook with a comfortable armchair, floor lamp, and small table, and shelf after shelf of books and other reading material. "Wow, your aunt really did love to read."

"She bought a lot of the books at yard and library sales, so I'm pretty sure there isn't much of value, but that's kind of what I wanted someone who knows the market to tell me."

"I'm so very sorry for your loss," Angelica said sincerely.

"Thanks. Nobody expects a family member to die so horribly," Donna said.

"Will there be a service?" Tricia asked.

"Not a funeral. She was cremated. I thought we might hold a

memorial service in a couple of weeks. Sunday would probably be the best day for it. Pets-A-Plenty is closed and more of her friends might be able to come."

"Did she ever speak to you about what goes on at the shelter?" Tricia asked.

Donna shook her head. "As I said, we weren't all that close. Aunt Vera thought making candy was pretty frivolous."

"I've tasted your product from the Coffee Bean. It's anything but frivolous," Angelica said.

Donna smiled self-consciously. "Thanks. I know you ladies have stores to run. You should probably take a look at what Aunt Vera had."

Angelica was trying to peer around the corner and into what looked like the kitchen. "Did she keep her cookbooks in here or in the kitchen?"

"The kitchen. By the way, I'm Donna."

"And I'm Angelica Miles. As Tricia must have told you, I own the Cookery on Main Street."

"And Booked for Lunch and that new spa that's going up," Donna said.

Angelica smiled. "That's right."

"I'll show you where she kept her cookbooks."

While Donna took Angelica into the kitchen, Tricia wandered around the shelves in the living room, glancing at the titles. Vera had had an eclectic taste in reading material. Her collection was full of books on domestic and wild animals, which she kept in a tall shelf unit. Beside it was an entire bookshelf of fiction, which ranged from mystery and romance paperbacks to women's fiction and horror in the shape of every Stephen King novel ever published, the most recent in hardcover. Another smaller shelf held old copies of *National Geographic*, *Dog* and *Cat Fancy* magazines, and in labeled containers, newsletters from several animal rescue associations.

Tricia returned to the shelves with the mystery novels. Most of them were pretty beat-up and looked like they'd been purchased secondhand. She was able to pick out a few, but they were newer mysteries—nothing that could be called vintage.

She set them on the worktable and retraced her steps to look at the romances. Most of them were in good shape and probably something Joyce Widman might have liked for her shop, but it wouldn't be in good taste to suggest to Donna that a woman who was a person of interest in her aunt's murder investigation should come and have a look. Instead, Tricia entered the kitchen, where it seemed Angelica was having much better luck. Already there were at least ten vintage cookbooks piled on the worn white Formica countertop.

"Look what I found," Angelica exclaimed, brandishing a buff-colored book that was at least two inches thick. "*The Lily Wallace New American Cook Book*! Grandma Miles had this exact edition from nineteen forty-seven." She flipped through the pages. "Look, wine soup, planked chicken, and how about macaroni and chipped beef en casserole?"

Tricia wasn't sure she was eager to try any of those recipes.

"And look—there are sheets of paper with handwritten recipes, too. Gosh, I love to find them in old cookbooks. They were probably shared by a friend or neighbor or maybe copied out of a newspaper. They're like little pieces of history."

Tricia nodded. "Looks like you found more, too."

"You can buy them all," Donna said. "I'm not into vintage recipes."

"They're wonderful. Like a cookery time machine."

"Did you find much, Tricia?" Donna asked.

Tricia shook her head. "I'm afraid not."

"Do you mind if I keep going through these cookbooks?" Angelica asked.

"Sure."

"Your aunt seems to have been a big bird fan, judging by all the birdhouses out front," Tricia commented.

"There're even more in the backyard—although I suspect the birds prefer to build their own nests rather than use them."

"Would you mind if I had a look?"

Donna shrugged. "Help yourself."

The setup was the same as at Joyce's home next door. Sliding glass doors opened to a small covered patio, and several fruit trees dotted the yard. The big maple still domineered, despite its recent attack by a chainsaw-wielding tree surgeon.

Tricia was drawn to the maple and wanted to have a look at the door that led to Joyce's yard and inspect it from Vera's vantage point. It was closed. She pushed against it, but once again it had been bolted from Joyce's side of the fence.

Along the back side of the yard was a rather tangled garden filled with a large array of unkempt vegetation. Tricia was no gardener and didn't have a clue what most of the bushy plants were. The garden itself was unusual since Vera's home was tidy and her grass was well maintained. It wasn't until Tricia saw the milkweed plant that she realized what she was looking at: a butterfly garden. So, Vera was a friend to all kinds of animals and wildlife.

Was her first—and really only—impression of the woman in error? Tricia wanted to be in Joyce's corner. After all, Joyce had said that Vera stole her herbs. Tricia wished she could remember what she'd seen in Joyce's yard—and then it came to her. It wasn't mint that was growing in her herb garden; it was catnip. Frannie Armstrong had probably planted it for her cat, Penny—who now belonged to Mr. Everett. Bonnie had mentioned that Vera often brought catnip for the cats at Pets-A-Plenty. She must have liberated it from Joyce's yard. Frannie probably hadn't cared if Vera swiped it. Catnip seeds often traveled on the wind, and if one wasn't careful, it could take over a garden just like its cousin, mint.

Tricia ambled over to one of the fruit trees—apple by the look of it—and was once again scolded by a nesting purple finch. "Okay, okay. I won't hurt your babies." She backed off and headed for the house once again, glancing over her shoulder for one last look at the maple before reentering the kitchen.

"Oh, there you are," Angelica said from the counter, looking up from the checkbook she stood over. She looked back down and signed her name with a flourish. A large cardboard carton had appeared and Donna was in the process of filling it with vintage cookbooks. "Your books are in there, too, Tricia."

"Thanks."

"I'd be glad to carry the box to your car," Donna offered.

"Thank you." Angelica stowed her checkbook and pen back in her purse. "And thank you for letting us look at your aunt's collection."

Donna let out a breath and looked around the kitchen. "She was a bit of a packrat. When I think about how much work it's going to take to empty the place . . ."

"Couldn't you hire an estate liquidator?"

"I could," Donna admitted. "But they take such a large chunk of the proceeds, and I'm going to need every penny I can lay my hands on if I'm going to get my candy shop up and running."

"I've tasted your wares," Angelica said. "I think you have a bright future here in Stoneham."

"Thanks. I sure hope so. Do you have any advice on how to get rid of the rest of the books?"

"You might want to put together a flyer and either send it to or perhaps make a personal pitch to the booksellers on Main Street," Tricia said. "Detail what you've got and add your phone number. Then if they're interested, they can make an appointment to come to the house to have a look. If all else fails, the Stoneham Library has an annual sale and would be glad to take them."

Donna nodded. "Thanks. I'll remember that." She led the way back through the living room and out to the driveway. Angelica opened her trunk and Donna set the box inside.

"Thanks again," Angelica said, and she and Tricia waved to Donna, who started back for the house.

They got back into the car. "Did you have a nice look around the yard?"

"Yes. Very interesting, and I think I know why Vera was so angry with Joyce."

Angelica backed the car down the drive. "Oh?"

"I'm just wondering if I should confront her about it."

"Is it worthwhile? I mean, would it prove she killed Vera?"

"Oh, no—nothing like that. But it does shed some light on Joyce's character."

"And?"

"Maybe it's a good thing that we aren't more than acquaintances since I don't think I would want her to be my friend."

By the time Angelica pulled into the municipal parking lot, it was twenty minutes 'til noon—almost time for them to open their stores. That would give Tricia plenty of time to get the coffee going, put some cash in the till, and make sure everything was ready for the influx of book-buying customers she hoped to serve that day.

The sisters got out of the car.

"Want help hauling that box back to the Cookery?" Tricia asked.

Angelica shook her head. "I think I'll go back to the shop and get my dolly. It's too heavy for just one of us to carry very far, and especially not in these shoes." She pointed to her Jimmy Choo three-inch spikes.

"Wise decision," Tricia said. Angelica did, however, retrieve the mysteries and handed them to Tricia. They started across the lot, heading for the sidewalk, then turned the corner and passed the Patisserie. Tricia was in no mood for another distressing exchange with Nikki and kept her gaze straight ahead, but as they passed Joyce's romance bookstore, Joyce darted out the door to intercept them.

"Tricia, did you ever get a chance to talk to Chief Baker on my behalf?" Joyce asked eagerly.

"Hello, Joyce," Angelica said rather grimly, as though to remind the woman of her presence.

"Oh, hi, Angelica. I didn't see you there."

Angelica's gaze swung over to her sister, who wore flats and was at least two inches shorter than Angelica's Choo-extended height. She looked back to Joyce. "Lovely weather we're having."

"Uh, yeah."

Angelica pinned Joyce with her gaze. "It seems you have an important matter to discuss with Tricia. I'll just leave you two ladies to it." She looked at Tricia. "See you tonight at dinner."

"Right."

Angelica didn't bother saying good-bye to Joyce but did at least give her a nod in passing.

Joyce didn't seem to notice. "Well? Did you speak to Baker?"

"I did," Tricia admitted. "Unfortunately, he wasn't interested in a testimonial. What I *didn't* mention was that you and Officer Pearson seem to be involved."

Joyce's eyes widened and her breaths quickened. "What—what do you mean?"

"I saw the two of you at the Chinese restaurant in Merrimack the other day holding hands and gazing into each other's eyes."

"I—I . . ." But then Joyce didn't seem to have anything else to say.

Instead, she grabbed Tricia's arm and hauled her into her bookshop, no doubt to keep anyone from overhearing their conversation.

"How did that happen?" Tricia asked. She had no reason to think Joyce would actually answer the question. But then . . .

"Cindy came into my store, looking for something to read."

"Erotica?" Tricia guessed. She couldn't see the tough-looking cop reading historical romance.

"I don't sell it," Joyce reminded her.

"She's new in Stoneham. She probably didn't know it, either."

"No, she didn't. She wasn't embarrassed about her preference for that type of romance. Uh, we struck up a conversation and found we had a lot in common," she said, somehow sounding evasive. "I—I enjoyed our conversation. I didn't think anything else of it until she came back a few days later. We got to talking once again and . . . we became friends."

"And then it became more."

Joyce's cheeks grew pink. "Tricia, what are you implying? Cindy and I are friends."

Uh-huh.

"What are you going to do about it?" Tricia asked.

"I don't need to do anything," Joyce said firmly.

"I didn't mean whatever your relationship with Cindy is. I meant what are you going to tell Chief Baker? It might look suspicious if he stumbles across it during his investigation. Cindy could lose her job."

"We've done nothing wrong. We're friends," Joyce reiterated.

"You're a person of interest in a murder investigation. Cindy's an officer who's worked on that case. I can see where a lot of people might get the wrong impression."

"Well, they'd be just as wrong as you," Joyce said tersely.

"Have you told Roger Livingston about Cindy?"

Joyce frowned. "No."

"I think you ought to—to protect yourself *and* her."

"I'll think about it," Joyce said, but Tricia suspected she wouldn't.

"Was there something else you wanted?" Joyce asked pointedly. Had she forgotten she'd been the one to initiate the conversation, not to mention hauling Tricia into her store?

"I also think I figured out why Vera didn't want you to cut down the tree limb that hung over your yard."

Joyce stared at her blankly.

"It took me a while to remember exactly what it was I saw in your backyard. Something nobody but Vera—and you—would have noticed."

"And what was that?" Joyce challenged, annoyed.

"The bird's nest."

Joyce's eyes widened.

"Vera would no doubt have been upset to see her tree massacred, but she probably wouldn't have thrown a public hissy fit if you'd done as she'd requested and waited for the birds to vacate the nest. Am I right?"

"I don't know what you're talking about."

"When we first went into the yard, there were a couple of very upset purple finches fluttering around the tree. Their nest—along with their babies—was gone. Vera was an animal activist. She was incensed when she came back from her volunteer job at Pets-A-Plenty and found part of her tree—the limb with the nest—had been cut down."

"I never saw a nest on that limb."

"But you knew it was there—Vera told you. And then there was evidence of the nest on the ground in your yard after the wood had been hauled away and the smaller limbs had gone through the chipper."

Joyce turned away. "I had every right to have that limb cut down. It was only a couple of baby birds. My garden—"

"It was only a couple of insignificant birds in the grand scheme of things, but you knew how much they meant to Vera," Tricia said, unable to keep the disappointment she felt about her neighbor from her voice.

"I broke no laws," Joyce asserted.

"That's where you're wrong, Joyce. It's illegal to remove or destroy the nests of native bird species. When Vera threatened to take you to court, she knew what she was saying. She had the law on her side. If you'd known that—"

"Are you accusing me of killing Vera?" Joyce practically shouted.

"I'm just telling you how it would look to a jury."

"A jury! Tricia, you've known me for six years. Do you really think I'm capable of murder?"

"It's not me you have to convince," Tricia said firmly. "First, Chief Baker, and if they decide to charge you, twelve honest citizens called to listen to the facts and make a judgment."

"I did not kill Vera Olson," Joyce said grimly.

"I believe you." But Joyce had been responsible for killing those baby birds. Sure, many people wouldn't have cared, but Tricia did. And so had Vera.

"I suppose you're going to tell Chief Baker about that, too."

"I haven't decided what to tell him. Talk to Roger Livingston and do the right thing—on both accounts."

Joyce said nothing.

"I'd better get going."

"You've worn out your welcome," Joyce muttered.

"I'm sorry, Joyce."

Tricia left the store and knew without a doubt that though she and Joyce had been friendly in the past, they could now never be friends.

TWENTY-THREE

As Ginny had mentioned, since Angelica had started hosting weekly family dinners, Tricia found she, too, looked forward to every Sunday. It was a time to connect with her makeshift family. Okay, not quite so makeshift now that she knew that Angelica's so-called stepson, Antonio Barbero, was actually her biological son, which made him Tricia's nephew. And she'd been close to his wife, Ginny, who had also been her former assistant at Haven't Got a Clue. Now Tricia and Ginny were family, too. And, of course, there was their daughter, Sofia—the apple of Angelica's eye. Also in attendance were Grace and Mr. Everett. Ginny had long ago adopted them as her pseudo grandparents, and Tricia had looked up to them as replacements for the parents she knew had never truly loved her.

On that day, because of the whole Pets-A-Plenty fiasco, Tricia wasn't in quite such a jovial mood. That said, she was determined to swallow down her discomfort and enjoy some wine, the conversation, and, of course, a wonderful dinner.

Lately, Antonio and Ginny had been bringing Grace and Mr. Everett to the gatherings to save them from having to drive themselves home. Now that Ginny was a mom, she worried about everyone in her life.

And so the group arrived en masse: Grace and Mr. Everett filing into Angelica's entryway, with Ginny behind them carrying a tote with the wine of the day—the only thing Angelica would let her bring—and Antonio carrying Sofia. Sarge, of course, was nearly crazed with absolute joy! He delighted in seeing the whole family, too.

"Hello!" Angelica called, practically zooming out of the kitchen to intercept Antonio and take Sofia from his arms.

"Eh, Mamma—*anche io non conto*?"

"Of course you count, too, darling boy," Angelica said, and leaned over to get a kiss from her son.

"Hi, everyone!" Tricia called as Ginny handed her the tote with the wine bottles.

"Pour me a glass—quick!" Ginny said.

"Bad day?"

"Sofia has been wound up like a clock all day. I'm hoping she'll sleep like a rock tonight. She gets so excited about coming to see her *nonne* and Zia Tricia, and, of course, Sarge."

"Sarge, hush!" Angelica ordered, and the little dog instantly quieted, but that didn't stop him from gleefully dancing around their legs.

"Dear little Sarge," Grace called, and attempted to pet the Bichon Frise, but Sarge couldn't seem to calm down.

"Tricia, would you get the drinks and appetizers?" Angelica called.

"Sure thing."

"I'll help, too," Ginny volunteered.

While Angelica led the others—and Sarge—out onto the balcony, Tricia removed the sweating bottles from the tote. Angelica had already assembled the glassware, so Tricia uncorked the wine while Ginny grabbed the tray of yummies from the fridge and removed the plastic wrap that covered them.

"Are you nervous about Wednesday?" Ginny asked, and grabbed the pitcher of iced tea from the fridge for Mr. Everett, the teetotaler, and poured a glass.

"Wednesday?" Tricia asked, confused.

"The Bake-Off."

Tricia laughed. "Since I didn't do any practice baking today, I kind of put it out of my mind. I'm sure I'll be a wreck the day of the contest, but I'm feeling good about it."

"And your recipe?" Ginny asked.

Tricia stifled a smile. "It's a secret."

"I won't tell Angelica. Cross my heart and hope to . . . never tell a lie," Ginny said, and for a moment looked embarrassed at possibly bringing up the fact that Tricia had found Vera Olson.

"Let's join the others," Tricia said, hefting the tray.

The rest of the family had settled on chairs and the chaise, while Sofia squealed with delight at throwing the ball for Sarge and getting to do it all over again once he retrieved it.

Ginny winced. "Ugh. Dog spit." But Angelica was prepared, and on one of the glass-topped tables sat a plastic container of antiseptic wipes. Ginny set the plate down and handed the tea to Mr. Everett, while Tricia put her tray beside it and started pouring wine and handing glasses around.

"What's the conversation about?" Tricia asked.

Angelica looked a little apprehensive. "Mr. E was just telling us about his day off and his visit to the county lockup."

Tricia nearly spilled the glass of wine she'd been about to hand to Antonio. She turned to Mr. Everett. "Oh? I didn't know you were in contact with Frannie."

Mr. Everett nodded and took a sip of his already sweating glass. “She gets so few visitors. She contacted us after learning that we had adopted her cat, Penny, asking if we would keep her informed and perhaps send her a picture now and then.”

“How nice of you,” Angelica said, but her voice was subdued, her gaze drifting to watch her granddaughter at play. Of course, she had reason to still be angry with Frannie, who’d not only blackmailed her but had threatened to harm Sofia—as well as attempting to murder Tricia for figuring out her nasty little scheme.

“I thought someone should break the news of the death of her friend Ms. Olson in person. Ms. Armstrong hadn’t been told,” Mr. Everett said quietly.

“It must have been quite a shock,” Ginny said.

Mr. Everett nodded. “They had been neighbors and friends ever since Ms. Armstrong came to Stoneham—more than a decade before.”

Tricia sipped her wine and felt yet another twinge of betrayal, which was absurd. Mr. Everett had a heart as big as the ocean. He might not approve of the things Frannie had done, but he also had compassion for a fellow human being who likely would be locked up for the rest of her life without the comfort of her cat and now communication with Vera, who may well have been the only friend she had left.

“Did Vera Olson ever visit Frannie in jail?”

“On occasion. I understand they exchanged letters quite often.”

“Did Frannie ever mention how she felt about Joyce Widman buying her house?”

“It was not a happy topic. I did not bring it up,” Mr. Everett assured them. “Ms. Armstrong was upset that all her assets were sold to pay her attorneys’ fees. She sees herself as destitute and that all her treasures are forever gone.”

A small price to pay when one contemplated the life she took—and the lives she had disrupted because of greed and misplaced anger.

"I wonder what else Vera might have told Frannie," Ginny said.

"Something about Monterey something or other. The last time Ms. Armstrong saw Ms. Olson, the latter apparently went off on a wild tangent."

Tricia's ears perked up.

"About what?" Antonio asked.

"Dogs. Something about dogs. She didn't seem to remember much more, but thought it might be important."

"I've heard that company name before. Don't they have a plant outside of Concord?" Angelica asked.

"If they do, I've never heard of them," Grace said.

"They have something to do with animal experimentation," Angelica said. "I saw something about it on the news several months ago."

"Do you remember anything else about the report?" Tricia asked, deciding not to mention her conversation days before with Cori at Pets-A-Plenty.

Angelica shook her head.

Hmm. Tricia decided that later that evening she would spend some time on her computer and do another Google search on the company. "What else did Frannie have to say?"

"Ms. Armstrong became lost in her memories of her friend and not only got very upset, but she became disruptive. After she was advised by a guard to be quiet and did not follow orders, I was asked to leave and the guards took her away. A most distasteful experience," Mr. Everett admitted, and shook his head. Strong outbursts of emotion always seemed to embarrass and distress him. "In future, I think I shall refrain from visiting and simply mail her updates on Penny."

"It's very kind of you," Ginny said, but her expression more or less mirrored Tricia's thoughts. *And the moral is . . . don't kill someone and you won't end up in jail.*

"Can't we talk about something more cheerful?" Grace asked.

"I agree," Antonio echoed.

"How about the Bake-Off? Are you girls caught up in the competitive spirit?" Grace asked.

"I don't know how Tricia feels, of course, but I feel extremely confident," Angelica said. "I have *so* many years of baking experience behind me. But I do think it's terribly brave of Tricia to jump into the contest after spending such a short time behind an apron."

"Yes, I feel terribly brave," Tricia agreed and rolled her eyes, which caused all but Mr. Everett to laugh. "For my next cooking contest, I think I'll attempt an entry at the county fair. It's about time I started earning blue ribbons and all the acclaim that goes with it."

"County fair," Angelica groused, but then she looked thoughtful. Aha! Tricia had planted a seed. Angelica could never walk away from a challenge.

"What's for dinner?" Ginny asked, which was a welcome change of subject.

"Steaks for us, and a tube steak for Sofia—that is, if you don't mind."

"Sofia would eat hot dogs twenty-four/seven if I let her. They're the ultimate kid treat."

From then on, the conversations turned to more mundane things, which was a welcome relief. No one mentioned Pets-A-Plenty, and the subject of Vera Olson was laid to rest as well. Tricia was determined to enjoy the rest of their family gathering and put thoughts of the Bake-Off out of her mind as well.

She didn't need to feel anxious until the day of the competition.

If that was possible.

TWENTY-FOUR

When Tricia returned home from the weekly family dinner, she went straight to her computer to try to find the video clip Angelica had mentioned seeing on Monterey Bioresources. It came up on the second page of listings, which was probably why she'd missed it the last time she'd done an online search. The less-than-two-minute report was more about people protesting than about providing information on the company itself. Just another false lead.

After closing down her computer, she chose another book to lose herself in—this time, it was Erle Stanley Gardner's *This Is Murder*—and settled in the reading nook in her master suite with Miss Marple to keep her company. Her eyes grew heavy and Tricia turned in, but not before checking her phone. No missed call from Marshall, and no texts, either.

Tricia awoke early that Monday morning to the sound of roaring vehicles barreling down Main Street. With one look at the clock—

5:16—she threw back the covers and leapt out of bed, startling her cat, who had been snoozing at the bottom. Rushing to the window, she caught sight of the last of what looked like a convoy of trucks. Written on the side of the truck were the words GOOD FOOD CHANNEL and an obnoxiously large picture of Chef Larry Andrews.

Tricia hurriedly dressed in yoga pants and a T-shirt, grabbed her keys, and headed out the door, walking at a brisk pace and heading toward the high school, not really sure why, as it wasn't on her usual exercise route. *Pure nosiness?* she asked herself.

From two blocks away she could see a mass of cars and trucks already surrounding the school. The Eat Lunch food truck, owned by Nigela Ricita Associates, was parked nearby and was already doing a brisk business selling coffee, pastries, and breakfast sandwiches to the crew. Trust Angelica to think of everything. Tricia stopped to buy a cup of joe and crossed the street to linger and watch as a crew of men and women began to unload the truck with the Good Food Channel's logo on it and filled with television equipment, while another team set up a remote station in another of the trucks that bore no signage.

As Tricia angled to get a better view of the organized chaos ahead of her, someone tapped her on the shoulder. She whirled, grateful her coffee had a cap or else she would have spilled it.

"Sorry, I didn't mean to frighten you," Angelica said, looking so much shorter than usual thanks to the sneakers she wore—shoes Tricia hadn't known her sister even owned—and looking sweet in a pink tracksuit, which would be far too warm within an hour or so.

"Did the trucks wake you?"

"Who could sleep with all that racket?" Angelica craned her neck to get a better view. "Isn't this exciting? I wish *we* were going to be on TV for our portion of the Bake-Off."

"Not me. I'll be nervous enough just trying to bake, knowing a famous chef—and Grant Baker—are going to be judging my efforts."

"Grant's a judge?"

"Didn't I tell you?"

Angelica's face fell. "I'm doomed."

"Why do you say that?"

"The man can't stand me—never could."

"Oh, you're being silly," Tricia chided, but Baker had treated Angelica with less than the respect she deserved, and on more than one occasion.

Angelica sighed. "Well, it will be a strike against me—but I will win him over with my cupcakes. They will be divine."

"She said modestly," Tricia muttered.

"Self-confidence is a must in any competition. You have to believe you can win or you won't."

Six months before, Tricia wouldn't even have thought about entering any kind of cooking contest, but she'd been an apt pupil, eager to excel, and it had paid off. If she did well in the Bake-Off, maybe come September she really would enter the Hillsborough County Fair, and if she did well with that, maybe she'd try entering her cupcake recipe at one of the state fairs, too. It was something to consider.

"But there's more good news," Angelica said.

"I'm all for that," Tricia said.

"It seems the students have an in-school TV station and do a weekly report that's sent to the local cable company."

"Oh, yeah. I think I've seen it." Hadn't the temporary receptionist at the Chamber mentioned that, too? "But the rumor was that it was going to be shown on the local cable channel."

"Highlights only, dear. Even though school's out, they're going to be allowed to take part in the Bake-Off by televising it via closed circuit to the school's auditorium. For a ten-dollar fee, anyone can spend the day watching the pro contestants."

"I admit, I've watched more than a few of the Good Food

Channel's TV shows, but let's face it, they take hours—even days—of film and boil it down to an hour. Sitting there for the whole day might be as interesting as watching paint dry."

"Not for me."

"I guess it would depend if they have one static camera focused on the room at large, or if they're going to be allowed to switch points of view."

Angelica shrugged. "We won't know until the day of the shoot—which is tomorrow!"

"I wonder if you could pay for the day but slip in and out if you needed to." Or if it got incredibly boring.

"I don't see why not. But you'd probably lose your seat."

"Not if someone was saving it."

Angelica shrugged. "I'm going to stay the whole day, although I may want to pack a lunch. I wonder if they'd let you bring one."

"I can't imagine they would. There's the auditorium's upholstery to think of."

"Teenagers are messy. If I spilled something, I would at least know the proper agent to clean just about every stain imaginable."

"I'm sure the Eat Lunch truck will be well stocked to feed the crew and rubberneckers."

"They may bring in their own catering people—they certainly haven't called Eat Lunch, Booked for Lunch, or the Brookview to fill the need."

"Could any of them handle it?"

"Any and all." Angelica scowled. "Okay, it would be a little tough for Booked for Lunch since our short-order cook is *in* the competition, but I'm sure other arrangements could have been made."

"What's Tommy going to make?"

Angelica looked coy. "I've been sworn to secrecy, but I can tell you this—it's delicious. I think he's got a real shot at winning."

"Against Nikki?"

"Her cupcakes might be prettier, but they're just average in taste."

They were better than average, but maybe not spectacular. In fact, Tricia had never had a spectacular cupcake from the Patisserie. Now, some of Tommy's soups—*they* were truly spectacular.

More and more people seemed to be gathering in front of the school.

"I don't suppose there's much more to see," Angelica lamented.

"Why don't you come with me on my walk?"

"I really should get to work. I have a lot to accomplish today if I'm going to take tomorrow and Wednesday off. And besides, I've got Larry's book signing this afternoon."

She spoke of the chef as if they'd been friends for years. Still, Tricia envied her sister with a full day ahead of her. "Okay," she said cheerfully. She'd spend the time not only walking to get fit but thinking. Her daily walk always was the best time to ponder and brainstorm ideas for the future—or even the present.

The sisters left the area and headed south down Main Street.

"Um, I have the teensiest favor to ask of you," Angelica said.

"Oh?"

"We're expecting quite a crowd at the Cookery this afternoon. Would you be able to spare Mr. Everett to help out?"

"It's his day off."

"Oh, darn. I forgot."

"But I'd be glad to pitch in. What do you need?"

"If you could open the books and hand them to Larry to sign, that would be fantastic."

"And while I'm doing that—?"

"June will be on the register and I'll be coordinating things."

More likely she'd be sucking up to the chef. It didn't matter; Tricia had loads of time to kill. "Sure thing."

Angelica patted Tricia's arm. "You are just the best sister!"

"Don't I know it," Tricia said, but she appreciated the compliment nonetheless. "What time do you want me there?"

"Two thirty."

"No time for our usual lunch, then?"

"I'm sorry."

"No problem. I'll grab a bite at home. If nothing else, I've got tons of cupcakes in the freezer."

"Did I mention that you're the best sister?"

Tricia laughed. "Not nearly enough."

When they reached the corner of Main and Locust Streets, the sisters split off. Tricia headed west and Angelica carried on south to return to the Cookery.

The whole circus atmosphere surrounding the Good Food Channel's arrival in the village seemed to revitalize Tricia, who picked up her pace, arms pumping. Even if she didn't place in the competition, she felt the Bake-Off might just be the stepping-stone to some other aspect of her life. Too bad she had no idea what that might mean.

After returning from her walk, Tricia whipped up a strawberry smoothie for breakfast and sat down in front of her laptop to check her mail before starting the day. Happily for her, she'd received an e-mail from a fellow bookseller, Ken Drummond. Unhappily for him, he was holding a liquidation sale that began that morning. This particular store was not mystery oriented, but they did have a large new-and-used section and he was offering a good price for his stock. Was she interested? She wasted no time in answering, telling him she could be there in two hours. That would give her plenty of time to shower, change, and drive to . . . Concord.

Concord: the home of Monterey Bioresources.

After checking Google Maps to get directions, Tricia printed them out and considered her morning. She didn't have to be at Angelica's store until midafternoon, which would give her plenty of time to hopefully fill her car with books *and* take a drive by Monterey Bioresources. But then she remembered what Cori at Pets-A-Plenty had told her: You couldn't even see any of the buildings from the road. Tricia did a Google drive-by and found it was true. Though the area had been photographed some two years before, Tricia doubted much had changed. All that was visible were trees, long expanses of freshly mowed grass, iron gates at the end of the drive, and nothing much of interest to see.

The TV report had been made in April. Was it possible protesters still picketed the company?

There was only one way to find out.

Tricia texted Pixie, telling her about the book sale, and took off before her assistant manager made it into work.

The drive to Concord was uneventful, and Tricia listened to an audiobook to help pass the time.

Drummond's Book Stall was located in a strip mall that had seen better days. More than half the shops sported FOR RENT signs, and it didn't seem at all surprising that the shop would soon be joining those ranks.

The door was locked, but Tricia knocked on the glass, and soon a tall, gangly man emerged from the back of the store. Dressed in a bright yellow T-shirt that bore the name of his store, Ken Drummond had managed a welcoming smile, but the look in his eyes was infinitely sad.

"Tricia Miles?"

"That's me."

"Come on in. Thanks for coming."

"I'm sorry about the circumstances," she said sincerely.

Drummond looked around his rather messy store, which was filled with flattened cartons and piles and piles of books on the floor. It looked like he'd already sold off most of his display pieces. Thanks to Pixie, Haven't Got a Clue's business was booming, while this poor man's store had been decimated.

"The mysteries are over here," he said, and led her to the back of the store.

Tricia crouched to better take in the spines. The newer books tended to favor thrillers and bestsellers, with a small number of cozier reads. He had several copies of Fiona Sample's works, as well as Ellery Adams's earlier novels. Tricia immediately picked those. In fact, she took just about everything Drummond had on offer, feeling sorry for the man, and sorrier still about the price he wanted for the stock—low. Then again, there was no point in returning new books for credit if you were going out of business anyway.

It didn't take them long to box up everything.

"What can you tell me about Monterey Bioresources?" Tricia asked.

Drummond yanked a long strip from his tape gun and applied it to one of the cartons. "Not much. Every so often, a bunch of protesters goes out there and pickets. They're not militant, so they don't get the kind of coverage other animal activists get. I've heard of some pretty ruthless protesters in other countries sending nail bombs and mobbing companies, destroying windows and furniture and terrorizing the employees of firms that do animal experimentation."

"But Monterey doesn't experiment on the animals they raise."

"But they sell them to those who do."

Tricia nodded.

"Monterey employs over three hundred people. That gives them some clout. Forcing them to move or shut down would create quite a hardship for the people around here who depend on that paycheck—and from what I hear, they pay really well and have good benefits. That happy workforce shields them from a lot of flak."

Yes, it would.

Drummond fetched a dolly from the storeroom and piled it with boxes, then he and Tricia went out to her car with the first load. In all, there were seven boxes, which filled Tricia's trunk and the back seat of her car. Drummond gave her the total and she rounded it up to the nearest hundred. He gazed at the check. "Aw, you didn't have to do that."

"You've given me one heck of a deal. I really appreciate it."

He shrugged. "I might just break even if I can sell the rest of the stock before I have to be out of here at the end of the week. The owner has someone ready to move in at the end of the month."

"I'm surprised by that, considering how many other storefronts are empty."

"New management. The whole plaza will get a makeover before the end of the summer. They're aggressive and have already signed up three new tenants. I would have had to move anyway."

"Have you got any prospects?"

"My brother-in-law owns a McDonald's franchise up by the highway. He's willing to take me on as an assistant manager trainee."

"Have you ever worked in the food-service industry?"

"No, ma'am, but at my age, my options are limited."

Tricia nodded and offered him her hand. "I wish you all the best of luck. And I'll speak to some of my fellow booksellers to see if they're interested in contacting you."

"I e-mailed every bookstore in New Hampshire and northern Massachusetts. I've had a couple of replies." He raised his hand and crossed his fingers. "Thanks for coming."

"Good-bye," Tricia said, and got in her car. She watched as Drummond reentered his store and locked the door; then she turned the key in the ignition and drove away.

It didn't take long for her to travel the three or so miles to Monterey Bioresources. As she suspected, there were no picketers, the iron gates to the property were closed, and there was no sign of life anywhere around the property, which was surrounded by trees and grass—just as she'd seen online.

Tricia drove past and headed back toward the highway and home, hoping that Pixie would be pleased with the number of books she'd scored to restock Haven't Got a Clue's shelves. All in all, a successful morning for her—and devastating for poor Ken Drummond.

TWENTY-FIVE

Once again, Tricia parked her car in the alley in back of Haven't Got a Clue and struggled to cart the boxes of books up the stairs to sit outside the back door. She moved her car to the municipal parking lot and hurried back to bring the books into the store, arriving via the front door.

"Hey, Tricia—how'd the sale go?"

"Pretty well. I got the books for a good price and should fatten our inventory and keep us afloat for at least a month."

"Vintage books?"

Tricia shook her head. "Mostly new, but the covers are in good shape and it will help us to keep going until and if I can find us more vintage titles."

"We've got a lull going. Want me to help you sort through them?" Pixie asked eagerly.

"I was just going to take them down to the stockroom and start putting them in the inventory."

"Too bad Mr. E has the day off. That's one job he loves to do," Pixie said wistfully. "I guess he could start tomorrow."

Tricia was going to begin the task, but she suspected Pixie might also like to take some time getting to know the new stock. "Would you like to empty the boxes while I hold the fort?"

"Would I!" Pixie said eagerly.

"I'm afraid I can only give you an hour or so, though. Angelica's got a signing this afternoon with that TV chef and asked if I could lend them a hand."

"Yeah, I heard she'd managed to pull it off. Do you mind if we get started with those books right now?"

Between the two of them, they got the boxes into the dumbwaiter and sent them down to the basement storeroom in three trips. Tricia waited on three customers before Pixie's lunch hour. Once she'd returned, Tricia made her way up the stairs to her apartment to change and eat.

As it happened, Tricia did not have to settle for a cupcake for lunch. Instead, she whipped up an omelet, tossing in some frozen onions and peppers she'd thawed in the microwave. Simple, but pretty tasty.

Tricia figured her usual sweater set (light pink that day) would do and headed down the stairs to Haven't Got a Clue, which was as quiet as a tomb.

"Maybe we should put some music on," Tricia suggested.

"Oh, sure. I'll do it now," Pixie agreed. "You'd better hurry over to the Cookery for the book signing. And while you're there, see if you can steer some of their customers our way."

Tricia smiled. "I'll do that."

Tricia left her store and was surprised to find that the Cookery was nearly filled to capacity with eager customers. June was already busy ringing up sales, with a number of women waiting in line to buy one or more of the chef's books.

Tricia threaded her way through the throng of people to the large folding table that had been set up near the back of the shop. On it were stacked forty or fifty copies of the chef's hardcover cookbooks. She found her sister staring at the dumbwaiter, dressed to the nines, and about to grab another box. "Let me get that," Tricia said. "You'll get your pretty outfit all dirty."

"Thanks. I just took off my apron. I guess I should have waited." Angelica struck a pose. "Isn't this dress darling?"

"Are those new shoes, too?"

"Well, of course. I can't host Chef Larry in rags."

Since renovating her apartment, Angelica had made sure to have an enormous walk-in closet added to her boudoir, and she'd spent quite a bit of time filling it, too. She handed Tricia a box cutter.

"You have high hopes for this signing," Tricia stated.

"I do."

"And all these people arrived because of your social media posts?"

"Antonio got the chef's PR people to help spread the word, too," Angelica admitted.

Tricia opened the box and began to unload yet another title onto the table. "I take it the chef will arrive by three?"

"Yes. Antonio was assured he'd be here right on time, and I took a call from his press agent this morning, who said the same thing."

"Where's the chef staying? Not in the Brookview or the Sheer Comfort Inn—otherwise, I'm sure you would have told me."

"If I were to guess, I'd say he's holed up in a hotel in Nashua. He's a big-city kind of guy with restaurants in places like LA, Vegas, New York, and even in Dubai. He wouldn't want to stay in a backwater village like Stoneham."

"Ange!" Tricia admonished.

"I'm not saying Stoneham is a hick town—I'm assuming that the chef might think that of us."

"*We* are a tourist destination and we have nothing to be ashamed of," Tricia asserted.

"A year ago, I would have agreed with you, but since we have next to nothing in the way of support from the Board of Selectmen or the Chamber . . ." She let her words trail off.

The truth was the tourists visiting Stoneham would still be charmed by the village because Angelica—in her Nigela Ricita persona—had paid for all the beautiful flowers that once again graced Main Street. That she'd had signs erected to denote the donation hadn't diminished the thanks the merchants on Main Street felt and only engendered more goodwill toward the Nigela Ricita Associates brand.

A commotion at the front of the store drew their attention. The chef had arrived.

Angelica almost knocked Tricia down in her rush to greet her guest.

"Chef Andrews! Welcome to the Cookery. We're so happy you could join us today."

"Happy to be here," Andrews said, his gaze wandering around the store. His smile seemed to droop as he took in the shelves filled with vintage cookbooks. "What's with all the old stuff?"

"Uh, Stoneham is proudly known as Booktown. We're renowned for embracing vintage books."

"You mean *used*," he said with a sneer.

"We celebrate the past," Angelica answered honestly. "But we also embrace the present. And that's why we invited you to be here today."

Andrews scowled. "I don't make a nickel from used booksellers. Do you sell used copies of my books?"

Angelica hesitated. "We have a wide variety of books. But as you can see, we cater to the needs of people with a love of preparing food. We sell vintage and new utensils—everything we think our customers would use and enjoy. And we have a variety of your books here today."

"Used?" he again accused.

"No. They were ordered from our regular distributor—and whatever is sold today will be afforded your full royalty."

Andrews's scowl deepened.

Angelica tried again. "It was a great honor for me to meet you a year ago on the *Celtic Lady* Authors at Sea cruise."

"I'm sure it was," Andrews said dismissively. He looked at his watch. "I have an interview with *People* magazine in an hour, so I need to get out of here by three thirty. Make that happen," he said with a cold glare.

Tricia blinked and immediately felt sorry for her sister, and she saw Angelica swallow down pangs of anger and disappointment.

"Whatever you say, *Chef*." That last word was said in a tone Tricia had come to know and fear. Angelica was unhappy. Not just annoyed. But royally *pissed off*.

She led Andrews to the back of the store and he stood behind the table. All the women who'd assembled rushed to see who would be first in line.

Andrews continued to stand behind the table and gave a brief—a *very* brief—speech, which was little more than a commercial for his Good Food Channel television show, before he sat down and grabbed a pen, ready to start signing.

Tricia stepped up to hand him each book, title page open so that he could sign it. He didn't personalize any copy, just scribbling his name in an incoherent line and rushing each gushing woman along without a smile or a hint of gratitude.

"Could you make it out to Doris?" one woman asked. "It's for my mother. It'll be an eightieth birthday gift."

"No. We need to keep the line moving," Andrews said tersely, scribbled his name, and bellowed, "Next!"

The man must have woken up on the wrong side of the bed that morning, Tricia thought as she placed yet another cookbook before him. Even Gordon Ramsey had better manners than this piece of work. She'd seen Andrews's TV program, which had portrayed him as a benevolent kind of guy. Had it all been a sham?

"Mr. Andrews?" It was Muriel (or was it Midge?) Dexter who had stepped up to the table, holding on to the book she'd purchased days earlier, its receipt sticking out of the top and acting as a bookmark.

"*Chef* Andrews," the celebrity cook demanded.

"Chef Andrews," she corrected herself. "I'm Muriel Dexter, and this is my sister, Midge." On that day the twins were decked out in the matching sailor suits in white with blue piping that they'd worn on the cruise and looking smart in matching sailor caps perched upon their snow-white hair. "We're your biggest fans."

"Then why aren't you both holding books for me to sign?"

Midge blinked. "I beg your pardon?"

"If you're my biggest fans, why are you only asking me to sign *one* book instead of *two*?"

"Well . . ."

"They're sisters and they live together," Angelica explained.

"Not surprising," Andrews muttered under his breath.

Tricia held yet another of the heavy cookbooks in her hand and at that moment fought the urge to whack the guy over the head with it.

"Would you please sign it?" Midge asked as Muriel held out the book.

Andrews wrenched the book out of the old woman's hand, the movement sending her rocking on her heels.

"Excuse me!" Angelica said in that familiar tone once again. But

Andrews seemed oblivious, scribbled his name across the title page, and slammed the book shut. The Dexter twins backed away as though scalded, and several of the women in line began whispering among themselves.

Angelica bent down so that her mouth was next to the man's ear and muttered in a tone that only he and Tricia could hear, "I'm sure your mother didn't bring you up to be so rude."

Andrews swiveled his head in her direction and glared at her.

Oh, dear. Had Angelica just ruined her chances at winning the amateur division of the Bake-Off?

The sound of the little bell over the door drew Tricia's attention, and she saw the Dexter twins and several other customers flee the store. A woman in a beige suit, with a face frozen in what could only be described as disgusted resignation, signaled the author, who stood.

"I have to get going. I've got an interview with channel nine. Be sure to watch the news tonight," he called before he dashed out of the Cookery and into a long black limo that had double-parked outside the store.

Tricia caught sight of her sister, who stood off to the side, her expression grim. She moved to join her. "I thought he said he was talking to someone from *People* magazine."

"Who cares," Angelica muttered.

"Are you okay?"

Angelica's expression was tense. "I guess."

"I'm sorry," Tricia said.

"What for?"

"I know you admired that jerk."

"He's an extremely gifted chef," Angelica said, stiff-lipped.

"And he's still a jerk," Tricia insisted.

Angelica's wry smile was ironic. "Yes, he is. He could have at least signed the rest of the stock before he vamoosed."

A short line remained at the register and the stack of books on the signing table had dwindled, but the excitement at meeting the world-famous chef had completely disappeared.

"Are we on for martinis on your balcony tonight?" Tricia asked.

Angelica turned a sad face toward her sister. Somehow she managed a smile. "It looks like it'll be the best part of my day."

TWENTY-SIX

The first day of the Great Booktown Bake-Off dawned hot and hazy, which was not good weather if one wanted to make a meringue, but since that wasn't a task in Tricia's near future, she put that thought aside.

Tricia had hours to kill before she and Angelica were to meet to walk to the high school to witness the spectacle, so she had plenty of time for her morning exercise and to get ready for the day. What did one wear to observe a baking contest? Was the auditorium air-conditioned? Should she bring a sweater? In the end, she chose just another sweater set. This one was powder blue.

With her cat fed and money in the till to begin the day, Tricia left Haven't Got a Clue for what she figured would be most of the day and showed up at the Cookery to find Angelica waiting behind its door. "Let's grab a latte at the Coffee Bean," she suggested.

"Sounds good to me," Angelica agreed.

They entered the shop to find a short line. It was co-owner Boris

Kozlov, who usually did more of the behind-the-scenes work these days, manning the front of the house. "Vhat can I get for you ladies?" he asked.

They gave their orders, paid, and spoke to him as he prepared the drinks.

"Are you excited about Alexa entering the Bake-Off?" Tricia asked.

"Is not my nature to be excited," the thin, grim man admitted. "But if she vins, it vill be good for the shop. Vould you like a cupcake to go vith that?"

"Uh, not today. But I hope Alexa will add her entry to the menu beginning tomorrow," Tricia said.

Boris nodded. "Da. That vas the plan." He handed them their coffees. "Thank you for patronizing the Coffee Bean. Next!"

"That Boris—still a charmer," Angelica muttered as they left the shop.

The sisters walked up Main Street toward the high school and found they weren't the only ones headed in that direction. Despite the ten-dollar fee to watch the proceedings, which would be used to buy new television equipment for the school, a surprising number of people had shown up to watch the contest unfold.

Tricia saw the Dexter twins standing on the edge of the crowd and nudged Angelica. "I'm surprised they'd want to watch the proceedings after what happened at the Cookery yesterday."

"I'd better go over and apologize to them," Angelica said, and headed in the twins' direction, with Tricia following.

"Muriel!" Angelica called. One of the twins looked up and offered a weak smile. "I'm terribly sorry about what happened yesterday at the book signing. I do hope you'll accept my apologies."

"Your apologies?" Midge asked. "You have nothing to apologize for."

"*Mister* Andrews"—and Angelica emphasized the word, not his title—"was terribly rude to both of you. I don't condone that kind of behavior in my store."

"We don't blame you, dear lady. We've always had a wonderful time when we've visited the Cookery, and this incident won't keep us from coming back again."

"Thank you," Angelica said, her tone heartfelt.

"After that man's incredible rudeness, I'm surprised to see you ladies here," Tricia said.

"Our admiration for the chef may have dimmed, but we came to cheer on Nikki, Alexa, and the other local bakers," Muriel said.

"As a matter of local pride," Midge pitched in.

"Stoneham is very lucky to have such ardent community-spirited citizens," Angelica said sincerely, which caused both ladies to blush.

"We'd better get in line," Muriel said. "We'll see you later," she promised, and the twins waved and joined the throng heading up the steps to the school, while Tricia and Angelica hung back.

"Talk about gracious," Tricia said.

"Yes. Thank goodness. Come on. We'd better join the crowd."

Minutes later, they paid the entrance fee and were given flimsy neon pink plastic bracelets to wear. "This way if you need to leave the school for a while, you can get back in," said the cheerful teenage girl with a ponytail and wearing the school's cheerleading outfit—which, with its blue-and-gold sweater with a big white S, was far too warm for the early-summer day.

"Members of the marching band will be selling cookies, cupcakes, sandwiches, soda pop, and coffee at the breaks, so you won't need to go far."

"Thanks," Tricia said, and donned her bracelet, which clashed with her sweater set.

Angelica frowned and tugged at the ring of plastic around her wrist. "I'm sure Sofia would love something like this, but it doesn't go with my outfit." On that day she'd chosen an apricot linen suit and matching heels.

"You can finish your coffee, but there's no food or drink allowed in the auditorium," the cheerleader told them.

"No problem," Tricia said. She'd nearly finished her small, skinny latte. The sisters filed into the school. "I can get us seats if you want to finish your coffee."

"I'm nearly done," Angelica said, and took a mighty swig before dumping the paper cup into a nearby trash bin. Tricia ditched her cup as well.

As they entered the cavernous auditorium, they were surprised to find the lower level was already half filled. "Wow, this Bake-Off really is popular," Tricia said.

"And think of the PR opportunity it could have been for the Chamber had Russ Smith shown the slightest interest in the event," Angelica lamented, shaking her head in consternation.

"Speak of the devil," Tricia said as they walked down the aisle. She nodded in the direction of the front row. There sat Russ alone in the aisle seat, with shoulders slouched, looking uncomfortable. "Do you think he wants to see Nikki win?"

"More likely lose," Angelica muttered. "He probably came to make catcalls and boo at her."

"According to Pixie, everyone's betting she'll take home the trophy."

"Not me. I hope it's Tommy or Joann from the Brookview," Angelica said of her employees.

"But if that happens and they go to California to compete on the chef's TV show, *you* might lose them."

"It would be a wonderful opportunity for either of them. I would never try to hold them back. They both have unique talents. Why wouldn't I want to see them succeed?"

A surge of pride in her sister swelled through Tricia as they paused about six rows from the front of the auditorium, sidling by several other villagers to sit mid row and stare at a large blank screen that had been lowered from the top of the stage.

"I feel like we should have disgustingly big tubs of popcorn saturated with butter-flavored oil to munch on," Angelica said.

"You heard the cheerleader—no food or drink."

Angelica looked around and lowered her voice. "I brought a couple of boxes of Sofia's animal crackers—just in case we get desperate."

Tricia was pretty sure she wouldn't get *that* desperate.

Just then, the darkened screen came to life, but the lights in the auditorium didn't dim. The camera focused on the culinary rooms, which seemed to have gotten a refresh since Tricia and Angelica had visited them the week before. The walls were now painted a bright white, and new counters—which looked like granite but were probably Formica—had been installed, as well as new, sparkling-white stoves and refrigerators. The Good Food Channel had done well by the school. The camera took in two of the kitchenettes, and a woman with a clipboard seemed to be counting the various gadgets, spoons, and other paraphernalia at each site.

"Looking good so far," Angelica commented, then she squinted. "Rats! The stoves are still electric."

"Maybe they didn't want to risk a gas explosion," Tricia suggested.

"Shhh! Don't say such a thing! Do you want to have us kicked out of here?"

It was obvious that no one on the "set" was ready to perform, what with the cables lying around, darkened areas where the hot lights had yet to be lit, and the lack of the talent—Chef Andrews. Bored-looking technicians and cameramen came and went, and there was a lot of muttered "testing, one, two, three, four" for sound checks. Tricia looked at the clock over the auditorium's side exit. They weren't supposed to start filming for at least another forty-five minutes. She should have brought a book to read. Then again, she could read from an app on her phone. She should have thought about downloading a new-to-her book to read. Then again, her phone could access her collection of e-books from the cloud.

Unlike Tricia, Angelica seemed riveted. "Isn't this exciting," she said.

No, it was boring. "It doesn't look like they're going to be ready anytime soon. I may as well take a walk."

"What if you miss something?" Angelica demanded.

"You can fill me in later. Save my seat."

Tricia got up, squeezed past the other people in the row, and walked up the aisle and out into the area outside the auditorium. It couldn't be called a lobby—too small—and she made her way back out of the building and into the air, which was already hotter than it had been when she and Angelica had entered the school not long before. She took off her outer sweater, tossed it over her arm, and started to walk.

For a while, her head just felt empty as she started up Hickory Street and away from the school. But then her thoughts wandered back to the day she'd found Vera Olson. Vera had been on her mind a lot lately, but Tricia tried not to dwell on the memory of actually finding the woman's body. Maybe that had been a mistake.

Poor Vera had lain on the grass behind Joyce's vegetable garden. No puddle of blood had mired the grass. Vera's blue eyes had been wide open, and the pitchfork had stood upright, piercing her middle.

That last thought made Tricia wince. Vera's arms had been cushioned by the grass, her palms down. Someone very strong, or very determined, had probably had to straddle her body to push the pitchfork through her. She could imagine a heavy booted foot thrusting hard against the top of the steel tines until they had penetrated the woman's torso. That task was difficult to do in the hard, dry earth, let alone a fat-and-muscled body.

Surely it had to be a man who'd killed Vera. Few women possessed that kind of strength. Tricia seriously doubted Joyce did. But what about Officer Pearson? She was much younger than Joyce and was tall and buff. To get hired by the police department, she would have to have passed some kind of physical fitness test.

And what about Toby Kingston? He was tall and looked capable of the kind of strength it would take to stomp on the lethal garden tool. And why do that? Vera was dead before she was pierced. Had it been done as a message to others? But if so, to whom?

Vera had had problems with Toby Kingston. Was it Bonnie Connor or Rebecca Shore who'd mentioned that Vera had had a private meeting with Toby and had left his office very upset? Was there something really fishy going on at Pets-A-Plenty? That seemed logical. Perhaps it was the reason Toby hadn't welcomed Tricia with open arms. Was that because she'd had nearly as much—or perhaps even more—experience running a nonprofit organization? Okay, her skills might be a little rusty, but she could have polished them up in no time. And Cori Haskell, the Pets-A-Plenty volunteer, had talked about her distrust of Monterey Bioresources and anomalies that went on within Pets-A-Plenty. Did Vera know something about the company and tie it to the pet rescue, too?

But who had told Nikki about Grace trying to influence Toby and the board to take Tricia on? What if it had been Toby himself? For what reason? And if so, how could she prove it?

Tricia turned the corner at Poplar Avenue and started walking south.

What did she really know about Toby Kingston, anyway? He had come to Pets-A-Plenty a year or so before, but she wasn't sure what kind of administrative work he'd done in the past. He was definitely not a people person, so she couldn't imagine he had an affinity for animals, either. And worst of all, he didn't like her. But did that make him a killer?

No.

What about the most obvious suspect: Joyce?

Joyce apparently had had the opportunity, but what was her motive? She'd had the large limb on the maple tree in Vera's yard removed. It had been Vera who'd threatened Joyce—and in front of witnesses, too. It would have been pure stupidity for Joyce to have killed Vera. If it had been Joyce who'd turned up dead, Vera would have been the prime suspect. But as far as the witnesses in Joyce's store were concerned, the altercation between Joyce and Vera had been initiated by Vera. It was Joyce who'd been threatened, and no one would have been surprised if she'd been the victim of violence.

Supposing Joyce's innocence, the door in the south side of the tall wooden fence had to have been opened by someone other than Joyce. It had been bolted on her side of the yard, and the chain-link gate to the front yard had been padlocked, but it wasn't particularly high, either. Just about anyone could have easily scaled it and gained entry to the yard and then opened the wooden door that separated the yards. Who could have known about it? Or was that thought a dead end?

What if Vera herself had scaled the chain link to get more catnip from Joyce's herb garden? Or could she have been confronted by her killer in her own yard? That seemed the best scenario. Could there have been traces of catnip on Vera's hands or under her fingernails? Would the medical examiner have noted it? Tricia could ask Baker, but he might think her question frivolous—as he now seemed to regard her. His loss.

Baker was to be on hand for the Bake-Off's judging. They were keeping the spectators away from the culinary rooms where the

Bake-Off was being filmed, and also away from the judges and contestants. But there might be an opportunity when she could corner the man and ask. Tricia would have to see what she could do to make that happen.

With that in mind, she turned onto Main Street once again and started back toward the school, not that she was in a hurry. It would likely be hours before the competition came to an end and she could track down and speak to Chief Baker.

Tricia made peace with the fact that it was likely to be a boring day, but maybe by the end of it, she'd have some answers.

Unfortunately, she didn't feel all that hopeful.

TWENTY-SEVEN

By the time Tricia returned to the school, brandishing her pink bracelet so that she didn't have to pay the entrance fee once more, she found that the contest had already begun in earnest.

"What did I miss?" she whispered to Angelica after taking her seat.

"Everybody running for their ingredients. They're filming the actual Bake-Off in real time. I thought it was going to be an all-day event," Angelica said, sounding disappointed.

"Wow."

"They'll be doing pickup shots at the end," she continued, and actually sounded like she knew what that meant.

The audio feed seemed to be malfunctioning, as only a loud hum was broadcast over the auditorium's sound system. In addition, the student-run camera was focused on only one of the rooms, and on two of the contestants: Nikki Brimfield-Smith and the Brookview's pastry chef, Joann Gibson. Both were French trained, and both had a shot at winning. Dressed in chef whites, they both looked good on camera, but it was Nikki who, every so often, gave sly looks in Larry Andrews's direction.

"She could be a little less obvious," Angelica quipped.

"I'll say."

With the static camera angle, the competition was pretty dull, but Tricia consoled herself with the fact that the money the school collected would buy new equipment to help its future moviemakers and broadcasters and those sponsoring the contestants would be giving money to local charities.

Several times Tricia found her head drooping, as it was hard to stay alert with the lack of action and sound and the rising temperature in the auditorium. She felt sorry for the kids who had to endure assemblies during the warmer months of the school year.

When the hour had passed, the bakers were given a signal, and their arms flew into the air. Time was up. The bakers surrendered their cupcakes to the judges and then finally a break was called while they set up the shots for the judging. A screech of feedback assaulted their ears, and then the sound was finally available again. The audience broke into cheers, whistles, and a hearty round of applause.

"About time," Angelica muttered.

They watched and heard many voices speaking over one another as the makeup crew descended and gave everyone a quick touch-up while the judges conferred off camera.

At last, the student camera was moved to take in the judging area, with more audio squawks before settling down once again. The judges stood in front of a green screen. That meant that before the network broadcast they were going to add a different background than the bland classroom behind them. They stood gravely in front of the linen-clad table covered with beautifully decorated cupcakes, and then the elimination began.

Tricia didn't know the first four contestants, who must have come from restaurants and bakeries from the greater southern New Hampshire area. She watched with growing agitation as Booked for Lunch's short-order cook, Tommy, came up to be judged. She was pulling for him. All his baked goods at the little retro café were more pedestrian than what Nikki or Joann made, but they were delicious just the same. Alexa from the Coffee Bean was next, and, of course, her entry was a mocha cupcake. Nikki and Joann were next, and just as Tricia had expected, the real competition was between the two of them.

The three judges were poker-faced during the segment, but then finally Andrews stepped forward. "It's been a tough decision. Everyone put forth a cupcake worthy of praise, but two of the contestants stand out. Nikki Brimfield and Joann Gibson, will you please step forward?"

Tricia could only imagine the looks of disappointment on the other contestants' faces, but thanks to the static picture, the audience wasn't privy to that view. Nikki and Joann moved to stand in front of the judges.

"Joann, your hibiscus, mango, peach, and rum cupcake was a tour de force of taste, but the judges felt you got a little carried away with the rum."

A definite "aww" echoed through the auditorium, but everyone knew what that meant. Joann's head dipped ever so slightly, but she forced a smile. "Thank you, Chef."

Andrews turned his attention to the other finalist. "Nikki, your crème brûlée cupcake was a breath of fresh air in this hot and stuffy kitchen. The taste was there, and the custard center hit the bull's-eye. Therefore, you, Nikki Brimfield, are the winner of the professional portion of the Great Booktown Bake-Off."

The applause was sincere, but it was obvious that despite the popularity of her bakery, Nikki wasn't the audience's darling. And there was no mistaking the rather snarky smile that crossed her features. As the applause died, Tricia saw Russ Smith get up from his seat and trudge up the aisle. His expression was dour. Was he unhappy that his former wife had won the professional portion of the Bake-Off or that she'd dropped his surname?

Andrews handed Nikki a gold trophy in the shape of a cupcake and she held it up over her head in triumph.

The director called "Cut," and everyone "on the set" seemed to breathe a sigh of relief. The director then turned to the student camera to address the members of the audience. "We'll be having an impromptu press conference and picture-taking opportunity in front of the school in fifteen minutes. See you there." As his words died in the air, the big screen went dark.

"Well, that should prove interesting," Angelica said, but Tricia doubted she meant it.

Around them, people rose to their feet and started filing out of the auditorium. Tricia and Angelica remained seated. Who wanted to stand around in the hot sun for a quarter of an hour or more?

"Well, what do you think?" Tricia asked.

"I think I'm going to give Joann a raise just for putting up with that pompous Larry Andrews."

Aha! So Angelica had changed her mind and now thought the celebrity chef had feet of clay. It wasn't really surprising.

"And?" Tricia prompted.

"I'd sure like to try that cupcake she made."

"I meant what do you think about Nikki winning?"

"The way she made eyes at Chef Andrews? Well, if I was going to be catty—which I would never do—I'd say I wouldn't be surprised to find out she'll meet him for drinks—and more—at his hotel room later this evening."

"Meow," Tricia agreed. "Are you going to hang around for the picture taking?"

"And watch Nikki preen? No, thanks."

"I think I will."

"Going for a photo op with her?" Angelica asked.

"No way. I just want to see what happens."

"You don't think she or anyone else in the competition had anything to do with Vera Olson's death, do you?"

"Of course not. But Pixie has everything under control at Haven't Got a Clue, so I won't be missed if I stay away a little bit longer."

Angelica eyed her sister. "No, I don't suppose you will."

Tricia was about to ask for further clarification on that, but then Angelica stood. Tricia rose, too, and followed her out of the auditorium and into the cooler corridor, where the students were hawking the last of their breakfast leftovers. They passed by them and filed out into the hot, trampled schoolyard.

"What are you going to do now?" Tricia asked.

"Head to the day spa. I'm sure I can find something to do there, and, of course, I always have tons of e-mails, contracts, and sales catalogs to go through for my other businesses."

"Are we having dinner together?"

"Darling girl, when do we not?" Angelica asked.

Tricia smiled. "I'll see you later."

She watched as Angelica started down the sidewalk before gravitating to the shade under one of the large maples that populated the front of the school. The crowd that waited was a lot smaller than she had anticipated, and she didn't find any familiar faces among them. To kill time, she took out her phone to check her e-mail and phone messages and, to her disappointment, found nothing pressing.

It was just about the estimated fifteen minutes after the competition had ended when most of the contestants filed out of the building. It looked like several reporters—probably from Nashua or Concord—had made it to the Bake-Off and would probably be filing stories, possibly with pictures, but it didn't take long for the losers to be dismissed as unimportant, and none of the newspeople seemed particularly interested in meeting and interviewing them.

"Tricia," said a familiar male voice, and she turned around to find Antonio standing behind her.

She couldn't help but smile. "What are you doing here?"

"I came to congratulate my pastry chef for coming in second. I consider it an honor and I wish to convey that sentiment to Chef Gibson as well."

"Were you in the auditorium for the whole Bake-Off?"

"Just for the last ten minutes or so." He flashed his pink bracelet to show that he, too, had coughed up ten bucks to benefit the students' television arts campaign.

"You should have come and sat with Angelica and me."

He waved a hand. "It would have been disruptive."

She nodded. "You must have stepped out as soon as it ended."

"Yes, I needed to make some calls." He looked up. "Ah, and here she comes now. Would you mind taking our picture? I would like to share it with the rest of the kitchen staff."

"Of course."

Tricia followed her nephew to the bottom of the stairs, but a reporter intercepted the Brookview's pastry chef and they had to wait two or three minutes before Joann was free to join them.

Antonio greeted his employee, introduced her to "my dear friend Tricia," then handed his cell phone to Tricia. She took several shots before handing his phone back.

"I'm so sorry your entry didn't come in first, Joann. It sounded fantastic."

"Some of our customers like it," she said modestly.

"Which is a lie. Everyone loves it. The last time it was served at a bridal shower, the guests begged for the recipe," Antonio said.

"And did you give it to them?"

"Of course not. It's my strategy to entice the bride to book her wedding reception with us."

They all laughed and then Antonio turned to Joann. "May I walk you back to your car?"

"Sure thing, boss."

"I will see you later, Tricia," Antonio said.

"It was nice meeting you, Joann," Tricia said, and then watched them walk to the sidewalk and head south for the municipal parking lot.

Just then, Tricia recognized another familiar face in the crowd—Rebecca Shore from the Pets-A-Plenty shelter. "Rebecca! Rebecca!"

Rebecca turned at the sound of her name and Tricia hurried over to intercept her. "Hi. You're just the person I was hoping to run into."

"Really?"

"I wanted to let you know that last week I spoke to one of the volunteers at Pets-A-Plenty and she had some serious concerns about Monterey Bioresources."

Rebecca's mouth thinned with displeasure. "You're talking about Cori Haskell?"

"Why, yes."

Rebecca nodded. "She's no longer with us, I'm afraid."

"Why not?"

Rebecca sighed. "She was spouting all kinds of conspiracy theories about Pets-A-Plenty and Monterey that were just pure fantasy. Toby asked her not to return."

Tricia wasn't sure what to make of that statement. Vera had thought something was fishy about Monterey Bioresources and might have died because of it. Cori Haskell had reservations about the company and now she'd been dismissed by the shelter.

"Oh, look!" Rebecca called and pointed. "It's Nikki Brimfield and Toby."

Tricia glanced in their direction. Sure enough, a smiling Toby stood next to Nikki—who had apparently not only ditched her married name for the contest but had done it for all aspects of her life as well. They seemed rooted to the school's top steps, with his arm around her shoulders, but it was Patti Perkins from the *Stoneham Weekly News* taking the photo—not Russ Smith. Was it because he couldn't stand to see his soon-to-be ex-wife with another man—or he just couldn't stand her?

"Don't they look cute together?" Rebecca said, beaming at Toby and waving enthusiastically.

"I guess," Tricia said. "I didn't know Nikki was dating."

Rebecca turned and gave Tricia a puzzled look. "Dating? Toby?"

Tricia nodded.

"They're not dating. They're cousins."

And then Tricia understood why Nikki had taunted her with the information about Grace pressing to get Tricia the Pets-A-Plenty board position. Had Toby asked his cousin for information on Tricia? Nikki would have been only too happy to put the worst possible spin on things, and he must have told her about the Everett Foundation's donation and the stipulation that came with it, knowing she would taunt Tricia—just to make her miserable. Unfortunately, it had worked.

"I'm so thrilled for Nikki. Imagine going to California to try out for the next Big-Time Chef competition. I think she's got what it takes to win and get her own TV show. Wouldn't that be a boon for Stoneham?"

Not that Tricia could see—or was that just sour grapes on her part because Tricia and Nikki's friendship had not only cooled but was totally in the freezer?

Rebecca's eyes shone with delight. "I think I'll try to join them. Would you mind taking my picture with them?" She dug her phone out of her purse.

Swallowing her pique, Tricia forced a smile. "I'd be delighted."

Rebecca started worming her way through the crowd until she reached the school's steps, which she quickly ascended. She spoke to Toby and Nikki, who seemed to find her request more palatable than Tricia did. Tricia stepped up closer and held the phone up. "Smile!" She clicked a few shots and then Rebecca trotted down the steps to retrieve her phone.

"Thanks. See you later," Rebecca said, and practically bounded back up the steps to rejoin Toby and to bask in Nikki's glory.

Tricia turned and was surprised to see Angelica waving to her from the back of the crowd. She quickly joined her.

"I thought you were going to the day spa."

"I did, but Randy has everything under control for now, although he asked me to come back later this afternoon to talk to one of the distributors. As I hadn't seen you pass by, I decided to see if you were still here."

"I was just about to leave."

"Ready for lunch? Bobby worked today so Tommy could compete, but his soup special is just as good."

Tricia consulted her watch. "It's earlier than we usually eat, but it sounds okay to me."

"I was so hyped, I skipped breakfast, but now I'm ready for something."

"You mean you didn't snack on Sofia's animal crackers when I took my walk?"

"I was far too engrossed watching the action."

Action? For Tricia, watching Nikki and Joann bake—with no sound and no narration—had been painfully mind-numbing.

"Then we'd better get you some sustenance before you keel over," Tricia said, and the sisters started off.

"What a long morning," Angelica commented, but sounded oddly satisfied.

Yes, it had been. And somehow not only dull but anticlimactic as well.

Clouds were beginning to clutter the sky, Tricia noticed. A storm might be brewing, which did nothing to heighten Tricia's mood. She already had too many dark thoughts whirling through her mind and wasn't sure where they might take her.

TWENTY-EIGHT

During their walk to Booked for Lunch, Angelica chatted about the Bake-Off. Like Rebecca, she, too, thought Nikki might have the chops to take on other wannabe chefs angling for a TV cooking show of her own and just couldn't seem to stop talking about it. Tricia was contemplating shoving one of Sarge's squeaky toys in her mouth when they finally reached the retro café.

Bobby, the weekend short-order cook, had whipped up gazpacho to go with a vegetarian sandwich made of avocado, cucumber, and lettuce with a lemon vinaigrette that sounded light and refreshing after the far too many cupcakes Tricia had ingested during the past few weeks.

Tricia ate her lunch only half listening as Angelica speculated about how the Bake-Off would differ for the amateur chefs the next day.

"And, of course, I've got an uphill battle to win."

"Why's that?" Tricia asked.

"Because I've got two judges who've taken a dislike to me."

"I think you're probably overreacting."

"We'll see," Angelica said.

The sisters agreed to meet later at Angelica's for happy hour and dinner and parted in front of Haven't Got a Clue.

Tricia reentered her store.

"Ms. Miles," Mr. Everett greeted her with enthusiasm. "How did the Bake-Off go?"

"It went," she said unenthusiastically.

"And the winner?"

"Nikki Brimfield."

"Ah, as suspected," he said, nodding.

Mr. Everett peppered her with a slew of questions, while Pixie listened and nodded. She seemed subdued, not unlike how Tricia felt.

"It seems I may have a better shot at winning than I thought," Tricia said.

"Why is that?" Pixie asked.

"Angelica is convinced that two of the judges might not be supportive of her efforts."

"How come?"

Tricia shrugged. "She and Chief Baker have never exactly been pals, and Chef Andrews was rude to Angelica's customers at the signing yesterday and she called him on it."

"He was rude?" Mr. Everett asked, appalled.

"Especially to the Dexter twins."

"Those sweet old ladies?" Pixie asked.

Tricia nodded.

"There's no excuse for rudeness," Mr. Everett said solemnly. "I went to several of his demonstrations on the Authors at Sea cruise and he seemed perfectly nice."

"Yesterday must have been an off day for him. I would hope all the judges would strive to be impartial when it came to choosing the best cupcake."

"Yes," Mr. Everett said, looking troubled.

The door opened, and Pixie and Mr. Everett immediately went into hospitality mode. Tricia quietly bowed out and retreated to her office down in the basement, where there were no windows and not much to do. Mr. Everett had attacked the task of updating the store's inventory spreadsheet with everything but the cost of the books. Tricia glanced at the prices he'd assigned to each and found them acceptable. She then divided the total cost by the number of books she'd purchased to come up with her base cost and filled in that field.

With that done, Tricia decided to go on eBay and look for more books to stock the store. That was something that could prove to be a time sink, but on that day she welcomed it.

She'd put bids on more than twenty books by the time the store closing rolled around, and she mounted the stairs to consult with Pixie before the store was shuttered for the day.

Mr. Everett had already left, and Pixie was gathering up her purse when the door opened and Angelica stepped inside.

"What are you doing here?" Tricia asked.

"I'm back from the day spa and I came to collect you."

"I'd better be going," Pixie said hurriedly. "Good luck at the Bake-Off tomorrow," she called. "Both of you." And she was gone.

"Wow. I wonder what's gotten into her," Tricia said at her assistant manager's abrupt departure.

Angelica didn't answer; instead, she queried, "Are you ready for happy hour?"

"Just let me close the blinds and lock up."

A minute later, they exited the store. The wind had picked up, the sky was an angry steel gray, and the air felt heavy with humidity as they walked over to the Cookery, which had already closed for the day. June had left a note on the door to the stairwell saying she had let Sarge out just after closing the store, which meant Tricia's martini wouldn't have to wait. Of course, Sarge was ecstatic to see his dog-mom, and despite her orders to hush, it was only three biscuits that finally quieted him.

"I just can't get over what an interesting day it's been—and in more ways than one," Angelica commented as she washed her hands at the sink.

"Well, I can," Tricia said, and marched straight to Angelica's liquor cabinet to retrieve the gin and vermouth.

"Oh, let me do that," Angelica said, while Tricia got the olives out of the fridge and jabbed them onto frill picks. "I'm sorry there are no goodies to go along with our drinks, unless you want crackers."

"I'm fine. Let's sit out on the balcony and watch the weather."

"Sure. There's nothing like a good thunderstorm," Angelica agreed. She picked up the tray and followed Tricia to the balcony, set the tray down, and unfurled the awning, which would keep them dry once the rain began. They sat down and Angelica handed Tricia a martini. "While we were having lunch, Randy interviewed a new candidate for one of the spa's nail-tech positions. Cheers."

They raised their glasses. "I thought you'd already hired a couple of them."

"Yes, we did—but Randy wanted me to consider a third person. He described her as an older woman and a rather *colorful* character. From her crazy red hair to a gold canine tooth, and dressed like one of the Andrews Sisters."

Tricia's mouth dropped. That was an apt description of Haven't Got a Clue's assistant manager, Pixie!

"Why on earth would Pixie need a second job as a nail tech? I pay her a good wage. And she's constantly telling me how happy she is working for me."

"Well, she and Fred now have the little house on Maple Street. I gave her a good deal on it, but we don't know what other expenses they might have incurred. Maybe just decorating it put them over budget."

"Pixie is a thrifter. I doubt she'd go into hock to buy anything new when she adores everything vintage—and has a nose for bargains," Tricia pointed out.

A rumble of thunder sounded above them.

"Maybe you should talk to her about it."

"And say what?"

"Why are you interviewing for another job?"

"Wouldn't that sound like I'm spying on her?"

"Do you want me to ask her? I *am* the spa's owner—and I consider us to be friends, too."

"Maybe she didn't consult with you because she didn't want it to look like she was asking for a favor."

"Maybe. But we've all seen how nicely she keeps her own fingernails. I'm sure she'd be just as good at doing it professionally as she is selling vintage mysteries."

There was no doubt about that.

"Why don't you call her right now?" Angelica suggested.

"Pixie just put in a full day. I don't want to bother her at home. And besides, the way she bolted from my store, she probably knew you were going to tell me about it."

"Then text her and ask her to come in early so you can talk before we have to be at the Bake-Off in the morning."

More thunder rumbled above them, and a crack of lightning split the clouds to the east as fat droplets fell beyond the fringe of the awning.

Tricia didn't have to be at the school until ten o'clock, the exact time Pixie started work at Haven't Got a Clue. Asking her to come in early shouldn't be that much of an imposition. She could let Pixie leave early, since without the TV coverage, the amateurs' portion of the Bake-Off was sure to be over far quicker than the professionals' competition had been. It wouldn't give them much time to speak, but enough to have one question answered.

Why?

The storm had passed and the sky had cleared and was darkening to indigo when Tricia returned to Haven't Got a Clue. She'd had a lot to think about during the preceding hours, and instead of heading upstairs for her apartment, she went down to her basement office and fired up her computer once again. Besides her upcoming conversation with Pixie, thoughts of Cori Haskell and her dismissal from Pets-A-Plenty played on her mind. She did a Google search, but nothing came up for the woman. Next, she tried looking for her via the online White Pages. Unfortunately, unless she had a paid subscription to the site, they weren't going to give up any information.

Tricia sat back in her chair and wondered if Cori was on social media. If so, which platform was she likely to use?

First, she tried Instagram and came up with three people with the same name, the same spelling. The icons were too small to decipher, so she clicked on each and—bingo!—came up with a positive on the third try. Unfortunately, Cori's account was set to private. Forget that. Next, she tried Facebook and came up with five possibilities. She clicked on the face that matched that of the woman she'd spoken to. They weren't Facebook friends, so Tricia couldn't leave a comment—but she did try to private message the woman. Sometimes that worked; sometimes it didn't. It depended on if the not-friend looked in her inbox. Tricia reminded Cori of her name and the circumstances of their meeting at Pets-A-Plenty.

Tricia didn't expect a reply but thought she ought to stay online for a while—just in case. To kill time, she pulled up her sales spreadsheet and clicked to make a graph. No doubt about it, since Pixie had taken the job as Haven't Got a Clue's manager in January, overall sales had improved. She had suggested and, upon Tricia's approval, taken on projects to make that growth happen. Considering that for the first four months of the year sales were usually dismal, they were more than 10 percent above the previous year's figures. Pixie was damn good at her job. She came in every morning with a smile on her face and an off-key song in her heart. She delighted and educated customers with her encyclopedic knowledge of vintage and current mystery authors. There was no way Tricia could afford to lose her. Not that there wasn't dignity in being a nail tech, but Pixie had proven herself in the managerial position. She had seemed to thrive on the work. There had to be a serious reason for her to contemplate leaving Haven't Got a Clue, and Tricia wanted to know what that was.

Her computer gave a ping and Tricia looked up to see that Cori had indeed received her message. Tricia wasted no time in replying.

Would you be willing to speak to me about what happened at Pets-A-Plenty and why you were asked to leave?

No way.

Can I ask why?

Because I don't want to end up like . . . you know who.

Tricia guessed Cori hadn't meant the villain from the Harry Potter stories, Lord Voldemort.

Could we meet?

No. I'm leaving town. Please don't contact me again.

Tricia stared at the words on her screen. On impulse, she typed Cori's name into the search bar and hit the little magnifying glass. The various profile pictures came up on her screen once more, only this time the Cori Haskell from Milford, New Hampshire, was no longer there. Tricia had been blocked.

Had Toby Kingston threatened Cori? Was she so scared she'd decided to leave town? And if so, could Tricia really blame her?

The uneasy feeling in Tricia's gut seemed to grow, and she wasn't sure what to do to make it go away.

TWENTY-NINE

Sleep didn't come easy, and despite the blackout drapes covering the windows in her bedroom, Tricia was still up at sunup and wasn't sure if the anxiety she felt was because of the upcoming Bake-Off or confronting Pixie. Either way, she wasn't about to veer from her usual routine and fed her cat, dressed, and headed out for a brisk walk before breakfast.

But it wasn't just the events of the day that had her thoughts in a jumble as Tricia power walked down the empty sidewalk along Main Street. The memory of Vera Olson's dead body never seemed to leave her. Despite being a person of interest, Joyce had not been arrested, but there hadn't been any news, let alone rumors, about other suspects. Was there a chance Tricia could talk to Chief Baker before or after the Bake-Off? The day before, he'd been surrounded by the TV crew and the other assorted people associated with the contest, and it would have been impossible to catch a word with him. Was he aware of Joyce's liaison with Cindy Pearson? If not, was it Tricia's place to tell him? And what about Toby Kingston? Everything about him seemed shady. And now it appeared he'd threatened Cori Haskell because she'd spoken about a possible connection between Pets-A-Plenty and Monterey Bioresources.

By the time Tricia returned to her apartment, her stomach was unsettled and she decided against making coffee. On a day like the one she was facing, the last thing she needed was caffeine to make her feel even more jittery. To kill time, she took a leisurely shower and fussed with her hair and makeup—despite the fact that the only camera she was likely to face that day was from the *Stoneham Weekly News*—not that Russ would allow any photo of her face to appear in its pages. If she won the Bake-Off, he'd probably highlight someone else or kill all references to the amateur portion of the competition out of spite.

Next, Tricia returned to her basement office and fired up the computer. This time, her Google search was centered on Toby Kingston. The first thing that popped up was the Pets-A-Plenty website About page. The paragraph about Toby was brief, just saying that he had come to the pet rescue after work in the "agricultural industry."

That covered a lot of ground.

Tricia logged into her LinkedIn account and searched for Toby. His profile came up almost immediately. His résumé was quite a bit longer than what Pets-A-Plenty was willing to convey—and rather enlightening, too. Toby had started his career working at a meat-processing plant near Cedar Rapids, Iowa. Hogs came from Iowa. Monterey Bioresources raised pigs for the medical industry and Big Pharma. He'd worked his way up from an entry-level position to management during his ten years with the firm. Obviously, he hadn't been all that interested in animal welfare back in the day. Had something happened to give him a change of heart, or was a white-collar management job just a paycheck and it didn't matter what kind of widgets he was passing around as long as he kept to a budget?

The other Pets-A-Plenty board members had to have known about his background before they agreed to hire him. What if donors to the rescue found out about Toby's former career—would they want to run him out of the rescue on a rail? She certainly didn't like the idea that someone in his position had been responsible for the deaths of potentially millions of pigs.

And then she again thought about her own hypocrisy. She really did love bacon, even if she had avoided it for most of her life—and not because of the taste, but because of the fat content.

Tricia's cell phone gave a ping and she removed it from her slacks pocket to see she'd received a text from Marshall.

Good luck with the Bake-Off.

Thanks.

Nervous?

You bet.

Call me later?

I will.

Dinner?

Sounds good.

And then Marshall sent a thumbs-up emoji.

Tricia smiled and glanced at the clock. Pixie would be arriving at any minute. She put the computer to sleep, pocketed her phone, and went up the steps to her store to get the beverage station up and running for her employees and customers.

As Tricia had asked, Pixie arrived at Haven't Got a Clue early—exactly twenty minutes before her workday was due to start. Despite the warm summer day, she was dressed in a black suit—almost as though she was in mourning. Her expression was dour, and on this day she'd gone easy on her makeup. Her bright red hair was twisted into a chignon and she wore no jewelry—nothing to brighten her appearance.

"I'm here," she said wearily as she closed the store's door behind her, the tinkling bell sounding absurdly cheerful in contrast to Pixie's appearance.

"Are you going to a funeral later today?" Tricia asked, concerned.

"No."

Oh, dear. That didn't bode well.

"Let's have some coffee and sit down," Tricia said, and poured two cups. They stood at the beverage station, not speaking, as they doctored their brews, and then Tricia led the way to the reader's nook.

"What did you want to talk about?" Pixie asked as she sat down across from Tricia.

"I think you know." When Pixie didn't comment, Tricia tried again. "Angelica told me you'd visited the day spa."

Pixie wouldn't look at Tricia and just stared at her coffee cup.

"Are you unhappy working here? Is there anything I can do to—?"

Pixie shook her head. "No. I've loved working here since the day I started."

"Then why did you put in an application to become a nail tech at the new day spa?" There was no way Tricia could call it by the name Angelica had proposed.

"I really think we should talk about this on a day when you haven't got so much on your mind," Pixie said. "I want you to have a real shot at winning that Bake-Off."

"How can I do my best when this is hanging over my head?" Tricia asked. She didn't even dare think about the other dark clouds hovering over her.

"Because my explanation is probably going to take longer than the ten or fifteen minutes we've got."

"If you need more money—"

"You pay me extremely well."

"Then . . . ?"

"Later, please," Pixie insisted, sounding close to tears.

Tricia looked into her friend and employee's dark brown eyes. "Okay. But we *will* speak about this later." She got up from her seat, walked to the washroom, and dumped her untouched coffee. Then she went upstairs to retrieve her purse and the bag of supplies she planned to use in the Bake-Off. By the time she got back to the front of the store, Pixie had moved to stand behind the sales counter, her posture straight, and had regained at least a portion of her joie de vivre.

She gave Tricia a big smile. "Now, you go get your sister and you two skedaddle to the high school and make the best damn cupcakes in the world."

"Better than Nikki's?"

"She may have won the professional portion of the contest, but she didn't win any hearts."

That was certainly true.

"Now, go. And I want a full report later today."

Tricia smiled. "Okay."

Tricia headed for the exit. Upon opening the door, she looked back, but Pixie was facing away from her.

There wasn't anything else to say. Tricia left the shop, closing the door behind her.

Angelica was waiting just inside the Cookery and practically burst through the door before Tricia could even reach for the handle. "Well, what did Pixie say?"

"I don't even get a hello?"

Angelica closed the door behind her and grabbed Tricia's elbow, steering her north up the sidewalk. "Hello. Now, what did Pixie say?"

"She didn't say anything except that what she had to say would take longer than the time we had before I needed to get to the school for the Bake-Off."

"Well, that's a disappointment."

"Tell me about it. She said she didn't want me to think about it until after the competition was over."

"Thoughtful of her—except now that's probably *all* you're going to be able to think about."

Not true. Tricia had a lot of other thoughts whirling around her brain, but it was time to focus.

"No, I'm going to try to put it out of my mind," Tricia said as they approached the corner and the crosswalk. "I can't be distracted if I want to beat you in this competition."

"At least I know you'll try your best," Angelica said.

Tricia gave her sister a sour look but decided not to continue that conversation.

Only one van from the Good Food Channel remained parked in front of the school, and the chaos from the day before had pretty much diminished now that the main thrust of the professional portion of the contest had concluded. There would be no live feed to the auditorium, and even the Nigela Ricita food truck, Eat Lunch, had disappeared from the site.

"In contrast to yesterday, it seems like we're a pitiful afterthought," Tricia muttered.

"That doesn't mean I don't intend to win," Angelica asserted, then sighed dramatically. "Despite my long odds."

Oh, yeah? Tricia thought, and brightened. Despite Angelica's theatrics, Judge Grant Baker was someone Tricia definitely wanted to speak with.

As they approached the school from the south, they saw Mr. Everett approach from the north. The sisters waited for him to catch up, and Tricia greeted him with a smile. "Mr. Everett, what are you doing here? Did you come to watch the contest?"

"Why, I'm going to compete in the Bake-Off. Pixie gave me the day off."

Tricia blinked in shock. "But why didn't you mention it to me before now?"

Mr. Everett looked sheepish. "I didn't want to steal your thunder."

"I didn't even know you baked," Angelica said.

"When I owned my grocery store, I needed to know every job just in case one of my employees couldn't make it in on any given day. Out of necessity, I learned a lot about baking, albeit in large quantities. That's why I chose one of my first wife's recipes." He smiled fondly. "Alice would have jumped at the opportunity to participate in the Bake-Off. So in her honor, I've entered her maple walnut recipe in the contest."

"Well, isn't that sweet," Angelica quipped. She sounded sincere, but Tricia had no doubt Angelica had calculated that her chances of winning had just gone up another notch.

Mr. Everett offered his elbow to Tricia. "Shall we go in?"

She gave him an affectionate smile. "Yes."

They climbed the stairs that led to the building and entered the school. The corridors were empty, and they made their way to the culinary rooms on the second floor.

"Are you excited, Mr. E?" Angelica asked, apparently unable to hide her own anticipation.

The older gent shook his head. "Grace was disappointed that there was no way she could come and watch, but I told her if they allowed it, I would bring one of my cupcakes home for her to try."

"That's sweet of you," Tricia said. "I hadn't thought about having leftovers."

"I saw on one of the Good Food Channel's baking shows where contestants were terribly confident and only made one or two cupcakes, only to have them fail," Angelica said.

"I'm baking as many as the muffin pan will hold," Tricia said. "Just in case."

They entered the culinary rooms, which Tricia and Angelica were already familiar with, but which now looked so much nicer after the Good Food Channel's spruce-up and even better than what they'd seen projected on the screen in the auditorium the previous day. It was also much hotter than it had been on the day they'd visited the week before. It had to have been stifling the day before, with all the extra lights for the cameras. No wonder they had stopped for a makeup touch-up before the winner was announced.

A bored-looking young woman with a clipboard handed out numbers to the contestants that corresponded to the kitchenettes, along with a full-front apron that said GREAT BOOKTOWN BAKE-OFF.

"Oh, look," Tricia said, indicating the bottom of her apron, where the logo for the Armchair Tourist had been printed. "Marshall told me he was a Bake-Off sponsor. It looks like these were his contribution."

"They're darling," Angelica said.

"And a nice souvenir of the day," Tricia agreed.

Tricia and Angelica were assigned to Room 1, while Mr. Everett was given a number for Room 2.

"Good luck," Tricia wished him.

"And to both of you, Ms. Miles," he said, nodding in the sisters' direction.

They split up and the sisters took their places before their counters, where Nikki and Joann had performed the day before, tying on their aprons.

The kitchenettes were equipped with new, state-of-the-art standing mixers in a variety of colors, ranging from lime green to neon pink, sure to thrill the heart of any young wannabe pastry chef. Tricia looked at the rest of the mixing bowls, spatulas, measuring cups, and everything else she needed to prepare her cupcakes. The contestants were also allowed to inspect the ingredients cupboard so as not to lose time once the competition began.

Tricia was on her way back from the cupboard as two more contestants arrived: Toby Kingston and Rebecca Shore, each carrying a plastic grocery bag. Every contestant was allowed to bring some of their own ingredients and utensils, but first, each had to be approved by the woman in charge.

Toby's gaze strayed in Tricia's direction, and she could swear his upper lip began to curl. "Tricia," he said by way of greeting.

"Toby," she said brightly. "It's so nice to see you."

He didn't echo the sentiment.

"Hi, Tricia," Rebecca said. "Going to win today?"

"I sure hope so."

Rebecca laughed. "I'm going to give you a run for your money."

"I wouldn't expect any less."

The woman with the clipboard cleared her throat and called for all the contestants to gather in the first room. Aside from Mr. Everett, the other contestants were strangers to Tricia.

"I'm Lara Morris and I'll be the liaison working with you throughout the contest. Before we get started, I need to check out all the ingredients and utensils you brought into our contest kitchen, and then we'll go through the rules in case any of you hasn't read through them. Okay? Right. You, number five"—she pointed to Angelica—"you're first."

Angelica snatched up her enormous purse, walked over to Lara, and pulled a large plastic bag from it. Tricia's mouth dropped open in horror as Angelica extracted the exact mold Tricia had borrowed from Donna North. Also in the bag was a plastic container filled with what looked like white candy melts as well as a big bag of nuts.

Oh, no! I'm doomed, Tricia thought upon seeing the mold. Would Angelica be making lemon cupcakes as well?

Toby was up next. He had a large brown shopping bag, and again Tricia cringed as he, too, pulled out the same book mold and white chocolate candy melts. And so she wasn't surprised when Rebecca did likewise.

Tricia was almost embarrassed when she was called up front and brought out her candy mold, too. She could tell Lara wasn't impressed.

"Looks like great minds do think alike," Rebecca said, and laughed hollowly.

Toby merely scowled.

Tricia returned to her station and Angelica hissed, "Why didn't you tell me you were making chocolate books?"

"You didn't tell me, either," Tricia whispered right back.

When it was his turn to appear before the judges, Mr. Everett pulled a small bottle from his pocket, which turned out to be walnut extract.

The others had brought colored jimmies, sprinkles, and edible glitter, but nothing out of the ordinary. Tricia scrutinized her competition. Because the bakers from the second room hadn't brought anything spectacular to embellish their cupcakes, she determined that her real competition was Angelica, Toby, and Rebecca. She had tasted Angelica's baked goods so many times during the past year that she deduced Angelica was still the one to beat. Yet, what if Toby and

Rebecca had entered other competitions in the past and had won? They were both unknown entities.

Out of the corner of her eye, Tricia caught sight of Chief Baker standing in the wings, alongside the Booktown Ladies Charitable Society's leader, Adelaide Newberry. She gave Baker a wave and he forced a smile. Was there a chance they'd take a break before the competition started so she could talk to him?

Lara went over the rules before motioning to the two judges to join her.

"Contestants, I'd like you to meet two of your judges, although they may already be known to you. Stoneham Chief of Police Baker, and Mrs. Adelaide Newberry."

"Hello, everyone!" Adelaide called happily, and gave a cheerful wave.

"Mrs. Newberry would like to say a few words," Lara announced, not looking all that thrilled about it.

Adelaide stepped forward. "Welcome, welcome, and thank you for participating in this wonderful charitable event. The professional portion of the Bake-Off raised over ten thousand dollars from Stoneham's citizens and local businesses. Charities benefiting from this generosity include meals for seniors and children, medical research, and animal welfare. The ladies from the society want to thank you for participating and encouraging your friends, families, and co-workers to sponsor you in the event, too. Now. Let's bake some cupcakes!"

Everyone applauded politely, but Lara looked chagrined. "Uh, unfortunately, there'll be a slight delay in the contest. It seems our *talent*—Chef Larry Andrews—has been held up. Therefore, we won't be starting the competition until he gets here. You're free to use the restrooms, down the hall and to the right, or to get some coffee.

We've got a station set up out in the hall. If you want to chill here, just sit at the tables between the kitchens. There's Wi-Fi, so feel free to check your phones. I'll call you when we're ready to begin. Thanks."

The group broke up, with Mr. Everett and his fellow contestants heading back to their room, while Toby and Rebecca settled at one of the tables and took out their phones.

"Do you want some coffee?" Tricia asked Angelica.

She shook her head. "If I've got a few minutes, I can text Antonio and Randy and get some work done."

"Okay."

By now, Tricia felt the need for a caffeine boost, and she left the room in search of coffee. She saw Chief Baker standing near the coffee station. He must have snuck out of the culinary room during Adelaide's speech. Perfect!

While Baker had seemed to be enjoying his judging duties the day before, for the professional portion of the competition, he looked downright irritable to be wasting his time for the second part of the contest.

"Hi, Grant. We haven't had a chance to speak since last week."

"I've been busy," he practically growled, and turned back to his phone.

"As have I."

"And now that overrated chef is going to be late. Why didn't they just have you guys start baking and then call us in?"

Tricia shrugged. "Protocol?"

Baker's scowl intensified.

"Um, Grant, there's a delicate matter I need to discuss with you."

Baker raised an eyebrow.

"It concerns Joyce Widman . . . and Officer Pearson."

Baker's gaze intensified and he grabbed Tricia's elbow and steered her away from potential eavesdroppers farther down the empty corridor.

"Okay, spill it."

"Well, it's just that . . . they seem to have a relationship."

"And you know this because?"

"I saw them in a restaurant in Merrimack. They were gazing into each other's eyes and holding hands. It seemed a little strange under the circumstances."

Baker did not seem pleased. "Anything else?"

"Not about Joyce."

"If you must know, Officer Pearson came to me the day after Vera Olson's death. Except instead of intimating a lesbian relationship with a possible suspect, she admitted that Joyce Widman was her stepmother."

"Stepmother?" Tricia echoed. No wonder Joyce had been so angry with Tricia. But then why didn't she just admit what her real connection to the officer was? And why had she been keeping it a secret?

Baker's gaze was penetrating.

Tricia offered a weak smile. "Boy, I really stepped in it, didn't I?"

"I'll say. Do you have any other brilliant tidbits to offer me?"

"Well, just one. I spoke to a number of the volunteers at Pets-A-Plenty, and one of them—who has been asked to leave—mentioned that Vera was very interested in Monterey Bioresources and that something fishy was going on between them and the animal shelter."

Baker's eyes narrowed. Aha! He hadn't heard about *that*. "Go on."

"I myself noticed that one woman seemed to be adopting an awful lot of animals. I saw her leave the shelter with a couple of beagles. The Pets-A-Plenty volunteer said that often all the ferrets and guinea pigs would disappear all at once. Monterey Bioresources sells all those kinds of animals to their clients, claiming that they were bred to be disease-free for experimentation by the medical and pharmaceutical industries. It seems Vera had a thing for beagles, and Pets-A-Plenty has a deal with a Massachusetts beagle rescue to find homes for their dogs. Potential owners are vetted through Pets-A-Plenty and the dogs placed in their forever homes. But from what the woman I spoke to said, there was no vetting. The dogs came in and went so fast it was like they'd passed through a revolving door."

"And just who is this person who told you about the situation?"

Tricia frowned and looked around. "Cori Haskell," she whispered. "She was frightened the last time we spoke. She thought Vera might have uncovered evidence about the shady dealings and was killed for it."

"Have you got a suspect?"

"Toby Kingston."

Baker looked skeptical. "How long has it been since you heard this information?"

"Thursday," she answered sheepishly.

"Why didn't you immediately come to me?" he berated her.

"I wanted to tell you yesterday, but I didn't run into you. What will you do with the information?"

"Our department will look into it. But I don't want you talking about this to anyone. Understand?"

Tricia nodded. He must have thought the news was worthy of consideration or he wouldn't have issued such a warning.

"I'm going to talk to Lara to see if I can get a reprieve and leave until the actual judging starts. Stay out of trouble," Baker said, and headed for the culinary rooms. As he went in, Rebecca came out.

Tricia busied herself by pouring herself a cup of coffee. "Can I get you a cup?"

"Are you kidding? It's way too hot for that. I was heading to the ladies' room. Where did Lara say it was?"

Tricia pointed down the corridor and Rebecca went on her way. As Tricia approached the culinary room, she found Toby nearly blocking the doorway, his expression one of irritation.

"Good luck," Tricia said.

"Good luck to you, too. You're going to need it," he said, and turned away.

It almost sounded like a threat.

THIRTY

The coffee had been a big mistake, Tricia decided by the time she'd drained her paper cup and discarded it. By then, Lara and the chief had finished their conversation, and then Lara spoke with someone else on the phone for several minutes. She stabbed her phone's end-call icon and called the contestants together once again.

"I'm sorry for the delay, but it seems Chef Andrews is going to be later than he anticipated."

Several of the contestants groaned.

"So, we're going to start the competition without him, which will also give Chief Baker an opportunity to check in with his officers."

"Thanks," Baker said. "Give me a call when you want me back. I can be here in five minutes." And off he went.

"Speaking of phones, would everyone please silence your phones so that they aren't a distraction during the competition."

Tricia turned off her ringtone and placed her phone in her purse, and then placed her purse in one of the cabinets in her kitchenette.

"If everyone's ready, let's get started." Lara pulled a little bell from a pocket of her jeans and a stopwatch from the other. "When you hear the bell ring, you will have ninety minutes to prepare your cupcakes. Ready, set—"

Ding!

All eight contestants dashed for the ingredients cupboard and fridges to secure flour, butter, eggs, and flavorings, as well as grabbing nuts and other embellishments to top their cupcakes. Once back at their cooking stations, they immediately turned to their ovens to preheat them before starting to work on their batter. Again Tricia lamented the fact that the school wasn't air-conditioned, and in no time the room became unbearably warm. Tricia wondered if upon finishing her decorating her chocolate books might melt. Well, if hers melted, the same would befall the other three contestants who'd had the same idea as her.

She measured her ingredients, prepared her lemon zest and squeezed the juice, and was ready to go. And though Tricia had little time to observe Toby or Rebecca, she did catch glances of Angelica whipping around her kitchenette and preparing her cupcakes with what seemed like incredible speed and efficiency. She had her cupcakes in the oven long before Tricia and was working on her chocolates before Tricia had poured the batter into the paper liners in her muffin pan. Once they were in the oven, Tricia decided she might want to embellish her cupcakes with some colored sprinkles and went to the cabinet, but there were none left.

"Is it all right if I borrow some sprinkles from the other contestants?" she asked Lara.

"Sure."

Tricia checked the workspaces of the contestants and was given a small amount of both green and yellow crystalized sugar. She peeked around the corner and saw Mr. Everett working slowly and methodically. She gave him a wave and a nod and smiled. The others just ignored her.

Returning to her kitchenette, Tricia got straight to work on her chocolates, noting that Toby and Rebecca were now ahead of her, too. Still, she wasn't going to let that rattle her. A glance at the clock on the wall told her she still had plenty of time.

Once she'd melted the chocolate in the microwave and filled the mold, she popped it into the freezer to set and let out a weary breath. The stress from concentrating on her work made her feel jittery, and she wished she'd gone for decaf instead of the caffeine-laced stuff. But now she found she needed to visit the ladies'—or more probably marked in a school—the girls' room.

"Five minutes," Lara called out from her position between the two culinary rooms.

Tricia took her chocolate from the freezer and saw ice crystals on top. Had she left them in too long? She set a dish towel on the counter and turned the mold over it, giving it a smart thump. Nothing happened. She gave it another whack and the chocolates went flying—with five of them hitting the floor and shattering. That left her with only four, but thankfully they were perfect. She looked around and saw that Angelica's white candy melts had been tinted a deep green. Green books? Tricia didn't have time to think about it.

She patted dry her already sweating chocolates. She'd already picked out four of her prettiest cupcakes and had frosted them, piping the icing into a mountain of citrus joy. Now all she needed was a few careful shakes of the yellow crystalized sugar and to set the chocolate books at a jaunty angle in the mounds of lightly tinted frosting. She did the same to the three others and carefully set them on a plate. Voilà! Three flawless cupcakes to entice the judges, and one extra.

"Time's up!" Lara called, and, like they'd all seen on the Good Food Channel's cooking competitions, the four pseudo chefs in the room threw their arms into the air—hands off!

Just then, Larry Andrews showed up. "And I've arrived right on time!" he proclaimed smugly.

Lara, who must have worked with the chef countless times before, merely shot him a glowering look before turning back to her charges. "If everyone could bring their cupcakes up to the table in front, we'll take some photographs of the group and the food, get the chief back here to judge, and then we can all go home."

Well, she certainly knew how to take the fun out of things.

Tricia was the first to set her cupcakes on the table. Lara placed a small paper with each contestant's number before the offerings. The frosting on Angelica's cupcakes was green, but much lighter than the little tinted "chocolate" books that sat on them. "What kind did you make?" Tricia asked.

"Pistachio—totally flourless. It's a surefire winner!"

"You hope," Tricia muttered.

The others had all embellished their cupcakes with intricate frosting and/or fondant roses and other flowers. And then there was Mr. Everett's entry. His cupcakes were covered in a slightly off-white frosting with only a solitary walnut on top as decoration. Poor Mr. Everett. He didn't stand a chance against the other beauties on the table, but he looked pleased. He had honored his late wife and her recipe. He saw Tricia's gaze upon him and gave her a shy smile. She smiled back.

Adelaide, who'd been flitting back and forth between the rooms throughout the contest, watching and offering encouragement, clapped her hands in delight. "You've all done marvelous work. I'm sorry you all can't win, but I want you to know that you are all winners because you've asked your sponsors to back you. Every dollar you earn for your chosen charity will help those among us who have little hope. You'll help others—and there can be no greater gift from the heart. Thank you."

During Adelaide's impromptu speech, Lara had been on the phone. She stabbed the end-call icon and called for everyone's attention. "Chief Baker will be here in about ten minutes. Let's get these pictures taken, and then everyone is free to take a bathroom or smoke break—whatever—before the judging starts."

Everyone assembled behind the table and in front of their cupcakes while Lara took some pictures on her phone and a member of the crew pulled out a larger-format digital camera and took a few more. Once the pesky humans were out of the picture, he took more of the cupcakes themselves.

"I need to go to the ladies' room. Do you need to go?" Tricia asked her sister.

Angelica shook her head. "You go ahead. I want to see if I can talk to Lara—to pick her brain."

"Okay."

Tricia left the room and started down the hall. She pushed through the door to the john and found Rebecca had gotten there before her and was washing her hands in front of one of the white porcelain sinks.

"Some contest," Tricia quipped, and headed for one of the stalls.

"Too bad it's over."

"We've still got the judging," Tricia said.

Rebecca shook her head, reached for the paper towel dispenser, and pulled one out, wiping her hands. "I'm afraid you won't be able to attend."

"What do you mean?"

Rebecca reached into the pocket of her apron and brought out a tarnished, silver-handled paring knife. It looked old and had apparently been sharpened many times, for the blade had been whittled down and the point was ultrasharp—reminding Tricia of a stiletto. The hairs on the back of her neck bristled.

"What's going on?"

"I heard your little conversation with Chief Baker earlier this morning," Rebecca said.

It took a moment for Tricia to recall the gist of their discussion. Rebecca could have no interest in Joyce and her relationship with Cindy Pearson, so . . .

"How are you involved with Monterey Bioresources?" Tricia bluffed.

"You're a woman with all the answers . . . or so you think."

Tricia thought about what she'd seen at Pets-A-Plenty. "The shelter clears out at noon. When I was there, it was just you and the receptionist. Am I right in assuming you set up the volunteer schedule?"

Rebecca merely shrugged.

"And the woman who takes the animals away—Cheryl—does she drive them directly to Concord and Monterey Bioresources?"

Rebecca said nothing.

"Vera Olson figured out what you guys were up to—selling dogs, ferrets, and guinea pigs for research from the strays and surrendered animals at Pets-A-Plenty. The shelter is affiliated with a beagle rescue in Massachusetts. They give Pets-A-Plenty the dogs not knowing they all go to Concord, too."

Still, Rebecca said nothing.

Tricia looked down at the knife. "The animals Monterey sells are supposed to be disease-free and specially bred for experimentation."

"And who can tell when they aren't?" Rebecca asked.

"But why would you do that?"

"For the money, what else? Besides, everybody makes such a fuss about animal experimentation. They're dogs and rodents—period. The Bible says man shall have dominion over the animals. We're just exercising that right."

"You and who else—besides Cheryl and the receptionist Doreen?"

Again Rebecca shrugged.

"What happens next?" Tricia asked.

"You had to stick your nose into business that doesn't concern you, and now you're going to end up like poor Vera. Come on, we're going to take a little walk."

"And go where?"

Rebecca nodded toward the washroom's door and jerked her free thumb in its direction. "Out!"

Tricia turned and Rebecca was suddenly at her side, with the tip of the knife poking through her thin sweater and touching her skin. Rebecca rested a hand on Tricia's left shoulder and gave her a small shove. "Go," she said, practically in Tricia's ear.

Tricia pushed through the washroom's door. There were people just down the corridor. People meant safety. All she needed to do was give a shout and—

"Say a word and you're dead," Rebecca growled.

Wait, Tricia told herself. *Wait for an opening.*

As difficult as that might be, she did just that as Rebecca guided her toward the stairs.

Chief Baker was on his way. If they ran into him, Tricia would be safe—or at least he could subdue Rebecca. What organs were near where the knife rested against Tricia's side? The liver. The blade was only about four inches long—but if Rebecca twisted it, it could still do lethal damage.

As they reached the bottom of the stairs, Tricia started to turn left, but the hand on her shoulder pushed her the other way.

"Where are we going?"

"Not outside, that's for sure."

"Then where?"

"You're going to take a little swim."

For a moment Tricia didn't understand. And then she remembered the school's big, empty twenty-five-meter pool—which had no water.

THIRTY-ONE

Tricia's and Rebecca's footsteps echoed as they continued down the empty and eerily quiet corridor, heading toward the gymnasium and pool.

Keep her talking, Tricia thought.

"How did Vera find out about your little operation?" she asked.

"It was those damn dogs. She had a thing for beagles. She took special note of when they came and went. She brought them treats and toys. It was hysterical to see how much she loved them, spoke baby talk to them, and how much she wanted to pet them but couldn't because of her allergies."

"I suppose you taunted her about that?"

Rebecca laughed. "Why not?"

"How did she end up in Joyce Widman's yard with a pitchfork through her middle?"

"Now, that's an interesting story," Rebecca said, and laughed again. "Vera called me at Pets-A-Plenty last Monday and said she had taken pictures of Cheryl's license plate and of her loading her car with the ferrets and guinea pigs. She said she was going to take those pictures to the police."

"But she never got the chance."

"I drove right over to her house. There was no answer when I rang the bell, so I walked around to the back and found her coming through the gate that connected to her neighbor's yard. She had a handful of catnip. She dried it and made toys for the shelter cats. Stupid."

No, caring.

"Did you argue before you strangled her?"

Rebecca grinned. "Maybe just a little. But she was a lot smaller than me. It didn't take long."

"But why did you drag her into her neighbor's yard? What was the point of running the pitchfork through her if she was already dead?"

"As a warning."

As Tricia had suspected. "But she'd already mentioned the scheme to Cori Haskell."

Rebecca's voice was deadly calm. "She's next on my list."

If she hadn't already left the area.

They came to the door that led to the locker rooms and pool.

"Open it," Rebecca ordered.

As before, the door was unlocked. Rebecca gave the knife just the smallest of jabs, which prodded Tricia to move forward.

Unlike the previous week, the concrete deck around the big pool was littered with supplies to repair cracks on the sides and bottom, along with gallons and gallons of a special rubberized paint labeled for pools. With everything in place, why weren't any workers on-site?

"Unlucky for you," Rebecca said with a sneer, "the school suspended work on the pool until after the Bake-Off."

Well, that answered Tricia's unspoken question. Now what did

Rebecca intend to do, make her walk the plank—or rather, the diving board?

Rebecca kept pushing Tricia closer and closer to the deepest end of the empty pool.

"What's your plan for me?" Tricia asked.

"Just a little accident."

"Little?"

"Well, fatal," Rebecca admitted, sounding positively gleeful. Tricia could just imagine the smug smile on the woman's face. They advanced until Tricia's feet were just inches from the edge of the pool. The ceramic tile in front of her toes had a small lip, something for swimmers to grab on to to help pull themselves out of the water.

Rebecca's hand closed tighter on Tricia's shoulder. "Turn around."

With clumsy feet, Tricia managed to turn to face her assailant. She had an inkling of what came next. "And?" she prompted.

"I'm sorry to see you go, dear Tricia, but sadly, it's your time." Rebecca reached out her arm but wasn't prepared when Tricia grabbed it, twisting it until the knife in Rebecca's other hand went flying and the momentum made them whirl so that it was Rebecca whose back now faced the pool. But the tussling continued.

"Stop!" Tricia commanded. "Or we'll both end up at the bottom of the pool."

"Better to take you with me," Rebecca taunted, then twisted and sent the two of them careening into the void. Tricia thrust her full weight to one side just before they hit the hard concrete, the jolt causing an explosion of pain in her right arm that sent a scream from her throat that seemed to echo over and over again in the cavernous space above them.

Waves and waves of excruciating pain traveled through her and Tricia fought the urge to vomit. She rested her head on the cool cement and waited for what seemed like eons for her breathing to slow so that she was no longer gasping, and gradually awareness began to seep back into her brain.

Rebecca lay beneath her—or at least half of her did. It was Rebecca's body that had softened her landing, but a look at her right arm told Tricia all she needed to know when she saw the jagged edge of bone protruding through the skin of her forearm—the same arm she'd injured the previous autumn. It was then that what was left of the coffee in her stomach came up and she found herself retching until she was left with the dry heaves.

The stench of sour coffee made Tricia shudder, but it also helped bring her back to her senses. With a horrible jolt of pain, she managed to sit upright, her sight wavering until she thought she might pass out. It took another minute or so for her muddled brain to understand what had happened. She looked down at Rebecca, who was staring openmouthed at the ceiling, her body spread across the white concrete at odd angles. But it seemed she wasn't dead, because of the spreading pool of blood around her head.

"Rebecca?" Tricia called, but there was no answer. Still, Tricia knew that corpses didn't bleed. She swung her gaze to take in the edge of the pool above them. The metal ladder had to be at least eight or nine feet above them. Her gaze traveled the length of the pool to see steps and a rail that led from the shallow end to the pool decking. She was going to have to walk the length of the pool—almost twenty-five meters—to get there. And then what? She'd left her phone in her purse in the second-floor culinary room. The Good Food Channel truck had been parked outside the school, but she assumed the limited crew had all been inside with the contestants. The results of the contest might already have been announced, but at that moment Tricia didn't give a damn who won.

Rolling onto her knees, her right arm hanging uselessly at her side, Tricia somehow managed to crawl over to the wall some five or six feet distant, and then braced herself until she could stagger to her feet. Leaning her left shoulder against the tapered cement wall, she pushed herself forward on wobbly legs.

It took seventy carefully counted footsteps until she reached the base of the stairs in the shallow end of the pool. Unfortunately, the rail was to her right, so she turned, grasped the cold metal in her good hand, and mounted the steps backward. Once she reached the top, she leaned down to rest her sweating brow against the cool steel—but for only a few seconds. She needed help. More important, Rebecca needed assistance if she was to live to stand trial for the murder she had committed, and the one she had tried to commit.

The pain was an agony like nothing Tricia had endured before, but if she was going to get help, she had to move. Pushing herself away from the rail, she staggered across the concrete decking until she got to the door to the anteroom between the locker rooms and the corridor. Once through the door to the hall, she had another decision to make. Cross half the length of the school to go to the office, or climb the stairs to the cookery rooms and ask for help.

Although harder to navigate, the stairs were closer, so that's the direction she took.

One foot in front of the other.

Keep staring ahead.

Keep your goal in mind.

Get to Angelica. She will somehow make things right.

Tricia slogged ahead and rounded the landing halfway to the second floor before she realized how close she was to her goal. "Angelica," she croaked, but her voice sounded no louder than a harsh whisper. Where was she? Why hadn't she come looking for Tricia? It must have been ten or fifteen minutes since Tricia had left the culinary room for the john—which reminded her, she still needed to go.

But she needed other help first and had to use all the strength she could muster to haul herself up those last ten steps.

Once in the corridor, Tricia could hear the sound of voices ahead. No one stood out in the hall or by the coffee stand. Leaning against the wall, step by step she slogged along the passage until the culinary room's doorway loomed just steps away.

"On behalf of the Good Food Channel," Larry Andrews was saying, "it's my pleasure to award the trophy to the winner of the Great Booktown Bake-Off!"

Suddenly Tricia forgot about her broken arm—forgot about the woman in the empty pool possibly bleeding to death. The memory of her beautiful lemon cupcake with the crystallized sugar and the little chocolate book flooded her mind.

"And the winner is—"

Tricia leaned against the doorjamb, gasping for breath—and not just because of the painful, useless arm hanging at her side, but in anticipation of the answer—

"William Everett!"

Mr. Everett? Mr. Everett's unattractive cupcake? The little cupcake that had less than a quarter of the frosting of the other entrants? The cupcake with only a walnut as decoration?

"Oh, my goodness!" someone called.

It was Angelica, of course.

And that's when Tricia fainted.

THIRTY-TWO

Tricia's usual happy hour was almost sixty minutes away by the time she arrived at the back entrance of the Cookery the next day. She'd undergone surgery the evening before and now sported a metal rod and a couple of screws to secure her broken ulna, along with a pretty lavender cast. She'd taken a little white pain pill earlier in the day but had decided to forgo the next dose, preferring gin as her chosen anesthetic.

She'd also decided to stay the night with Angelica rather than go home to Haven't Got a Clue, but only because she didn't want Mr. Everett and Pixie to make a fuss over her. And she still had that difficult conversation with Pixie looming ahead and didn't feel up to facing it on that day. It could wait until tomorrow.

Angelica was like a mother hen helping Tricia safely up the stairs to her apartment. When she'd renovated her home, Angelica had forgone a huge master suite and instead had installed a second bedroom on her third floor. Now that she was a grandmother, she was looking forward to having sleepovers with Sofia and had decorated that other room to accommodate a fairy princess—what Sofia aspired to be. Tricia was sure she wouldn't even notice all that purple and pink once she closed her eyes and went to sleep.

Sarge—ever happy to see Tricia—was disappointed not to be immediately given a couple of dog biscuits, but Angelica fetched some and let Tricia toss them to him, which instantly quieted the always happy dog.

After settling Tricia on the end of the sectional in the living room, Angelica entered the kitchen to make them both a drink.

Tricia heaved a sigh and adjusted her arm in the sling, wishing the discomfort would settle down. Maybe she'd regret her decision to forgo the pain pill. She caught sight of a large vase of more than a dozen cheerful pink roses and baby's breath on the coffee table that she hadn't noticed when she'd entered the room.

"Who sent you flowers?" she called.

"They're not for me. They're for you. Pixie sent them over."

"They're from Pixie?"

"I don't think so."

Angelica came back into the living room, retrieved the card from the clear plastic pick that held it in place, and handed it to Tricia, who fumbled to open it.

"Oh, they're from Marshall."

"What does the card say?"

"Didn't want to bother you until you felt well enough for visitors. Lunch, dinner, or anything you want, anytime you want. Call me." She smiled. "Aw, he's so sweet."

Angelica raised an eyebrow, sizing up the large bouquet, and then turned to go back into the kitchen. A minute or two later, she returned to the living room and set down a tray. In addition to the pitcher and glasses, she had prepared a large plate of pepper poppers.

"You know how to treat a girl when she's been knocked down by life," Tricia said.

"Knocked down by a killer, you mean."

Still, Angelica had barely stirred the pitcher of martinis before her ringtone sounded. She grabbed it. "Yes, June? What?" Her features collapsed into a scowl. "Okay, send him up." She tapped the end-call icon. "Chief Baker is on his way."

Tricia grimaced. "I don't want to talk to him again."

"You may as well get it over with," Angelica advised and poured their drinks.

"Well, don't offer him any of my pepper poppers."

Angelica grinned. "No fear."

Sarge heard the footsteps on the stairs, leapt out of his bed, and started barking, the noise threatening to cause Tricia's frayed nerves to completely unravel.

"Sarge! Hush!" Angelica ordered, and the dog instantly quieted, but he waited behind the door to the apartment, and even from where she sat on the sectional, Tricia could hear his menacing growl. Sarge and Baker would never be friends.

Angelica picked up her dog and greeted Stoneham's top cop with subdued annoyance. She and Baker would never be friends, either. "Come this way, but do try not to upset poor Tricia. She's had a very bad twenty-four hours and needs peace and quiet."

"Then muzzle that dog," Baker barked, and stepped inside, without waiting for Angelica to show him the way. Instead, she set Sarge back in his basket with a command to stay and joined the two in the living room.

"Hello, Tricia."

"Hi, Grant."

"Are you up to making a statement?"

She stared at the man. He could have at least inquired about her injury. "I had surgery less than twenty-four hours ago, my arm hurts like crazy, and I'm feeling very crabby right now."

"Oh. Well, I guess I can understand that."

"What can I do for you besides sign a statement, and as you can see by my arm in this sling, I really can't do that right now, either."

"It's okay about the statement. You can do that tomorrow or even next Monday."

"Thank you."

"I thought you might want to know about Rebecca Shore."

"Someone at the hospital told me she was in pretty bad shape."

"She fractured her skull in the fall, as well as half the rest of the bones in her body. There's a possibility she could be paralyzed for life."

"Life in prison I hope," Angelica muttered, and handed Tricia a glass.

"Very likely," Baker admitted. "But she was able to talk this morning, and cursed your name."

That was a given.

Tricia raised her glass and addressed Angelica. "Cheers."

Baker frowned and cleared his throat. "We were able to locate Cori Haskell. She'd gone to stay with her sister in Albany. She was happy to hear that Rebecca couldn't threaten her anymore, but she doesn't want to return to New Hampshire until we can assure her that those working with Rebecca aren't liable to come after her."

"And how are you making out in that regard?"

"We've made three arrests: two at Pets-A-Plenty, and a worker at Monterey Bioresources. They promptly fired the man when they found out he'd been taking in animals from the shelter and possibly contaminating their stock."

Stock? He made the poor animals sound like items in a stationery store.

"One of the women, Doreen Mitchell, waived her rights and told us the whole scheme. It pretty much matches what you told me yesterday morning."

Tricia had to bite her tongue not to say *"I told you so!"*

"Anything else?" Angelica asked, sounding bored.

"We got a search warrant and went through Rebecca Shore's home. We found Vera Olson's cell phone."

"Did you find the pictures she took of Cheryl stealing the dogs and loading them in her car?"

He nodded. "The picture of the license plate helped us corroborate her part of the operation." Baker's focus shifted to the pepper poppers. "Can I have one of those?"

"No," Angelica said firmly.

Baker glowered at her.

"I spoke to Joyce Widman," he said.

"And?" Tricia asked cautiously.

"She's relieved to no longer be a person of interest in Vera Olson's death, but she has no great love for you, either."

"I didn't think she would. And Officer Pearson?"

"She faces disciplinary action for not immediately reporting her relationship with Ms. Widman at the start of the investigation. As she's on probation, it could mean the end of her short career with the department."

"I'm sorry to hear that."

"No more than me. But . . . we'll see."

"Anything else, Chief?" Angelica asked. "As you can see, Tricia and I are in the middle of happy hour, and your presence isn't making my dog happy. And when Sarge isn't happy, I'm not happy, either."

And for effect, Sarge growled loud enough for them all to hear.

"I guess that's it for now."

"What? No lecture? After something like this happens, you've usually taken the time to reprimand me," Tricia said.

"From what I understand, you never confronted Rebecca. She came after you."

Tricia nodded. She hadn't confronted Rebecca, but only because she hadn't put all the pieces of the puzzle together before the woman *had* come after her. But Tricia was pretty sure she would have eventually figured it out.

"I'd better get going," Baker said. "I hope you feel better soon, Tricia. Call me when you're ready to make that statement."

"I will. And thank you, Grant."

He nodded and turned.

"Close the door on the way out," Angelica called cheerily.

He did.

Tricia settled back farther into the depths of the sectional and sipped her martini. "With all that's happened, I'm not clear on the sequence of events of yesterday afternoon. Can you fill me in?"

"Of course, although now I'm even more annoyed with that pompous idiot, Chef Andrews."

"Why?"

"Because even though we couldn't find you and Rebecca, he insisted on naming the winner of the Bake-Off. He said he had an appointment back at his hotel he had to keep. Yeah, I'll bet he did. And I can probably guess with whom."

Tricia didn't want to pursue that conversation.

"Just how did Mr. Everett win?"

Angelica shrugged. "He had the best cupcake. It wasn't showmanship; it was just darn good baking."

"You were pretty sure *you* were going to win."

Angelica sighed. "As you know, Chief Baker and Larry Andrews were predisposed against me, but ultimately it was my ambition that did me in. It was pure genius of Mr. E to go the simple route, and in a way, I shared in his victory."

"What do you mean?"

"It was my recipe for maple frosting that topped his winning cupcake," she said, then raised her glass to toast herself and took a sip.

"What?"

"Mr. E took the frosting recipe from my first cookbook." She shrugged, her smile smug. "What can I say? We make a great team!"

Again, Tricia wasn't up to disputing the claim.

"So who came in second?"

Angelica positively grinned. "Why, you, little sister."

So startled was she by the news that Tricia nearly spilled her drink.

"I guess the judges preferred lemon over pistachio."

Tricia frowned. Had Angelica realized she'd just negated her own argument of the judges being biased?

It wasn't worth fighting about.

Tricia let out a breath. "Well, I'm glad to have impressed them with my baking, but I wish Pets-A-Plenty could have received the bigger share of the money."

"Oh, but they will. The Everett Foundation is matching not only what the bakers brought in, but Mr. Everett's chosen charity was also Pets-A-Plenty."

"I'm glad of that. And that the rot in the organization will be eradicated." And then Tricia thought about its director. "What did Toby Kingston have to say about Rebecca and her terrible mission to send pets to Monterey Bioresources?"

"He called me to inquire about you. He was pretty embarrassed. He rather sheepishly told me that you'd be a welcome addition to the Pets-A-Plenty Board of Directors—especially now that there are two openings. What do you think about that?"

Tricia frowned. "I'm not sure I want the position if it means working with Toby."

"You don't think the rescue is going to rethink his employment when they find out he worked with the meat-packing industry?"

"Somebody had to know about it—and pushed it under a rug." Tricia shook her head. "I'll have to seriously think about it."

Angelica shrugged. "You do that. In the meantime, have a pepper popper," Angelica said, and reached for one.

"I can't reach them and I can't really hold one, either."

"Then I will hold your drink while you have one. It's the least I can do."

"You've already done a lot."

"Not at all. You would do it for me. In fact, you did when I broke my ankle."

Yes, she had. It seemed like such a long time ago.

"Well, it's been a tough day or so, but now everything has worked out and you can forget all about this nastiness."

Tricia took another sip before exchanging her glass for a pepper popper. She took a bite and considered her badly broken arm, and worse—facing Pixie the next morning.

Feeling heartsick, she dreaded the day to come.

THIRTY-THREE

Since Angelica had a lot on her plate on that bright Friday morning, she carried Tricia's little duffel bag next door and got her settled in at Haven't Got a Clue's reader's nook, making a fresh pot of coffee and feeding a very needy Miss Marple, who'd been deprived of Tricia's company for two solid days.

"Are you sure you don't want me to be here when Pixie arrives?"

Tricia shook her head.

"Promise you'll call me right after your conversation?"

"I promise," Tricia said wearily.

Angelica reached down and squeezed Tricia's hand. "Whatever happens, you know I'm here for you."

"Yes, I do."

"Okay. I'll talk to you later."

Tricia watched her sister leave, her stomach feeling rocky. She'd almost prefer to have her other arm operated on than lose Pixie to work at Angelica's day spa. There had to be a compromise. There just had to be.

Though it was almost an hour before Haven't Got a Clue was to open, the door swung open and Pixie walked into the store. "Tricia!" she called happily. "I was so worried about you." She rushed over to the reader's nook and looked like she wanted to give her boss a hug, but held back. "Are you okay? Mr. E told me all about the Bake-Off and what a terrible mess your arm was. I was so worried about you. I wanted to come to see you yesterday, but Angelica said it would be better to wait until today."

"She's always looking out for me," Tricia said.

"Yeah, she does."

Pixie's careworn face seemed older than Tricia had ever seen it. She let out a breath. "It's time for us to talk."

"Yeah," Pixie agreed sadly, and sat down opposite Tricia. She didn't seem in a hurry to speak up.

"Now, please tell me why you wanted to interview for the nail-tech job."

Pixie's head drooped and her eyes brimmed with tears. "Because . . . it's time for me to leave Haven't Got a Clue."

"Why?" Tricia implored.

"Because you're not happy. This is *your* store and you love it. It's been breaking your heart for months making yourself stay away, hiding in the basement or up in your apartment when you'd much rather be standing behind the register taking care of customers."

"I didn't want you to think I was hovering."

"Hover? You've practically been invisible," Pixie declared.

"I don't want you to go."

"And I'm not sure I can stay. I've had a taste of management and I like it."

"Are you hoping to work your way up to managing the day spa?"

Pixie shook her head. "Nothing like that. But it's not unheard of that people working for Angelica end up with their dream jobs. Just look at Ginny."

"Some think she got her job because of nepotism. And Ginny doesn't work for Angelica. She works for Nigela Ricita Associates."

Pixie shook her head. "Tricia, just about everybody knows Angelica *is* Nigela Ricita."

"Well, if they do, they haven't said so."

"And spoil a good thing? Most people around here know what side their bread is buttered on. And Angelica somehow manages to bring out the best in everyone who works for her."

Yes, she did.

"I sure wouldn't mind that kind of opportunity to learn, to grow."

"But a nail tech?" Tricia asked.

"I'm good at it," Pixie said, and brandished her bloodred nails and perfectly kept cuticles.

"But you love vintage mysteries," Tricia insisted.

"Who says I have to stop loving them? I might be your very best customer."

Tricia shook her head. "No. I don't want to see you take a step backward."

"But what if it's something *I* want to do?"

"How about if we compromise? You can still be my assistant manager. You can have an extra day off a week—or go part-time. Then you could do two things you love. How does that sound?"

"I don't know. I've kind of already made up my mind."

"Have you spoken to Angelica about it?" Tricia asked, already knowing the answer.

"She said you'd kill her if she poached me from you."

"She's right," Tricia said, nodding, but then she let out an exasperated breath and shook her head. "Angelica knows I'd never stand in your way."

"She suggested the same compromise as you."

"And what do you think about it?"

The sound of the door rattling open and the little bell above it captured their attention. Angelica stood in the open doorway.

"I thought you had a busy morning," Tricia said, just a tad annoyed.

"Well, I do. But you're my sister and you've got a problem." She moved to join her sister. "*We've* got a problem. I'm here to help . . . if you'll let me."

Tricia swung her gaze to Pixie. "I guess it's your call."

Pixie's gaze shifted to the big square coffee table in front of her and she bit her lip. "Well, I certainly can't leave you with your arm like that. You really do need me right now."

"That's right," Tricia said, hoping a little guilt might help Pixie see things her way.

"But maybe at the end of the summer, once Haven't Got a Care is up and running, I could work there part-time—just to see if I like it."

"You can have as many or as few hours as you like," Angelica promised.

"Then, okay." Pixie managed a small smile, with not a glint off her gold tooth.

Tricia let out a pent-up breath. "That's a relief."

"And I've got another piece of good news," Angelica said.

"And what's that?" Tricia asked.

"I changed the name of the day spa. The sign goes up this afternoon."

"And what did you name it?"

Angelica frowned. "Booked for Beauty."

Tricia's brows drew downward as though in a frown. "Don't you think that conflicts with your restaurant?"

"I did think about your point about it being too close, but then I thought . . . why not? One might think of it as branding two of my businesses—they are on the same street—and even the same side of the street. My employees at the day spa can say, 'Don't forget to go to our sister business, Booked for Lunch, to eat,' and Molly can tell people who visit the café to get pampered at Booked for Beauty."

What she said made sense.

"I like the name," Pixie said.

"It'll grow on me," Tricia grudgingly admitted.

The shop door opened once again, the little bell tinkling merrily, and in walked Mr. Everett carrying a plastic container. "Ms. Miles, it's so good to see you," he said in greeting, his eyes bright and his smile wide. "I do hope you are recovering."

"Yes, thank you, Mr. Everett."

"Grace and I were so worried."

"It'll take a few weeks"—this was a bald-faced lie; her recovery would take five or six weeks, if not more—"but I'll be just fine. And what have you got there?"

Mr. Everett removed the lid from the container and set it down on the coffee table. Inside were a dozen of the prize-winning maple walnut cupcakes he'd made for the Bake-Off. "I knew you wouldn't be up to baking for the shop for some time, so I thought I might follow in your footsteps for just a bit."

"Why don't I pour us some coffee?" Pixie suggested and got up from her seat. "Do you want some, Angelica?"

Angelica looked tempted, but then her head dipped. "No, thank you. I don't want to infringe on you all."

"I would consider it an honor if you'd taste my cupcakes," Mr. Everett said sincerely.

Angelica looked toward Tricia, who gave her a nod and a smile.

"Well, maybe just for one cup of coffee and a cupcake."

"I'll get some napkins," Mr. Everett said, and moved to join Pixie at the beverage station.

"Sit down," Tricia encouraged, gesturing to one of the empty chairs in the nook with her good arm.

Angelica chose the seat to Tricia's left.

Pixie returned with a tray filled with cups of coffee, sugar, and creamer, and Mr. Everett set a wad of white paper napkins on the table. Once the coffee had been poured, Pixie and Mr. Everett each selected a cupcake. Angelica took two, peeling the paper liners off and handing one to Tricia. "Down the hatch," Pixie said, and took a bite, chewed, and groaned in what sounded like ecstasy. "Good grief, no wonder you won the Bake-Off, Mr. E. This is fantastic."

Angelica took a bite and her brows shot up in amazement. "Mr. Everett, this is the best cupcake I've ever eaten in my entire life."

"Your icing recipe is the crowning touch," he said modestly.

"You are too kind," Angelica said sincerely.

Tricia tasted her cupcake and had to admit, she agreed with the other women's opinions. "I'm so proud of you, Mr. Everett. And I'm sure Alice would have been proud, too."

Mr. Everett's head dipped. He wasn't accustomed to being the center of attention and humbly demurred.

Angelica took another bite of her cupcake and slowly chewed before swallowing. "Mr. Everett, when I pull my next cookbook together, I would dearly love to honor you and Alice by including the recipe. It really should be shared with the world."

"That would make me very happy, Ms. Miles."

"I would love to hear a play-by-play of the whole Bake-Off," Pixie said, then looked at Tricia's arm, a blush reddening her cheeks. "I mean, if it's not too painful to talk about."

"I'd love to compare notes. After all, if I'm going to win next year, I want to know both your secrets," Angelica said, her gaze bouncing from Mr. Everett to Tricia.

"Who said I won't win next year?" Tricia asked.

"I guess that depends on if Mr. Everett enters again," Pixie said.

Angelica frowned. "You've got a point," she conceded. "But first, Mr. Everett, tell me more about Alice—and did she leave behind more magnificent recipes?"

Tricia polished off her cupcake, sipped her coffee, and listened as Mr. Everett spoke with touching fondness about his late wife, and she was pleased by the genuine interest Pixie and Angelica showed as they listened intently to his answers.

She might have a badly broken arm, but at that moment, Tricia could only feel very lucky to have the love and respect of the three other people who graced that room.

Who could ask for more?

THE CUPCAKE RECIPES

Tricia's Lemon Cupcakes

½ cup (1 stick) unsalted butter, at room temperature
1 cup granulated sugar
2 large eggs, at room temperature
1½ teaspoons pure vanilla extract
1½ cups all-purpose flour
2 teaspoons baking powder
½ teaspoon salt
½ cup milk
Zest from 1 lemon
Juice from 1 lemon
Crystallized sugar (optional)

Preheat the oven to 350°F (180°C; gas mark 4). Line a 12-count muffin pan with paper or foil liners. Set aside. Using a handheld or stand mixer, beat the butter and sugar together on medium-high speed in a large bowl until creamed (about 2 to 3 minutes). Scrape down the sides and bottom of the bowl as needed. Add the eggs and vanilla. Beat on medium-high speed until everything is combined, about 2 minutes. Continue to scrape down the sides and bottom of the bowl as needed. Set aside.

In a medium bowl, combine the flour, baking powder, and salt. Slowly add the flour mixture to the butter mixture in three additions, beating on low speed. The batter will be thick. Beat in the milk, lemon zest, and lemon juice on low speed until just combined. Do not overmix the batter.

Spoon the batter evenly into 12 cupcake liners, filling them about two-thirds full. Bake for 18 to 22 minutes, or until a toothpick inserted in the middle comes out clean. Remove from the oven and allow to cool completely before frosting.

Frost the cooled cupcakes with lemon buttercream frosting. Sprinkle with crystallized sugar, if using. If topping with lemon zest, do so right before serving.

LEMON BUTTERCREAM FROSTING

3 tablespoons butter, at room temperature
2 to 3 teaspoons lemon extract
1 teaspoon milk (more as needed)
5 drops yellow food coloring (optional)
1 cup confectioners' sugar (more as needed)
Lemon zest (optional)

Beat the butter, lemon extract, and milk together until smooth. If using, add the yellow food coloring lemon zest. Beat the confectioners' sugar into the butter mixture until desired consistency is reached. You may decide to add more sugar at this point. Note: You will want to at least double the recipe if using an 8B tip to pipe the icing.

Yield: 10–12 cupcakes

Angelica's Pistachio Cupcakes

1½ cups pistachios
1 cup granulated sugar
3 large eggs, separated
2 tablespoons grated lemon zest
1 teaspoon baking powder
½ teaspoon baking soda
¼ teaspoon salt

Preheat the oven to 350°F (180°C; gas mark 4). Line a 12-count muffin pan with paper or foil liners. Place the pistachios and sugar into a food processor and chop until finely ground. Transfer the pistachio-sugar mixture to a large bowl and stir in the egg yolks, lemon zest, baking powder, baking soda, and salt. In another bowl, with an electric mixer beat the egg whites on high speed until stiff peaks form. Fold the egg whites into the batter. Spoon the batter into the baking cups, filling each three-quarters full. Bake for 15 to 18 minutes, or until a toothpick inserted into the center comes out clean. Cool the cupcakes in the muffin pan for 5 minutes before removing to cool completely on a wire rack.

CREAM CHEESE FROSTING

8 ounces cream cheese, at room temperature
½ cup (1 stick) unsalted butter, at room temperature
3 cups confectioners' sugar, plus an extra ¼ cup if needed
1 teaspoon vanilla extract
⅛ teaspoon salt
Green food coloring (optional)

In a large bowl using a handheld or stand mixer, beat the cream cheese and butter together on high speed until smooth and creamy. Add the confectioners' sugar, vanilla, and salt. Beat on low speed for 30 seconds, then switch to high speed and beat for an additional 2 minutes. If you like your frosting a little thicker, add the extra ¼ cup of confectioners' sugar. If you want your frosting to match your cupcakes, add several drops of food coloring to the frosting and mix well. Add more if you want to tint the frosting a deeper color. Yield: approximately 3 cups.

Yield: 10–12 cupcakes

Alice's Maple Walnut Cupcakes

1 cup chopped walnuts
½ cup (1 stick) unsalted butter, softened
1⅓ cups granulated sugar
2¼ cups cake flour
1 tablespoon baking powder

¼ teaspoon salt
2 tablespoons pure maple syrup
4 egg whites
1¼ cups milk

Preheat the oven to 350°F (180°C; gas mark 4). Line a 12-count muffin pan with paper or foil liners and set aside. Place the chopped walnuts on a parchment-lined baking sheet; bake for 6 to 7 minutes. In a large bowl, cream together the butter and sugar until light and fluffy, 2 to 3 minutes on medium speed of an electric mixer.

In a separate bowl, mix together the cake flour, baking powder, and salt. Add the maple syrup, egg whites, and half of the flour mixture to the butter mixing bowl. Mix on low speed just until combined. Add the remaining flour mixture and mix on low until combined. Add the milk and mix on low until the batter is fully combined. Fold in ½ cup of the chopped walnuts. Fill each muffin liner approximately two-thirds full. Bake for 26 to 28 minutes, or until a toothpick inserted into the center of the cupcake comes out clean.

ANGELICA'S MAPLE BUTTERCREAM FROSTING*

1 cup (2 sticks) butter, softened
2¾ cups confectioners' sugar
2 tablespoons brown sugar
2 tablespoons maple syrup
¼ cup chopped walnuts or walnut halves (optional)

Place the softened butter in a large bowl. Beat with an electric mixer for 30 to 40 seconds until whipped. Scrape the sides of the bowl. Sift the confectioners' sugar into the bowl. Beat with an electric mixer for 30 to 40 seconds. Scrape down the sides of the bowl and add the brown sugar and maple syrup. Beat for 2 to 3 minutes or until the mixture is fluffy, scraping the sides of the bowl as needed. If using, scatter the ¼ cup of walnuts on the frosted cupcakes as a garnish or top with the walnut halves.

Yield: 10–12 cupcakes

**Angelica's Maple Buttercream Frosting first appeared in* A Fatal Chapter *with her carrot cake recipe.*